T0013374

Truffles and Traffic

Susan M. Baganz

This is a work of fiction. Names, characters, places, and incidents either are the product of the author's imagination or are used fictitiously, and any resemblance to actual persons living or dead, business establishments, events, or locales, is entirely coincidental.

Truffles and Traffic
COPYRIGHT 2023 by Susan M. Lodwick

All rights reserved. No part of this book may be used or reproduced in any manner whatsoever without written permission of the author or Pelican Ventures, LLC except in the case of brief quotations embodied in critical articles or reviews. eBook editions are licensed for your personal enjoyment only. eBooks may not be re-sold, copied or given to other people. If you would like to share an eBook edition, please purchase an additional copy for each person you share it with. Contact Information: titleadmin@pelicanbookgroup.com

All scripture quotations, unless otherwise indicated, are taken from the Holy Bible, New International Version(R), NIV(R), Copyright 1973, 1978, 1984, 2011 by Biblica, Inc.™ Used by permission of Zondervan. All rights reserved worldwide. www.zondervan.com

Scripture quotations, marked KJV are taken from the King James translation, public domain. Scripture quotations marked DR, are taken from the Douay Rheims translation, public domain.

Scripture texts marked NAB are taken from the *New American Bible, revised edition* Copyright 2010, 1991, 1986, 1970 Confraternity of Christian Doctrine, Washington, D.C. and are used by permission of the copyright owner. All Rights Reserved. No part of the New American Bible may be reproduced in any form without permission in writing from the copyright owner.

Cover Art by *Nicola Martinez*
Prism is a division of Pelican Ventures, LLC
www.pelicanbookgroup.com PO Box 1738 *Aztec, NM * 87410
The Triangle Prism logo is a trademark of Pelican Ventures, LLC

Publishing History
Prism Edition, 2023
Paperback Edition ISBN 978-1-5223-9913-1
Electronic Edition ISBN 978-1-5223-9909-4
Published in the United States of America

Dedication

To all the first responders,
especially law enforcement,
who serve and protect with honor.
Your lives matter.

Other books by Susan M. Baganz

Orchard Hill Contemporary Romances

Pesto & Potholes

Salsa & Speed Bumps

Feta & Freeways

Root Beer & Roadblocks

Bratwurst & Bridges

Donuts & Detours

Truffles & Traffic

Black Diamond Christian Gothic Regencies

The Baron's Blunder (Prequel) novella

The Virtuous Viscount (Book 1)

Lord Phillip's Folly (Book 2)

Sir Michael's Mayhem (Book 3)

Lord Harrow's Heart (Book 4)

The Captain's Conquest (Book 5)

Home Grown Heroes Romantic Suspense

Whitney's Vow

Madi's Secret

Christmas Novellas

Fragile Blessings

Love's Christmas Past

Gabriel's Gift

The Doctor's Daughter

Sugar Cookies and Street Lamps

Pixie's Almost Perfect Christmas

Slam-Dunk Christmas

A Tangled Christmas

Short Story Compilation

Little Bits O' Love

1

THE GREATEST TRAGEDIES WERE WRITTEN BY THE GREEKS AND SHAKESPEARE... NEITHER KNEW CHOCOLATE.

SANDRA BOYNTON

OCTOBER 2014

"Suspect is armed and dangerous."

Jo March's pulse sped up as she spied the target the dispatcher had described. She flipped the sirens on, radioed dispatch, and took off in pursuit. The vehicle had distinctive detailing that made it stand out from the crowd of other blue vehicles out there, the metallic nature of the design catching the overhead lights from the center lane on the divided highway. Why pick a car that would stick out? It smelled of desperation.

"Car nine. Ten ninety-nine. Stolen car. Ten-eighty. Chase pursuit in progress." She repeated the car make and license number. She hoped this would end well. Adrenaline rushed through her as she skillfully wove in and out of the traffic on the highway, just as she'd been trained to do.

"Sending backup," dispatch replied.

"Car eight. Ten-sixty. I'm close and on my way." The voice of her partner, Sergeant Geoffrey Ross, rang out on the radio, strong and confident.

Good. She wouldn't face this alone.

Highway 41 was slick from the recent rain. Heading south, the driver exited at Good Hope Road. She gained on him. Blaring sirens and flashing lights, warned other drivers to move out of the way. Most complied, but she still had to swerve around a few vehicles. The suspect's vehicle pulled into a residential area, but made a turn too wide on the wet, leaf-covered road and slammed into a parked truck.

Jo hit the brakes and put her patrol car in park. She unbuckled her seat belt, jumped out, and removed her gun from the holster as the suspect exited his car and began to run on foot.

"Police! Stop!" she yelled. Adrenaline surged. Great, she needed to give chase. Good thing she was fit. She didn't like that she was the only one on the scene. There could be collateral damage in this residential neighborhood. Not if she could help it. Fortunately, with the rain, civilians were indoors.

She stepped from the shelter of her car to pursue the man.

He turned and fired his pistol.

A bullet whizzed past her ear. She aimed and fired as Geoff pulled up. She missed and fired again as a bullet struck the door of the patrol car. The suspect fell but still held his weapon. Geoff raced forward with his own weapon raised.

He blocked Jo's vantage point. She couldn't get another shot off if Geoff needed her.

"Drop it!" Geoff shouted as the man aimed at his new target.

The young man, shrouded in a hoodie and with the streetlight behind him, disregarded the warning and struggled to his feet, managing to pull the trigger again. Geoff crashed to the ground. With a clear shot, Jo aimed her own weapon again and fired a second before the suspect's next bullet struck her. Pain tore through her as she dropped to the cold, damp concrete. Her head hit hard, jarring her teeth. She shook her head and blinked to clear the stars from her vision and then check on the shooter. The perpetrator had fallen and no longer moved. The ordeal was over.

She rolled her head to try to see Geoff, but he was hidden from view. A shiver rippled through her, and she closed her eyes to stop the barrage of images, lights, noise, and rising nausea. More first responders flooded the scene. She longed for the sirens to stop their whining. They soon did. Chaos surrounded her, but an officer knelt by her side while motioning for the paramedics.

"Where are you hurt?" Sheriff's Deputy Alverez asked.

"My shoulder aches. I think he got me where my vest doesn't cover." Her head also throbbed from hitting the ground. "How bad is it?"

The officer glanced at Jo's shoulder using a flashlight. "You did take a hit to your shoulder. A second ambulance is on the way." She reached up to grab a warming blanket from another officer and covered Jo with it.

"How is Sergeant Ross?"

"He's alive and the paramedics are with him. The perp is dead."

The nausea she'd been fighting forced bile up, and she struggled to lean over to throw up. Pain shot through her, and the deputy eased her back to the pavement.

The officer offered Jo a tissue to wipe her face as paramedics finally arrived for her.

The medic moved the officer aside. "Excuse us. We need to assess her."

"How is my partner?" Jo asked of anyone who would listen. She could see the blanket covering the body on the moving stretcher but couldn't see his head.

"He's alive. I don't know much more than that. Let's worry about you now, OK?" The man smiled at her with his eyebrows raised. She shifted her focus back to him. "I guess I should let you do your job, right?"

The paramedic nodded. "It makes it easier."

The other ambulance sped off, with lights and sirens sending another shiver through her body. The men helped her to her feet and onto the stretcher.

"Thanks." She reclined as they covered her back up.

"I still need to get a statement," Officer Alverez told him.

"We can give you a minute," the paramedic

responded. "She's stable, but we need to tend to this wound."

"Can you tell me what happened?" the deputy asked.

Jo gave as many of the details as she remembered. "Was he the man?"

"As far as we can tell, yes. He'd already killed two people. Simultaneous shots, huh? You must have scored high on marksmanship to do that well under pressure."

"Thanks." Jo gave a weak smile.

"I'm sure you'll have more questions coming your way after they watch the dash cams." Jo handed over her gun and the other officer put it in an evidence bag.

"I suppose. And administrative leave while they investigate."

"You need time to heal. For whatever it's worth, you did your job, and you did it well."

"I appreciate that. Who was the guy?"

"We haven't identified him yet."

"I couldn't make out anything about him. It was dark. His hood shadowed his face. It's hard to pay attention to details when someone is shooting at you. I'm surprised he could see well enough to hit me. My lights were on, but that should have blinded him and made it more difficult."

"Just a couple of lucky shots."

"Time to get her to the hospital." The paramedic gently nudged the other officer aside. She saw the shadow of the man by her head grabbing his end of the stretcher. Before she realized it, she was in the ambulance alone with the first medic.

"No sirens, please?"

"Why? That's half the fun, Officer March. And we need to get you taken care of." He sat on the bench next to her. "You realize you're a hero now, right?"

"Oh, please." Jo closed her eyes as the rocking truck raced through the streets of town. The last thing she wanted was the notoriety of her name being in the papers and flying all over the web. How soon could she call her parents so they wouldn't worry? Would Geoff really be all right? If only the first shot had been a kill shot, Geoff would never have been hurt.

~*~

Jo struggled into clothing another officer had snagged from her apartment. She was not spending the night in the hospital. No way. No how. Thankfully, the officer was wise enough to bring a buttoned shirt. With the ding to her collarbone, pullover tops would be out of the picture for a while. The doctor said healing would take time. Wear the sling. Don't work.

Ugh. Worst thing ever. Well, not really…after all, she didn't need surgery, and it could have been far worse…she needed to stop any sort of pity party.

Jo sat down to rest as the nurse left. She picked up her mobile phone and dialed her parents' phone number.

"Hello?" her mother answered.

"Hi, Mom. I'm OK. Sorry to call in the middle of the night, but I wanted to let you know before you saw the news."

She heard rustling. "Wait. Let me put you on speakerphone so your father can hear this too. You are OK?" Anxiety colored her mother's voice.

"I'm injured but I'll recover. I'm going home soon." This was taking way too much effort.

"What happened?" her dad asked.

"I trailed a bad guy, had a shootout, and got hit."

"Did you get him?" he asked.

"Yeah, Dad. I got him. He won't hurt anyone else."

"Save the system some money at least," her mom mumbled.

"It's not justice, Mom. I'm meant to bring them in, not kill people." Horror shook her. *Murderer!* her conscience cried out.

"You did your job. I'm glad you'll be OK. We love you. Keep in touch," her dad said, his voice gruff.

"Do you need anything?" Mom asked.

"Rest. I'll be fine, it'll just take time to heal. Thanks for asking, Mom."

"Go get some sleep then, sweetheart. We love you."

"Thanks. Sleep well. Love you too."

The call disconnected.

Jo took a few deep breaths, grateful for the pain medication that took off the edge. One more call to make—to her big, firefighting brother, Ki.

"Hey, sis. Why're you calling at this time of night?" Ki answered with a yawn.

"You're not working tonight?"

"Nope. But you wouldn't call just to ask me that, so what's up, little sister?"

She really was little compared to her brother. "Just wanted to assure you that I'm OK so that when you watch the news in the morning, you're not worried about me."

"Did you get yourself in trouble?" A tinge of humor characterized his tone.

"No, but someone else did. There was a good ol' shootout, and the good guys won without fatal injuries on our side."

"Not fatal. But that means those were not minor injuries either."

"No. Both Geoff and I were shot. Clipped my collarbone, but I'll be headed home soon. Geoff had surgery."

"How is he?"

"I'm going to his room soon to find out. He's out of surgery and in recovery now."

"You gonna be OK? I don't need to take time off to come and babysit you?"

"I'll be fine. I always am, aren't I?"

"Wouldn't hurt to let others help once in a while. If you head up this way to see Mom and Dad, let me know and we'll go out." His yawn was loud.

"I'll let you get your beauty rest, Ki. Talk soon."

"Love you, Jo. Glad you're safe."

"Thanks. Love you, too."

Jo set the phone down as the nurse arrived with her discharge papers. She had something else to do before heading home to the comfort of her bed.

2

CHOCOLATE MELTS AWAY ALL CARES, COATING THE HEART WHILE SMOTHERING EVERY LAST ACHE.

ANONYMOUS

The monitors by Geoff's bed hummed. She'd resisted a stay overnight but had come to wait for her partner to awaken. He'd come through surgery fine and had been awake in recovery but rested comfortably for now. His strong face was pale against the white pillowcase. She wasn't used to seeing him so still. It unnerved her.

Geoff gasped for air as his eyes opened.

"Hey, big guy," Jo whispered.

He turned to look in her direction. "Jo? What—?"

"You were shot, and they operated. The doctors say you'll recover fully, but you'll be off work for a few weeks."

He groaned. "Five years with no incident and now this? Did I get the guy?"

Jo shook her head. "No. You never hit your target."

"Don't tell me he got away."

"No. He's dead." Her hands shook and she clasped them together. Was this a nightmare? Had the shooting really happened? She shivered. He frowned as he studied her face. She couldn't hide the weariness that weighed her down. She must look awful.

"You killed him?" he asked.

Jo nodded. The events of the evening replayed in her mind as if on fast forward…get to the good part of the movie kind of thing but then as she pulled the trigger it was as if her memory dragged it into slow motion. Could she have done anything differently? Better? Was there any other choice she could have made that would have avoided injury? And death?

"Were you injured?"

She pointed to the sling on her left arm. "After some time off to recover, I'll be pulling desk duty."

"Thanks for saving me."

Jo shook her head. "If I'd done my job right, he'd never have survived to shoot you. You distracted him enough that when he turned to shoot me, I still managed to hit my target. The kid was quick."

"Kid?"

"Eighteen. So sad to see someone so young make such poor choices He possessed a nice stash of heroin in the car he stole, as well as large sums of cash from the ATM after holding up two men. He killed them both."

"I trained you well."

"Yes." She smiled softly. "I'm grateful. I was upset when you fell. I'm sorry I didn't finish him with my first shot." She clenched her jaw, resulting in a throbbing in her head, a just punishment for her failure.

"It happens. Did you only try to wound him?"

"Yes. My mistake. I aimed intentionally for his leg to keep him from running. I didn't anticipate that he'd try to shoot again and I was too far for the Taser both times. If I'd killed him the first time, you wouldn't have ended up here."

"You can't second-guess yourself, Jo."

"It's hard not to, given the outcome." She hung her head, shame washing over her at the pain evidenced in Geoff's grimace.

"You'll be fine, as will I, as far as I can tell since I'm awake and chatting with a lovely woman. You saved lives. You did your job. Don't sweat it."

"Hard to let it go when it plays over and over in my head like a B-rated movie."

"It will be interesting to view the dash-cam footage."

"Yeah. I've not had the privilege yet. Wonder when they'll give us a look-see?"

"Don't sweat it, Jo. It's not worth the energy. I'm proud of you, but I'm sorry I couldn't be there quicker."

"You came as fast as you could. I admit I was terrified at the idea of taking him down alone. We're used to chasing people on highways, not in city streets. Thankfully, no one was out walking their dog or anything like that."

"Small mercies, huh?"

"Yeah, I guess."

"Jo, you really should be home resting."

"I couldn't leave until I was sure you would be

OK."

He reached over with his free hand. "Aw, does that mean you care?"

She stood and gave his hand light squeeze with her hand. "Come on, Geoff. You're my partner and friend. Of course, I care. But you know I don't date fellow officers."

"Yeah, well, a guy can always hope, right?"

"It's futile." She shook her head. She never did understand what he saw in her. Hair always pulled back and out of the way, and the uniform and vest certainly weren't flattering.

"Could you do me a favor?"

Jo perked up. "Probably. What is it?"

"I get that we'll only ever be friends. I respect your boundary on that. But will you finally come to church with me? You don't have work as an excuse this time."

Her heart sank. She and Jesus didn't have much to talk about. Not that she understood anything about God and all. "I suppose. You promise it won't hurt?"

"I sincerely hope not. Kind of rare for people to be injured during a Sunday morning worship service from what I can tell."

"I have nothing else to do."

"You'll be back behind the wheels of a patrol car in no time."

"It'll take you a little bit longer, though. It won't be the same working a shift without you there."

"Maybe they'll put me on dispatch, and I can sweet talk you through." He winked at her.

Jo chuckled. "I can just imagine how the boss

would like that."

"Chin up, Jo. This is a bump in the road. In your career, there will likely be more. Things will get better."

"Thanks for the pep talk. As long as you recover. I was terrified when you fell. I didn't hesitate to kill the kid for that alone."

"You're a fierce warrior. Why didn't you decide to do FBI or some other law enforcement?"

"I don't know. Maybe I like the hat."

He started to laugh but stopped. "It hurts to even breathe."

"Sorry to make you laugh. I should leave. Gotta find a ride home."

"You don't have to stay overnight?"

"They tried, but I refused."

"Sometimes you're too strong-willed for your own good."

"As long as I'm not taking the pain meds, I can still drive and visit you."

"You'd better. I also expect some of your award-winning chili when I get out."

"More like chicken noodle soup for you. I doubt I'll be doing much cooking like that for a while."

Geoff shook his head. "I'm a beef guy all the way. Chili or nothing at all."

"You really want chili?"

"Yes. Anything to burn more than this this"—he motioned over his abdomen—"whatever it is that happened to me."

"I'll let your doctor fill you in on those details."

She stood and squeezed his arm.

"Go home and rest. Will I see you later?" he asked.

"Sure. I'll be back after I get some sleep. Heal up, Sergeant Ross. Work wouldn't be the same without you to watch my six."

He grinned. "Anytime, Trooper March."

Jo saluted and left the room. She found her way to the lobby, where a fellow officer was waiting for her. "Sergeant Cooper?"

"Captain told me to stay to give you a ride home."

"I appreciate it." She allowed him to open the door, and she got into the squad car. "Just no quick chases. Not sure I can handle any more at this point."

Cooper grinned. "Technically, I'm not on duty. I just wanted to stay to make sure you got home safe. Sorry for what happened tonight. I was miles away."

"It ended up involving the local police and sheriff's departments as well. What a mess."

"Relax. You're not on trial. We're all rooting for you and Geoff to heal and be back with us on the road as soon as possible."

"Thanks."

He helped her out of the car and stayed until she managed to sloppily get the key in her door lock and enter. Jo gave a small wave, and he was gone. She dropped her keys by the door as she turned to set the deadbolt. Sitting down, she undid the laces of her boots and pushed each one off with the other foot. She left them where they were. Her shoulder throbbed. Time for another pill and some rest. She filled a glass of water and took the medicine.

Her home was simple but cozy. Was this all life had become? Work, sleep, eat? Jo usually patrolled second shift, so she didn't often get the luxury of hanging out with others after eight or more hours on the job to shoot the breeze or play billiards or darts with some handsome man.

A face from her past flew through her mind. Blue eyes, sandy brown hair, and sizzling wit. OK, so attractiveness was overrated. Still, as lonely as she was, it was nothing compared to what she'd dealt with in her past.

Relax. Enjoy the peace and quiet. Alone by choice was better than alone by neglect any day.

Wasn't it?

3

SPARRING IS NOT SELF-DEFENSE.

T. BLAUER

The news report on the television caught Benjamin Elliot's attention as he made his coffee. The photo of his friend Geoff appeared along with Trooper Jo March. Hearing her name from the reporter's lips stopped Benjamin dead in his tracks. The report didn't say how she was, only that she and Geoff had both been wounded. Injuries weren't specified, but there had been shots fired.

He rubbed his left shoulder as a sudden pain stabbed him there. The discomfort was gone. Strange.

What was weirder was hearing Jo's name again after so long. He'd followed her career over the past few years from a distance, proud of what she'd accomplished. He prayed she'd not been seriously injured. Long ago he'd given up the right to be the first notified in the event of an emergency or the first person she'd see when she opened her eyes in the hospital.

He prayed for his friend Geoff as well.

Ben poured his coffee and took a sip. There were things he'd done in his life that he regretted. Losing Jo had been the biggest. He sighed. There wasn't much he could do about it now.

The phone rang.

"Hi, Mum." She was in England where it was mid-afternoon.

"Did you see the news?" she asked

"What news? I don't watch news from England." He sipped his coffee and went to the living room to sit.

"It came across my e-mail."

"Don't tell me. You have Jo March typed into your web browser to flag anything that pops up online about her."

"You mean you don't?"

"No," he lied.

"Shame on you, then. Did you hear the news?"

"That she was part of a shooting in Menomonee Falls?"

"Yes. Is she OK? I couldn't find any information about her well-being."

"I hope she is, but I don't have a clue. The only fatality last night was the guy who murdered two people, robbed an ATM, and stole a car."

"But two state patrol officers were wounded in the shooting."

"Why are you so worried about Jo? She's not been part of my life for three years now."

"Stupidest thing you've ever done."

"Maybe so, but the past needs to stay there."

"Don't be a fool," his mother chided.

"Hopefully, I've outgrown some of my foolish ways."

"I hope so. If you hear anything, send me a message."

"Fine, Mum. Love you." He shook his head as he slid the phone into his pocket.

Initially, his mother hadn't been too thrilled when he'd started dating Jo. They'd been so young. After his mother met Jo, his mom cared very much about her, and that never stopped, even after all that had happened between them. It didn't make sense. *Women.*

Benjamin sipped his coffee and glanced at the clock. He headed to his office, logged into his computer, and checked his e-mail. He found one from the church group requesting prayer for Geoff, who was recovering from surgery. He bowed his head and prayed for his friend again.

Ben prayed for Jo as well. He suspected she didn't know Jesus. His own faith was new to him. Geoff was a believer, so he was assured of his eternal home. But Jo? If she had been killed... He shuddered at the thought.

Concentrate. He had a job to do. Jo was no longer part of his life. None of his concern.

Soon he was on a conference call with a new client. Eventually, he'd go onsite to do some training for the software he was developing for their network, but for now, they had some bugs to iron out.

Jo still haunted him.

Lord, I hope Jo is well. And if You give me a chance to apologize for the past, I pray You'd make her ready to forgive me.

It was an awful lot to ask of Jo, but God? God

could handle anything.

~*~

After lunch, Benjamin decided to visit Geoff in the hospital. If he ended up finding out information about Jo in the process, where was the harm in that?

He gathered a small cardboard box in the kitchen and his keys and left the house.

Once through the hospital checkpoint, he detoured to the gift shop, paid for a child's toy, and headed up to Geoff's room.

Geoff's eyes were closed, so Ben tiptoed over to a chair near the bed and sat down.

"Hey," Geoff said, his voice gravelly. "Ben? Didn't expect you."

"How are you?"

"It's nearly impossible to sleep in here. Nurses coming and going all the time."

"Did I come at a bad time?"

Geoff shook his head. "Nah, it's good to have company. Keeps my brain from trying to replay what happened last night."

"Will you be able to get out soon?"

"As long as they have someone checking up on me at home."

"I can put in a call to Pastor Dan. I believe the parish nurses can assist."

"That'd be great. Thank you. Dan was here earlier, and I never thought to even ask him about that."

"You've probably got other things on your

mind…like pain."

"Right now, it's not too bad. What brings you by?" Geoff's eyes were wider now.

"We haven't been acquainted for very long, but you've been someone who always gave me a warm welcome when I first started coming to church. Figured I'd come and make sure you weren't on your deathbed like the news reports indicate."

"Drama, huh?"

"Yup, and you're the main attraction."

"Don't make me laugh. It hurts too much, and they only give me so much pain medication at a time."

"Sorry. I'll try to be more somber." Ben grinned.

"There you go again. I appreciate you coming."

"I brought you something." Benjamin handed over a stuffed teddy bear.

"A stuffed animal?"

"When my dad had heart surgery, they gave him a stuffed animal to hug to his chest when he needed to cough. He said it initially felt silly but helped a lot."

"Well, the bullet didn't quite hit my heart, but given your propensity for making me laugh, I'll accept the gift with gratitude even if it makes me look like a sissy."

"You're too hard on yourself. You wear a badge and carry a gun. Nothing sissy about that."

"Let's change the subject. How're you doing with your walk with God? Have you been finding time to slow down and be with Him?"

"How'd you know I struggled with that?" It was still very new to have men asking him about his faith, but he was coming to understand that it was all in love, not a way to judge. Accountability was a good thing.

"I think we all do to some extent. You seem a little hyper to me whenever I see you, always looking for what's ahead rather than relishing the moment.

"It has been hard. I've always felt that I should be moving or doing something. Maybe I have attention-deficit/hyperactivity disorder or something, but I began playing around in my kitchen."

"Playing around?"

"Yeah, making chocolate." Ben shrugged.

"Why bother when you can buy it in the store?"

Ben pulled out a small box and lifted the lid to reveal smooth, round balls of chocolate. "Try one."

Geoff reached for one and popped it in his mouth. He groaned in pleasure. "Are you sure making these isn't a sin?"

"How?"

"I don't think I've tasted anything so good before."

"Glad you like them. This batch is yours. I make them for fun, because the process slows me down, and I pray or meditate on Scripture."

"Cool. I personally prefer running as I pray. Clears away the cobwebs."

"I've been doing some of that, too. Figure if I'm making and perhaps eating chocolate, and given that my job is sedentary, I'd better get moving to keep in shape."

"You've come a long way in a short amount of time," Geoff said.

"Adult Ministries group helped."

"Have you made friends there?"

"I'm taking out someone Friday night for dinner."

"I said friends, not a date."

"It's only dinner. I'm not planning to start anything."

"Then why go?"

"Because I get lonely, and maybe God will show me someone who would be a good fit in my life."

"Sounds more like a date than dinner with a friend." Geoff eyed him. "The group isn't for matchmaking."

"True. Perhaps another area God needs to grow me in."

"As long as you keep making these..." Geoff popped a second one in his mouth.

"Pace yourself. I don't make them every day. It's a hobby to get me away from my computer and to slow me down."

"Glad you found something."

"Yeah, me too. I should get going so you can rest. Call me if you need anything."

"Thanks, buddy. But I still think you might need to confess some kind of sin in making these beauties. I appreciate you bringing them."

Ben rose and with a wave was out the door, almost bumping into a nurse who was about to enter. Once in the hallway, he sighed. He still knew nothing about how Jo fared. He'd steered clear of the shooting lest it upset his friend, who was already suffering enough. He'd continue to pray for Jo. God knew her better than anyone, so Ben would leave her to the Lord's care.

4

FAITH DOES NOT ELIMINATE QUESTIONS.
BUT FAITH KNOWS WHERE TO TAKE THEM.

ELISABETH ELLIOT

Jo tiptoed into the darkened hospital room. Good. No other visitors right now. She sat by Geoff's bedside and watched him sleep. He was ruggedly handsome. A big guy. Probably why the kid managed to hit him with that wild shot. Geoff got hit in the abdomen just under the vest which always seemed too short on him from her perspective. Large target. Geoff was a great officer, and he hadn't disparaged her capabilities when she'd started her job and rode around with him to get acclimated. Why couldn't she fall in love with a rock-steady man like him?

She shook her head. Nope. Jo couldn't envision a future with a law-enforcement officer. What if they had kids? Two parents going to work and never knowing if either one would come home? It wasn't fair to put a man in that situation. There were some aspects to wedded life she missed, but toward the end, the hurt outweighed the passion. She couldn't take that risk again. And Geoff? There was no spark there, only friendship. When he smiled, he was handsome. He had a big heart and a generous nature. Any woman would be lucky to find a guy like him.

She didn't know the full extent of his injury and prognosis for recovery. It didn't matter right now. Her mistake hadn't gotten him killed. It was a difficult time to be in law enforcement. Too many people thought police, and by extension, all law enforcement officials, were the bad guys. There were a few bad apples out there, but she didn't quite understand how that could happen. Wearing a gun was a responsibility, and the badge was a privilege she'd earned the hard way. Going through the paramilitary-type training at Fort McCoy had been challenging, but she had grown stronger in so many ways from the experience. It made her wonder if she'd have made a good soldier. Would she have been happy seeing the world from a military post?

No. She was happy with her job, and the people who served with her. Thankfully, most of the people she pulled over were non-aggressive. Sure, some had been mouthy at times, but that was it. She doubted Geoff got as much of that, since he was such a big guy. Did he still play rugby? Probably.

"Hey, you came," Geoff said. Drowsiness filled his tone.

Jo smiled. "You adopted a teddy bear in my absence. Appropriate since you really are one at heart."

Geoff grinned. "A gift from a friend in the hopes that if I cough or laugh it won't hurt so much."

"Does it help?"

"Not really, but I won't tell him that. It was a nice

thought. Also brought me truffles. They're on the table there. Try one."

"I can't eat your gifts."

"Sure, you can. Just one. Trust me. You'll thank me."

Jo picked up the round candy and popped it in her mouth. Her eyes grew wide and then closed in pleasure as she ate it. "Mmmm."

"See? Told you."

"Darn. Look at all I missed by being released right away. You got flowers, balloons, a stuffed animal, and chocolate? You're milking this for all you got, so I suppose I shouldn't feel so guilty about you getting shot."

"Would you stop it? You did your job. I thought I could take him out, but he was faster than I expected. I should have stayed behind the car door."

"I should have moved into position for a clean shot when I saw him aim at you."

"Things happen in a split second," Geoff encouraged. "Our minds play it back in slow motion. I doubt you had the chance to move. What's important is you did shoot him, and saved me from getting shot again. Just stop it. Let it go."

"Is it that easy for you? I close my eyes and it replays, and I watch you fall and my heart races, fear grips me, and…"

"Have you gotten any rest at all since last night?"

Jo shook her head. "Not much."

"Me, neither, but that's more because I'm here and the nurses keep coming in or the pain gets bad and I need to call for more meds."

"I'm sorry. Your suffering is far worse than mine."

"Don't minimize the trauma of what you went through. See a therapist. Get some help. And remember, you promised to come to church with me when I get out of here."

"Sure. I'll go. Not sure God has much interest in me, but if it will make you happy, I'll do it."

"It'd make me happy if you let me take you out to dinner too…"

"I appreciate the offer, but I already told you—"

"You don't date law enforcement officers," Geoff finished and winced.

"Pain bad?"

"Just where you kicked me in the heart. So, if I want a relationship with Jo March, I have to quit my job?"

"Right, and what else would you do? You were made to be a hero and a cop. It's who you are to the core, and you're a great one. You can't give that up, and I would never ask that of you, nor should any woman who loved you."

"But that woman wouldn't be you."

"Geoff, I'm sorry. I don't think of you that way. You're a great friend and I treasure that. You're the best partner, and I know you'll have my six but—"

"You won't date law enforcement officers."

"Right." Jo sighed. She hated to disappoint people, but it seemed that was all she was good at. "I'd better go so you can rest. Visiting hours are almost over anyway. Call me if you need anything."

"Seems to be the common refrain."

"What?"

"Every person who visits says, 'Call me if you need anything.' I'm getting tired of hearing it."

"Because you wish someone was just there for you."

"Right. And I'm the one who rescues people."

"I understand. Hard for the hero to be helped, huh?"

Geoff frowned.

Jo squeezed his arm. "Someday, my friend. If God has any mercy and loves like you say He does, He'll find the perfect woman for you. And she'll be worth the wait."

"And for you?"

Jo shook her head. "I had my shot and lost it. Not searching for it again. Sleep well, friend." She turned and walked out the door with as much dignity as she could muster. Once in the hallway, she stopped and leaned against the wall on her good shoulder.

Alone.

Always alone.

A tear fell. She wiped it away and headed home to her empty apartment. A perfect illustration of her heart.

5

IN LOVE'S SERVICE, ONLY WOUNDED SOLDIERS CAN SERVE.

BRENNAN MANNING

Benjamin took his usual seat at church for worship.

"Hey, Ben." Will Dalton greeted him as he slid into the row of theater-style seats for worship.

"Hey, yourself." Ben settled in to scan through the bulletin, thankful for the soft recorded music playing through the speakers and a chance to take a breath before the service began.

"How was Friday night?" Will nudged him.

Ben shrugged. "It was fine. Jessica's nice." His date with Jessica on Friday night had been interesting, but he wasn't ready to commit to sitting with her in church. She usually came for second service, saying she needed her "beauty rest." That was what would come of dating a cosmetologist. He had to admit her nails were works of art, but at some level they kind of scared him.

Will and Ben stood as the band started to play.

Sitting in church with his friends had become his new normal. Ben grinned. A few years prior, he was self-employed and embroiled in a disastrous legal battle with a former business partner. Will had been the one to first invite him to church and introduce him to Christ. The relationship had not only helped him start a new and successful business but also changed his entire focus in life. Ben had enjoyed doing some contract work with the FBI as well due to his relationship with Will. Along with that, Ben enjoyed worshiping here, and the messages were always relevant. Bit by bit, the sins of his past fell away.

He did feel, though, that the Lord was leading him to ask for forgiveness to those he'd hurt. But would Jo be willing to talk to him after the way he'd sinned against her? He bent his head during the final song to pray, asking for God to guide him in that and to give him the courage to wipe that slate clean. Not so much so he could be free, but so hopefully Jo could be as well.

The service ended and Ben headed to the cafe for a cup of coffee.

Geoff stood to one corner.

Ben headed in that direction. The man was tall, standing a head above most people in the room. Someone stood next to him but was partially blocked by the crowd. Geoff had a girlfriend? Good for him.

Grabbing his coffee, he approached Geoff's other side. "Hey, buddy. Good to see you up and around." Ben turned to take in the woman next to his friend. The sensation of blood draining from his face rattled him. It took all his strength to hold on to the coffee mug instead of dropping it.

"Can't drive yet, but I talked Jo into bringing me this morning. Jo works with me. Jo, this is my friend Ben Elliot. Don't let the accent fool you; he's an ordinary guy."

Jo's eyes were wide. "Hi, Benjamin. It's been a long time."

Geoff frowned. "You know each other?"

"Yes, but it's been a few years," Ben responded to Geoff but refocused his attention back to Jo. He fought to push down the wave of loss and grief. "You're looking great, Jo. Well, except for that sling. I was sad to learn you were injured."

"Yeah, but I'll recover in time. Geoff is the one with the longer healing process."

"She keeps beating herself up, but she did her job. She saved my life."

"You don't have to keep saying that, Geoff," Jo protested.

"You shouldn't protest when a man compliments you," Ben said.

"Oh. You wouldn't talk about me that way, though, would you?" She'd thrown down the gauntlet.

Ben squashed down the temptation to hurt her as he'd been hurt. She was a child of God, too. She didn't know he was different.

Show her.

He gulped. "I'd describe you as tenacious, stronger than you probably think you are, passionate about those you love, and underneath your strength is a tender heart of gold."

"Whoa," Geoff said, "you two must have known

each other well."

"Those were kind words, Benjamin. Thank you. I definitely didn't deserve or expect that kind of praise from you, of all people."

"It's only the truth." Ben turned to Geoff. "I'll see you around. If you need a ride somewhere or help with anything, I'm a phone call away."

"Thanks. I appreciate that."

"Nice seeing you again, Jo." He nodded, smiled, and hoped his own unrequited love wasn't evident in his eyes. He turned and walked away to greet some other friends.

~*~

Later at home, Ben picked up the phone, hoping it wasn't too late to call home. An eight-hour difference in time zones always made him stop and do the math.

"Hi, Ben," his father answered.

"How are you, Dad?"

"Doing well. Did you call to fill us in on how Jo's doing?"

"Yeah. She's up and about and wearing a sling. She's as beautiful as ever."

A click indicated his mother had picked up from another extension. "Benjamin?"

"Hi, Mum."

"He said Jo is well and looks beautiful," his dad stated.

"Oh, did you tell her we asked about her?" Mum asked.

"Mum—she was shocked to see me. Given the way things ended between us, I didn't want to expose too much of our previous relationship to a mutual friend."

"Take her to lunch or give her a call," Dad suggested.

"Flowers. Oh, and truffles. Send her some of your truffles. That'll melt her heart," Mum suggested.

"We're not even friends now. Why do you keep bringing her up?"

"We miss her, and she was perfect for you."

"She was, but I was horrible for her, and she's not likely to forgive and forget that any time soon." Ben almost regretted calling.

"Where did you run into her?" Mum asked.

"At the church I'm attending."

Dad coughed. "You're still going to church?"

"I've made new friends there. Remember? I told you I had become a Christian last year."

"What?" Mom asked. "I always took you to church."

"Mum, I had no relationship with God. I do now."

"He's dead," Dad countered.

"He died and rose again, Dad. He's the Creator of the universe, and He is the only One who can save us from sin and eternal damnation."

"Oh, my," Mum exclaimed.

"It's not a bad thing, Mum. My life has changed for the better since I've gotten to known Him. Remember me mentioning Roberto Rodriguez? He assisted me with my legal stuff. And Will Dalton? He was great at helping me get my business up and running and helped me get my accounting squared away. Both attend there. Roberto had mentioned it a few times, but finally Will convinced me to go. My close relationship with Christ has given me the peace I could never find anywhere else."

"Well, son, if that works for you, great," Dad said.

"Thanks." Ben winced as his parents started sharing other details of their lives and his mom's latest health issue. He loved them both, but when it came to his love life, or lack thereof, he was glad there was an ocean between them. When he hung up a short time later, he sighed and set the phone down.

Jo. He'd prayed for her at the end of the service, and God brought her to church. Ben hadn't exactly asked Jo for forgiveness, though, had he? It wasn't quite the time and place for that, and obviously, Geoff had no clue about their previous relationship. Jo had blushed deeply when Ben complimented her. Maybe little things like that would show her just how much God had changed him. When the time came to apologize, perhaps she'd see the difference, and they wouldn't just be pretty words that couldn't be believed.

He was still in shock from seeing her face to face at church. Where did all those strong emotions come from?

What if she started attending church and dating other men there? He groaned. He wanted her to be happy, but it would be a shot to the heart if she chose one of his friends to be her next husband. Perhaps he needed to get his own teddy bear to help with the ache he already experienced. Witnessing her with Geoff and the appreciation his friend had for Jo hurt. Not that she didn't deserve a man like that. She did. Ben had had his chance and blown it. There was no going back from that.

Was there?

6

FAITH IS A PLACE OF MYSTERY, WHERE WE FIND THE COURAGE TO BELIEVE IN WHAT WE CANNOT SEE AND THE STRENGTH TO LET GO OF OUR FEAR OF UNCERTAINTY.

BRENE BROWN

Jo went through a drive-thru for food and drove toward Geoff's home. She pulled into his driveway. Once inside she set the bag of food down on the kitchen table.

"Stay for lunch," Geoff offered.

"I should go. You need to rest." Jo urged. Her sleep was filled with nightmares, the shooting replaying in her dreams.

"I've rested as much as I want to." He grimaced.

"Same here." Jo gave him a bright smile. "Let's move past it."

"OK. I'm curious. How well are you acquainted with Ben?" Geoff asked.

She bit back a smile as warm memories flooded her thoughts. *Benjamin*. The guy appeared more gorgeous than he had in college. Confident, and for a hyper man, at peace. The hard shell around her heart cracked when he'd complimented her. He really viewed her as strong? Beautiful? Passionate? A heart of gold? She sighed before answering. "I haven't seen Benjamin in years."

"Obviously not a great friend if you'd lost touch for so long."

"Sometimes things happen that closes a door to a relationship."

"What? You don't date computer geeks, either? How long is your list of men you won't marry?"

"At the moment, the list includes any and all jobs. I'm not in the market for a husband."

"Well, at least it's not just me, then."

"This discussion is over." She patted his arm. "I'll call tomorrow to check on how you are."

"Finally, someone who isn't waiting for me to call them," he whined.

"Exactly. Eat and get some rest." She gave a salute and headed out.

~*~

Once she arrived home, she took out the soup she'd purchased for herself. It was already getting cold, so she dumped it into a bowl to heat it up. A chill ran through her. She was grateful that Benjamin hadn't told Geoff how well they were acquainted. She wasn't ready to share that part of herself with anyone. It was too private and humiliating to admit her failure in their relationship.

Surprise was a mild term for her reaction to his description of her. Too bad he hadn't said words like that years ago. But they weren't true then, were they?

She'd worked hard to get to where she was today.

Which was where?

Alone.

Shot.

Totally lost.

Geoff's church sparked something inside of her. She wanted to go back, even if it meant bumping into Benjamin occasionally. She'd put on her police trained bravado and deal with it. There was something in the worship this morning that drew her. And the music. She'd never heard anything like it. Their talk about God was different from anything else she'd ever heard. She longed to know more. She grabbed her phone and texted Geoff.

Where can I buy a Bible?

I've got a spare you can have.

I don't want to inconvenience you.

It's not. Stop by anytime to pick it up. It will be waiting for you.

Thanks.

She set the phone down. It beeped again.

You can get an app for your phone too. I'll email you the link. Start with the Gospel of John.

OK. Thanks again.

The e-mail came through. She clicked and downloaded the application to her phone. She opened it up and, per Geoff's instructions, started in the Gospel of John.

~*~

Jo continued reading the Bible. There wasn't much else for her to do right now. This Jesus had her curious. Perhaps He held the key to free her from her past. She didn't want to keep bothering Geoff about it. It was Monday. She called Orchard Hill.

"Hi, I'm wondering if there's someone I can talk to about God?"

"Sure. Pastor Dan is available. Would you like me to put you through to him?"

"Thank you. That'd be great."

One ring, and a man answered. "This is Dan."

"Pastor Dan?"

"Yes. How can I help you?"

"My name is Jo. I visited Orchard Hill for the first time yesterday. I started reading the Bible, and I have some questions. Can I come in and talk to someone?"

"I've got a few hours open this afternoon. What time is best for you?"

They set a time, and Jo went to prepare herself for going out in public. She grabbed her phone and notebook where she'd been jotting down questions. Then she drove to Orchard Hill. Only this time, it was without the security blanket of the tall sergeant. Parked outside the church, she took a deep breath. She was a state trooper. She was used to asking hard questions. That was how one came to uncover the truth. For some reason, this truth was important for her to understand.

Jo got out of the car and strode to the building. She approached the front desk. "Hi. I'm here to meet with Pastor Dan."

"Take a seat. He'll be right out."

No sooner had she sat down than a tall, blond man came her way.

"Jo March?" he asked.

She rose to her feet. "Yes."

He nodded. "I'm sorry I didn't get to speak with you yesterday. We can meet in my office."

She followed him down the hall, through some doors, and into his office. A guitar was off in one corner.

Pastor Dan turned. "I recall seeing you with Geoff Ross. You're the other trooper who was injured."

"Right. He invited me to church. I figured since it was my fault he got shot, the least I could do was come to church when he asked."

"Your fault? I thought he'd been shot by the kid."

"True, but if I'd killed the guy with my first shot, Geoff would never have been injured."

"Does Geoff or your boss hold you responsible?"

"No. They say I did my job the way I'd been trained to do it. But I didn't. The man shot at me and I should have killed him. I didn't think he'd still try to shoot after he'd been injured."

"So, you gave him a chance to redeem himself and face the justice of the legal system, and he didn't go along with your plan, forcing you to execute him before he did that to Geoff."

"Exactly. Well—" Jo had never looked at it that way. Had she done that?

"Listen, I can't relate to killing someone or being shot at, but if others around you said you did your job, then stop doubting yourself. I suspect if you'd killed him outright, you'd be plagued with even more guilt for taking his life. It sounds as though you tried to do the least amount of damage to protect others without taking a life. When that didn't work, you did what the job required you to do. Regrettable, but that's what you signed up for when you took that job. Right?"

Jo stared down at her hands. A tear dropped. She sniffed.

He handed her a tissue.

"Thanks."

"Not a problem. Is that why you wanted to see me? I thought you mentioned wanting to understand more about God."

"I do. I started reading the Bible last night and just kept going. I have so many questions. Geoff is healing, and I didn't want to bother him, so I called the church and got you."

The pastor grinned. "I'll do what I can to help."

"First, I'm a little confused about why Jesus would need to die for our sins."

"Let me see if I can explain it to you."

Pastor Dan picked up a Bible from the corner of his desk. "Let's start here in Genesis, where it all began."

~*~

Jo walked out the door of the church. Her mind whirled with all she'd learned, but she'd need time to think on it. Jesus was there waiting for her. All she had to do was admit her sin, her need for Him, and submit to Him. She understood following the rules and respected the chain of command. This grace thing didn't make sense to her. If God was handing out tickets, she'd be convicted and in jail for life. Right? Because she'd taken that criminal's life? There was no way she could erase the past, but He would. Or at least the stain left by her sin. That didn't fix everything, eliminate the consequences of her choices, or guarantee that her future would be wonderful. What a strange faith.

"Pray about it, Jo," the pastor had said. "Let God lead you to Himself as you read."

She drove home and went into her apartment. Dan had given her a Bible and put some colored sticky notes in spots he thought she might want to read next. He'd also given her the business card of a therapist he recommended to help her with the aftereffects of the shooting. Jo fingered the card. Wouldn't hurt, right? There was no shame in talking to a safe person about her problems. She dialed the number and made the appointment. She had nothing better to do right now anyway, and it would make her boss happy.

7

CHOCOLATE SHARES BOTH THE BITTER AND THE SWEET.

ANONYMOUS.

Benjamin closed the file he'd been working on. "Julie, I think we've got this up and running now. Call me if you have any problems or need to set another training day for those who couldn't be here." He stood and grabbed his coat. The tall, leggy blonde had been winking at him all morning. As if that would make him ask her out. *No, thank you.*

"Want to go to lunch, Ben? I can leave for an hour, and there's a cozy little spot not far from here."

Flag down on the play. He shook his head. "I appreciate the invite, but I don't go out with clients."

"When the install is done?"

"You'll still be a client. Bye, Julie." He beat a hasty retreat out the door to his car and locked the doors as he put on his seatbelt. It wouldn't have surprised him to have her running after him, even in her high heels. It had happened before. If only they understood what a loser he was in the relationship department, they would think twice. And while he used to seek pleasure where he could, he wasn't that man anymore, hadn't been since he'd first met Jo. Abstinence wasn't fun, but he'd lost interest in that kind of relationship anyway. He went to pick up an order at a fast-food noodle restaurant and drove over to Geoff's apartment. He'd promised to stop by with a meal. Another reason to reject Julie's obvious charms.

He rang the bell at the apartment address Geoff had given him when he'd made the promise.

Geoff buzzed him in without a word.

Ben headed into the apartment hallway to the inner door. It opened before he could knock. "I come bearing comfort food."

"Mac and cheese?" Geoff asked.

"It is what you requested." He placed the bag on the table and went to get plates and forks.

"You don't have to serve me like a waiter."

"Don't sweat it. I'll pray over our food." After the prayer, they dug into the meal.

"Jo was pretty tight about your past with her. What gives?" Geoff didn't mess around.

Ben shrugged. "It was years ago, and no one else's business but ours. If she doesn't want to share, I'm certainly not going to."

"I should have said she did, and asked for your side of the story."

"Wouldn't have worked."

"Why?"

"Because, I would have asked for specifics and you wouldn't have that information, so I wouldn't give any either. Think of it as if I had a non-disclosure agreement with a company and couldn't share their trade secrets. The point in life where Jo's path intersects with mine falls into that kind of confidentiality."

"You must have really loved her. You still do."

Ben frowned. "Why would you say something like that?"

"We strive to protect the ones we love. I'll assume it's nothing criminal, or she wouldn't have cleared a background check or the psych evaluation to get her job."

Ben remained silent and ate his food.

Geoff took a few bites too. "So, you really won't say anything else?"

"Why? If I admit it, you'll press for more. If I deny it, you'll say I'm in denial. There's no point in defending or affirming your statements. Jo knows the truth, as do I. That's all that matters."

"But you love her."

"Never said that."

"You didn't need to. The look on your face when you complimented her was more than a man saying something nice to a woman. It was a declaration of love."

"How many of those pain pills are you taking at a time? Leave it be, Geoff. It really doesn't matter if I love her or not."

"It doesn't?"

"Nope. She doesn't love me."

Geoff sighed. "Join the club."

~*~

Ben returned home, restless. Not unusual, given his natural hyperactivity. It was what made him good at his job. Hyper-focused. It was also why he jogged. He'd even finished a few half-marathons and toyed with the idea of training for Boston.

He walked to his bedroom, opened the top drawer of his dresser, and pulled out a small jewelry box. Why had he ever saved it? Had he anticipated losing Jo? He flipped it open to view the ring he'd purchased for her out of his first big paycheck. He removed it and could have sworn the white gold was warm, as if it had just been removed from the wearer's finger. Why hold on to it? He could never give it to another woman.

He put it back in the box and slid the drawer shut. After wandering to his kitchen, he assembled what he needed to make some truffles. The activity slowed him down and relaxed him. Unfortunately, all the questions about Jo bounced around in his head.

He'd been an idiot the night she left. If she'd asked, maybe then she'd have understood why she'd found him as she had. It was a horrible failure on his part and she'd had every right to walk away from their marriage. He'd been utterly stupid and beyond drunk when that woman had approached.

Self-medicating his failures led to the second biggest mistake of his life. The first mistake he'd made was going into business with a friend who'd robbed him and another client blind. The haze of liquor and lust shut his brain down so he only experienced pleasure, something he'd been denying himself too much in an effort to prove to his wife—*his wife*—that he wasn't a screw-up. That he hadn't lost most of their money and almost ended up in Federal prison.

And the woman? He never could remember her name. He regretted the day she came on to him and that he was too drunk to think clearly and walk away from the temptation she offered.

Ben never complained when Jo emptied half the bank account. She could have taken it all. He was utterly ruined as it was. She never asked for anything in the divorce either. She'd only given her forwarding address as her parents' home, but letters he wrote to her were returned. Not that his explanation of what happened was any consolation.

He'd ruined his marriage in tandem with ruining his business. His parents rescued him by helping him through the last months of school as he fought his legal battles with Roberto Rodriquez's counsel. Will Dalton had assisted him with some forensic accounting, and they'd become friends.

That led him to Orchard Hill and learning about Christ, the redemptive part of his story. He studied the photo he still had of him and Jo at Big Ben in London. She'd sometimes called him that, and the memory was sweet. Maybe they'd been a mismatch, but he had loved her dearly and wanted to prove to her that he was all she believed him to be—brilliant. He'd failed her. He compared the image in the photograph to the woman he'd seen in church on Sunday.

She was pale, probably as a result of the shooting and her injury, but she was more mature, more composed—and so much more beautiful than the young woman he'd married.

On Sunday, he'd walked away more to avoid embarrassing himself over his attraction to her than anything else. As much as she despised him, he desired her. Would she spill his sins before his new friends? Could he ever live that down? Would they still accept him if they realized how weak and idiotic he'd been back then?

Three years had passed since she'd disappeared from his life. She never came to court for the divorce, but a lawyer came in her stead. Given how badly he'd hurt her, would she ever be able to forgive him? It didn't matter that he never had sex with the other woman. They'd never left the comfort of the bar. She'd eased an ache in him by temporarily soothing his ego. In reality, he'd killed his marriage with his own idiocy.

After cleaning up the kitchen, he sat at his computer and began to type. Every one of his letters had been returned back then, but it might have been done by her parents. Perhaps he'd get her to read one now and find a way to beg her forgiveness.

~*~

Jo organized her sock drawer and washed out the inside of her refrigerator. It was slower with only one arm to do the work. The nightmares woke her up often. She went over every detail when she was awake, until she forced her mind to think on something else. She rested as her captain requested. She paced. She dusted.

And she came across an old scrapbook.

Don't do this to yourself.

She did it anyway.

She dropped into her only comfy chair and opened the book. Why had she even saved this, much less unpacked it when she moved here? This was something she should have burned instead. *Oh, why not torture yourself some more, huh?*

The first photo was of her and Benjamin side by side at the bar where they'd met. It had been taken on one of her rare nights off. She giggled at the image. They were so young. Benjamin was all of nineteen and she was eighteen, fresh out of high school and spending the summer working on a Department of Transportation road crew, mostly flagging drivers and placing cones. They'd had her mowing and digging, and she'd loved most of it. At night, she worked at the bar part-time. She'd been able to serve the liquor even though she wasn't twenty-one yet, the legal limit for drinking in the state of Wisconsin.

Another photo showed them leaning against the pool table where they'd spent time arguing over technique. Ben had a uniquely scientific strategy to getting his shots, and her strategy had been instinctual. Every game was close, and she often won. He'd been gracious in losing to a woman. She'd been enchanted by his accent and good looks. He was too smart for a woman like her, but she fell for him anyway. He never treated her as if she was stupid like some guys did. It was amazing how inappropriate men could be when they were drunk. He'd waited until the third date before he even kissed her.

Several photos showed them kissing. Again, at the bar. Their social life revolved around the bar scene. That fall, she started college in downtown Milwaukee at the University of Wisconsin, and Ben attended the Milwaukee School of Engineering. She was undecided, and he was working on a degree that complemented the education he'd already had in computer programming, which he'd earned on the side while in school in London.

They'd fallen for each other hard and fast and chose to marry quickly over Christmas break so they could honeymoon in the United Kingdom. Her family was present for the courthouse wedding, but his parents and sister were still overseas. A second small ceremony was held in England for their benefit.

She flipped through the few photos of their wedding at the courthouse and their trip abroad. They'd visited his parents, and she got to tour some of the sights. She loved the pace of the smaller town where he had spent his childhood.

The first year of marriage had been hard but good. He was either studying for classes or working with a small business from home. She spent her summers on the construction crew again and never left the job at the bar.

Some photos she'd forgotten about. He'd snapped one when she was in her orange vest, and several from work, as he often came to visit when she was on the job. He called it insurance, because other men hit on her. During the summer, his sandy brown hair turned blond from jogs he took to keep fit.

It wasn't until after she'd finished two years of college that things fell apart. Undecided about further education, she'd stopped school after receiving her Associates Degree and began working more. Benjamin seemed preoccupied. He was always at his computer working, often not coming to bed until after she'd fallen asleep.

That final, fateful day, Jo had worked out in the hot sun. Pop-up storms forced them to quit road work earlier than expected. She'd come home that Thursday night to find Benjamin gone. She'd showered and dressed nice and went to hunt him down at their usual hangout.

Jo would never forget what she saw that night. She closed her eyes tight and shook her head trying to erase the horror of the memory.

Ben never contested the divorce. That was probably what hurt more than anything else. He never pursued her.

Jo figured it was because she wasn't worth fighting for.

Memories only highlighted that Jo wasn't the kind of woman a man stuck around for. She'd never fall into that trap again, even though Benjamin's accent still caused her heart to flutter.

She closed the book and let the tears come. She shoved the memories to the back of her closet and reclined on the bed. Her lonely bed. *Buck up, Buttercup. It's better this way.* Why did she struggle to believe that?

8

FOR SOME, THERE'S THERAPY. FOR THE REST OF US, THERE'S CHOCOLATE.

ANONYMOUS

Benjamin was more than happy to pick up his friend and take him to his medical check-up. Self-employment gave him some flexibility.

Geoff drew near at a slow pace.

"What'd the doctor say?" Ben asked.

"I'm healing well, but it will be some time before I'm back on the job. I'll be able to drive as soon as I can stop taking the pain meds. He told me I'll still get tired easily, and to rest and heal."

"Hard to do for a guy as active as you."

"Yeah, but thanks to Jo, I'm still alive, so I'll take this over the alternative." Geoff grinned.

November was around the corner, but the air already held a briskness to it that chilled him. Ben pulled his coat tighter.

Ben drove them to lunch. It was good to be out of the house.

"Jo said she'd bring my groceries by this afternoon. Humbling to ask someone else to do that for me," Geoff tossed out as they sat down with their food.

"Yeah, I expect so."

"You've been kind of quiet today. Everything OK, Ben?"

Ben shrugged. "I have a favor to ask, but it's not a comfortable one."

"Well, ask already."

"It's about Jo."

Geoff's eyes widened. "Yeah…?"

"Things ended badly between us. I tried writing, but the letters were returned unopened. I'm a different person now, and all I want to do is apologize. I screwed up—in a big way. I don't want her to go through the rest of her life hating me, and I don't want my presence at church to be a stumbling block to her coming to faith."

Geoff blinked. "What do you want?"

Ben slid an envelope across the table. "Can you give this to her and ask that she read it?"

"Do you want her back?" Geoff asked.

Ben shook his head. "I'd never stand a chance after what I did. God forgives me, and perhaps Jo will too, but that doesn't mean she'd ever want anything to do with me again."

"That's sad."

"It's the truth." Ben bit into his sandwich, and Geoff took a bite of his own.

"I'll give it to her." Geoff sipped his soda. "I'll not pressure either of you for details, but you do realize God is in the business of miracles, right?"

"Yes. I'm aware."

"Maybe you need to tell Him what you desire

most, and let Him do the rest."

Ben frowned and avoided Geoff's gaze. "What if what I want isn't what I deserve?"

"That's why it's called grace," Geoff said.

They ate the rest of the meal in silence before Ben dropped Geoff off at home.

~*~

Jo schlepped the groceries into the apartment in two trips, given her ability to only use one arm.

"I could help," Geoff pleaded.

"Nope. Let me do this for you. I need something to keep me busy." She placed a bag on the kitchen table.

"Going crazy being off work?" Geoff pulled out a chair and sat down.

"Yeah, and I can't run or exercise with this shoulder. It's frustrating," Jo grumbled.

"How's your pain?"

"I'm off the heavy-duty meds and only on an over-the-counter anti-inflammatory." She shrugged with her good shoulder. "It works fairly well."

"So, other than picking up my groceries, what else have you been up to?"

"Watching television and catching up on all the great crime shows."

"I should watch some of those too." Geoff finished putting the last can in the cupboard.

"Sometimes I think it makes it worse."

"Still having nightmares?"

"Yeah, but I visit a therapist tomorrow, so I'm

hoping that helps."

"Good." Geoff walked to the table and slid an envelope over to her. "This is for you."

Jo picked it up and tapped it against her other hand. "From you?"

Geoff shook his head. "I'm only the messenger, but could you do me a favor?"

What was her partner up to? "What's the favor?"

"Read it. I don't need to know what it says, but please just promise me you'll read it."

"Do I need to pinky swear?"

Geoff shook his head. "Nope. You're a woman who keeps her word, so I trust you."

"OK."

"And another thing…"

"You're greedy for favors this afternoon."

Geoff winked. "Come with me to church again on Sunday."

"Do you need a ride?"

"Probably be good, if you don't mind."

"You're on my way, so sure. Be glad to. I stopped by Monday and talked to Pastor Dan."

"You did? Oh, yeah, I promised you a Bible."

"Thanks, but he gave me one. I've been reading it."

"And…?"

"I've got a lot to think about."

Silence hung between them for a few moments.

Geoff broke it. "Thanks again for bringing me my groceries. Next week, I should be able to manage on my own."

"Glad to help a friend. Have a good night."

"Remember to read that letter."

"I promise." She saluted him with it and left.

Jo went home and shrugged off her coat. She settled into her chair and looked at the envelope. Her name, typewritten on the front, gave her no indication of its author.

Only one way to find out.

She broke the seal and pulled out the typewritten letter.

Dearest Jo,

Since every letter I sent you prior to this was returned unopened, I'm praying you'll read this one.

She glanced to the bottom to see Benjamin's name scrawled there. Letters? He'd sent her letters? It was possible, but she had no memory of them. She looked back at the page. She'd promised Geoff she'd read it. It surprised her that Benjamin would ask for Geoff's help.

There are no excuses for what happened that night, and I won't make any. I was an idiot, but I would like to explain and apologize. This Friday night is the anniversary of when I proposed to you. I've sworn off alcohol since you left. I hope you're willing to let me explain what happened, apologize, and plead for your forgiveness face to face. Please. If you'll meet me at the café near our old apartment at 6:00 PM. My treat. It's not a date, just a way to honor what we had so that you can understand that the failure in our marriage was all mine. I want you to be happy, Jo.

My parents send their love. They knew I was to blame. If you ever want to contact them, they would love to hear from you.

Benjamin Elliot

Jo read the letter again. He was offering her closure and to tell her the truth of what happened. He didn't blame her? She was the one who'd walked out. She'd never given him a chance to explain. She picked up the phone to call her mother.

"Mom."

"Hi, darling. How are you healing?"

"I'm doing fine. Just bored not being able to work. I wanted to ask you a question about something that happened after I left Benjamin and moved to Tomah."

"Sure, honey."

"Did Benjamin ever mail me any letters?"

Silence hung on the line.

"Mom?"

"There were a few, but your father believed it was best to return them. You were so devastated by what he'd done. You were training to be a state patrol officer. We didn't want you distracted."

"But they were for me, and it should have been my choice whether to read them or not."

"We were only trying to protect you."

"I understand, but I'm an adult and I need to deal with life on my own terms. I'm not a child to be cosseted."

"As if we ever did that."

"No, you didn't. At least, not until the divorce."

"Well, we liked Ben just fine, but you got married too fast and too young. We never expected it to last, but we didn't say anything then."

"Good. I wouldn't have listened. I loved him."

"Maybe you still do, dear."

Her parents had been furious with Benjamin when she'd left. Why would Mom even suggest this? "Stop talking nonsense." Jo needed to change the subject. "How's Dad doing?"

The conversation turned to more mundane aspects of her parents' life.

After Jo hung up, she re-read the letter from Benjamin. It looked as if she had some apologies to make as well.

~*~

Jo walked into the waiting room of the therapist and found an empty seat. She closed her eyes, leaned her head back against the wall and tried to minimize the throbbing ache in her shoulder by slowing her breathing. She'd never done anything like this before. She'd always considered herself strong enough to not need help.

"Jo?" a woman's voice called her name.

Jo opened her eyes, rose, and followed the woman to a cozy office decorated in peach and teal. She settled into a floral-covered sofa, and reached for a pillow to prop her arm. *Ahhh*. It was as if her soul sighed in relief to be here.

"I'm Shirley. Why don't we start with you telling me what brought you here today?"

"I'm a state patrol officer involved in a recent shooting. I've been having nightmares and can't seem to move past it."

"Is that the only reason you're here?"

Jo frowned. "Sure. Why?"

"How about I ask a few questions to get to know you better?"

"OK."

After Shirley asked questions, jotting down notes on her paper, she looked at Jo. "Thank you for answering those difficult questions. It will help me as we continue forward. Our time is up today, but here's what I see: you have a hard time forgiving yourself for any failure, imagined or real. You tend to look at the negative and find yourself lacking. That is also what's making it hard for you to understand and accept the grace of God. I want to meet with you again, so we can explore this further. Before you leave, would it be OK if I pray for you?"

"I suppose that would be fine."

"Dear God, Jo is seeking Your peace and healing, and only You can truly speak to her heart the truth of how deeply You love her just as she is—imperfect and flawed—but beautifully designed by You, her Creator. Draw her to Yourself and give her the peace she seeks, so she can face the challenges in her life with Your grace."

Was she supposed to say amen? Jo looked up at the woman. Shirley's sweet words wrapped around her like a soft fleece blanket. "Thank you."

"I'll see you soon, Jo."

9

FAITH IS TAKING THE FIRST STEP EVEN WHEN YOU DON'T SEE THE WHOLE STAIRCASE.

MARTIN LUTHER KING, JR.

Benjamin swallowed hard as he entered the cafe where he and Jo used to enjoy occasional meals together in between classes. Had Geoff given the letter to Jo? Had she read it? Would she come? It was a crapshoot, given she'd returned all his previous letters. Had he been a coward not to have added his number to call him to confirm that she was coming?

When he first fell for her, he'd given her his number instead of asking for hers. He wanted it to be her choice. To not feel pressured. The pursuit of her had been both slow and way too fast, from the time he first saw her to when they'd wed. He sat at a small table where he had a view of the door and ordered a soda. Enough years had passed that he recognized no one in the place from his past. It was nice to be anonymous in case she didn't show.

He watched the people reading, studying, chatting, and eating.

He recalled falling for Jo. She'd fascinated him with her strength and her dignity as she served some of the rudest people at the bar where she worked and they'd first met. She'd had confidence that showed in the fact she didn't need to dress provocatively or flirt with customers to get better tips.

He even admired that she worked on the road crew part of the year to help pay for college and rent. She'd carried more than her fair share of the burden financially when they'd first married as he tried to get his business up and running while going to school. He was grateful that she'd not been there to witness it when everything fell apart. She'd always thought he was brilliant. She believed in his skill and his dreams more than anyone else had. She'd sacrificed herself for him in so many ways.

And how had he repaid her?

He betrayed her, shut her out, and let her go.

She never asked for any compensation. Not that he had it to give. He'd been on the verge of going to prison for a crime he didn't commit. As painful as it was to watch her leave, he never had to experience her pity or disappointment in him.

Instead, he'd failed her as a man. He'd fooled himself for a long while, thinking he had never gone as far as Jo thought he had. Now, it didn't matter how far he'd gone. Allowing another woman to touch him in any way—and he had acted very inappropriate that night—had been a betrayal of his marriage vows. He had cheated on his wife. And the business? The divorce had spared her from suffering the incessant worry, and it would have saved her from the fallout should he have been convicted.

A lot had changed in the past few years. While he longed for Jo's forgiveness, there was possibly another way to make restitution for all he'd taken from her. He wasn't rich, but he was doing well financially. And while money didn't cover his sins, perhaps it would help her. But how? He'd have to talk to Will about how to do that secretly. It would be meaningless if he did it to draw attention to himself.

~*~

"You are a coward," Jo said out loud. She paced her apartment and glanced at the clock.

5:30 PM.

She could depart now and make it downtown in plenty of time to meet Benjamin. But should she? He still set her heart aflutter with just a look. *Danger,* her heart told her. After the right words, she'd be falling back into his arms for one of his delicious kisses.

Stop it! Just stop it. After what he did, you'd never want him in your life again.

5:45 PM.

She could still make it but would be a little late. Jo dropped into her chair, jarring her shoulder. Ouch. Maybe that was a sign. Going would only hurt her in the long run.

There had been no mention of what he really wanted to tell her. She was curious, but… *No. You've moved beyond him.* There was no need to reopen old wounds by meeting with him. She closed her eyes. *God? Are you there? What am I supposed to do?*

Silence.

6:00 PM.

How long would he wait there for her? Was it wrong to leave him hanging like that? She didn't have his phone number, and she wasn't about to ask Geoff for it. She could still get there. She rose and paced again, picking up his letter and re-reading it.

I really should find out what he wants. Does it matter? It's over and we've both moved on. It was years ago.

6:15 PM.

She grabbed her coat and inserted her good arm and let the other side rest on her shoulder. Picking up her purse and keys, she reached for the door. *No. Go to the bathroom first.* She set her purse and keys down and shrugged off the coat. As she washed her hands in the bathroom, she stared at herself in the mirror. Dark circles under her eyes. She hadn't even applied makeup, but then she didn't usually wear any on the job because she wasn't there to look pretty. But she couldn't go and connect with Benjamin looking like this. Her shirt was older. She really should change first. She went to the bedroom to rifle through her closet. She didn't have a lot of nice clothing since she wore uniforms to work.

6:30 PM.

She picked up the clothes she'd dumped on the bed and hung them back up in the closet.

She returned to the living room and sat. Obviously, she was too conflicted to go. Part of her felt bad for leaving Benjamin hanging like that, but the other part believed he deserved it. He'd left her hanging years ago. No explanation would get her to forgive his cheating on her. She wondered how long it had gone on, and if there'd only been one woman. She probably didn't want that information.

Jo turned on the television and found a movie to watch to try to erase Benjamin Elliot from her thoughts and to lock Jo Elliot back into the closet she'd tumbled from. She'd given up Benjamin's last name when the divorce was final. Skeletons should stay put.

~*~

The music was soft and jazzy. The soft hum of conversations pricked at this loneliness. His hand on the table sensed the vibration. Energy in him that wouldn't be dulled by sugary soda screamed for solace. His nerves were stretched thin as he waited, and finally he gave in and checked his phone for the time: 7:15 PM. It was probably safe to say she wasn't coming. He rose and went to give a tip to the waitress and thank her. He took one more look around the café before leaving. What had he expected? That she'd suddenly find him worthy of trust? He'd burned that bridge long ago.

Head down, he walked out to the street to find his car. He drove home in silence and went into his dark apartment, entered the kitchen, and proceeded to make chocolate truffles. For whom? It didn't matter. He just needed to be doing something to ease the ache deep inside.

10

You can't know; you can only believe—or not.

C.S. Lewis

November 2014

Benjamin debated whether to attend church. The temptation to stay home and work on one of his contract jobs was strong. If Jo showed up again, could he act normally? He could always go to second service, but Jessica already tried to call him several times a day, dropping broad hints about another date. It smacked of desperation. He felt as if he were being hunted. Jessica attended second service, and he didn't want to bump into her.

He could always attend a different church. There were many in the area.

But Orchard Hill had become family.

He shook his head in frustration, grabbed his keys and Bible, and headed out. *Lord, whatever happens this morning, please help me.*

He walked into church and greeted a few people before finding his seat. Was Jo perhaps in love with Geoff? The thought shook him, and he swallowed the jealousy that rose as the music started for worship.

Stop. Focus on God. Leave Jo in His hands. Easier said than done.

Will joined him.

Ben leaned toward Will to speak to him. "I have a question for you after the service."

"You've intrigued me," Will said. The countdown video had begun on the screen. "You're keeping me in suspense?"

"Just wondering how I could pay a debt I owe without the person knowing it was me."

"What kind of debt are we talking about here?" Will asked.

"Student loan."

"Ah, from when you were married, right? Do you have the account number?"

Ben shook his head. "I know her social security number."

"Since that's the case, and the debts were acquired during your marriage, your name should be on them as well. Ultimately, if she fails to pay, you'd be responsible. I bet you can find out the information from the company. Those account numbers are often social security numbers. If you remember her password, you'd be set."

"I probably know it."

"Then it shouldn't be a problem."

"Can you keep this confidential?"

Will shrugged. "Sure. Why?"

"Because she's started coming to church here. And a mutual friend has been trying to figure out our relationship."

"Gotcha. Mum's the word."

"Silly word."

Will grinned as the worship team called them to join in singing.

~*~

After the service, Benjamin sipped his usual cup of coffee. He spied Geoff and Jo off to one side and opted to stay away from them today. He was surprised when someone grabbed his arm, almost spilling his drink.

"I came early so I could see you before second service," Jessica purred.

Ben shook her loose. "You almost spilled my coffee," he complained.

"Sorry. I was excited to see you. Want to sit through this service with me?"

"No. I have plans."

She pouted. She was an attractive woman, but she'd become clingy fast. As if one date promised a wedding ring. "Aw, come on, Benny."

He cringed. He'd always hated it when anybody other than his sister called him that, and few ever did. "You're a nice girl, Jessica—"

She pulled away from him, eyes wide.

He strode away, emptied his coffee, and tossed the Styrofoam cup in the garbage.

He spied Roberto near the coatroom with his little boy, Levi, in his arms. "Robbie."

The attorney grinned. "Benjamin. Good to see you."

"How's the little man?" Ben reached for Levi, who eagerly came into his arms.

"Hi, Ben!" the little boy exclaimed, giving him a big hug. His blue eyes were stunning with his dark hair. He looked just like his father.

"As you can tell, he's doing just fine. Filled with vim and vinegar, as my mother would say."

"Where's Stephanie?"

"Ah, little Lexi had a fever this morning, so Steph stayed home. Figured I'd take this little man with me, so she might get some rest."

"You're a great dad." Ben proceeded to tickle the little boy, who giggled and wiggled.

"How's the business going?"

"Thanks to you, Will, and of course, God, things are going well. I'm experiencing a healthy balance in life right now."

"You worked hard to get there."

"Hey, would your wife like some truffles?"

"Who wouldn't? Your hobby is helping?"

"Yeah. I'll drop some off at the house some night this week."

"Just not Wednesday night."

"Still attending your accountability group?"

"Yeah, even though I don't have much issue with pain anymore, I think once you have an addiction similar to narcotics, there's always something inside that requires monitoring. I know your drug of choice was alcohol, but if you'd like to join us sometime, we'd be glad to wrap you into the group."

"I'll seriously consider that. I've been thinking I

might need some accountability."

"And encouragement and prayer...we do more than hold each other's feet to the fire."

"E-mail me where you're meeting, and I'll come this week."

Levi reached for his father.

"I'll do that." Roberto grabbed his son.

"I can bring the chocolate for her then."

"Sounds good. You'll have the information today. I've already mentioned you to the guys, so the invitation is from all of us."

"Thanks." Ben followed Roberto into the coatroom to grab his own jacket.

Roberto wrestled his little boy into his coat.

Ben had always longed to be a father someday. That hope had died when his marriage crashed and burned. "Have a great afternoon. I'll pray for Lexi and Steph."

"I appreciate it, Ben." Roberto hefted his little boy in his arms and headed out into the cold, windy November morning. Ben exited a different door and made his way to his car. He sat down and buckled up. He'd avoided any uncomfortable interaction with Jo. He frowned while recalling Jessica. Might need to start skipping Thursday night's studies. Maybe Roberto's group would be just the thing to keep him moving forward in his faith. It wasn't as if he was shopping for a girlfriend. Although he did admit there was something special about women, he'd closed the doors on a relationship years ago. Dating had only been a way to fend off loneliness.

He drove home, thinking about how nice it would be to hold his own child in his arms. Parenting was hard work, but he saw the love between Robbie and Levi, and Ben's heart grieved that it was something he'd likely never know.

Shake it off, man. You're right where I want you at this point in time. Stop worrying about the future.

Sometimes a guy just needed God to slap him upside the head and remind him just Who was really in control.

~*~

Jo sat next to Geoff, mesmerized, through Pastor Andrew's message. Jesus had become an intriguing person for her to grapple with. When the worship band came back to the stage to sing a song they'd sung earlier, she hung her head and prayed. *God, I don't understand. Help me.*

It was as if she walked toward God in a fog with a veil over her face. She could catch glimpses, but not the whole picture. Her heart yearned for clarity and her mind struggled, but at least He was there.

The lights came up in the auditorium-like sanctuary, and she opened her eyes.

Geoff sat in the chair next to her, silent.

She leaned back and sighed. People were mingling, angling for access to the aisle as they made their way to the cafe or to leave. She caressed the Bible in her lap before turning to her friend. "Ready for some coffee?"

He nodded, and they both rose and made their way out behind the crowd. She found a tall table. "Why don't you sit here, and I'll get it for you." She set down her Bible, and before he could say anything, she turned to get the coffee.

She was coming back when she spied Benjamin out of the corner of her eye with a gorgeous woman. Not really a surprise. He was a handsome, intelligent, and, from what she gathered, successful man. She swallowed the green-eyed monster that roared up inside her, wanting to shout and scream how unfair it was.

Arriving at the table, she smiled at Geoff. "Here you go." She sat in the chair across from him, which enabled her to still see Benjamin out of the corner of her eye. It looked as if his girlfriend wasn't too happy with him. She turned to focus instead on Geoff.

"Deep thoughts after the message?" he gently probed.

"Yeah."

"Care to share?"

"No. Just something I need to work out for myself."

"I'd like to be your friend."

"You are my friend, Geoff."

"Can I ask you something?"

"I think you just did." She smiled and sipped her coffee.

"Did you read the letter I gave you?"

"Yes. Tricky, huh? Benjamin using you as a middleman? You can say no to him."

"Did he hurt you?"

"With the letter? No. It's fine."

"Can I ask what it said?"

"A girl has to have some secrets, doesn't she?"

Geoff sighed. "So do some guys I know. Whatever happened between the two of you isn't over. I don't know the story. Ben's locked up tighter than a safe, except for when he looks at you or your name is mentioned. And you? Jo, you aren't over him as much as you'd like to pretend."

"Right now, the only man I'm seeking is Jesus. Give me the space to figure that out first. Benjamin is history. There is nothing between us."

"Oh, there's something between you. I can see that. You both seem to be locking the lid down on those memories and emotions. But they'll come back to haunt you."

She frowned. "Can we change the subject?"

"Fine. Did you go to that therapist?"

"Yes."

"How was that?"

"I go back again this week. I think it'll be good. I like her." She sipped her coffee.

"That's it?'

Jo nodded. "Again, wanting my secrets?"

"You said we were friends," Geoff protested.

"We are. So, let me ask you this. How are you sleeping since the accident?"

He shook his head. "You play dirty."

"Taking my cues from you, buddy." She gave him a half-grin and a wink.

Geoff laughed. "Fine. I'm having trouble sleeping. I need to call a therapist as well."

"Good to hear. I want my partner back in top-notch condition when the time comes."

"You'll probably be back before me."

"Maybe so, but there's no guarantee they'll put me on patrol right away. You know how long some of those investigations can take."

"This one wasn't a gray area, though. We both did our job as we were trained to and with both our dash cameras videotaping."

"I always thought it would be different. That I would be proud of doing my job, happy to have saved some lives, instead of plagued with guilt for killing a murderer."

"Life never turns out quite as we expect, does it?"

"Guess not." She took in her partner. "You're fading fast. Let's get you home so you can rest."

"Thanks for taking good care of me."

She turned and spied Benjamin again, but this time he was talking to a man while holding an adorable little boy. She used to hope she and Benjamin would have children when they'd finished college, a dream that died along with their marriage. Benjamin handed the little boy back to his parent before striding out of sight. She sighed. If she continued to attend church here, she'd need to get used to seeing him.

Maybe Geoff was right. Maybe she really wasn't over Benjamin, and the skeletons in her closet were trying their best to escape.

~*~

Ben strode into his house. Leaves had accumulated in the yard, so he threw on sweats and a jacket, grabbed a rake, and headed out to take care of the task. The sun shone through the leaves still left on the trees, and he enjoyed the quiet of the late morning. Either people were sleeping or out to church. No neighbors were to be seen. The quiet was broken only by the rustle of the leaves. The raking was good exercise. He typically didn't run on Sundays since he'd started attending church.

It was supposed to be a day of rest, but this relaxed him. Something about the fresh scent of fall and the crisp air and the colorful leaves all conspired to settle him.

Ben looked at his pile and smiled. He leaned his rake against the house and let himself fall backward into the leaves. Gazing up at the sky, he sighed. Rest. Recharge. Play? When did he ever really let himself do this? He sat up and picked leaves out of his hair and brushed them off his shoulders. The only thing that could have made this better would be having someone to share it with.

Jo.

Children.

A family.

He rose to his feet, and with the joy in the moment gone, he coaxed the leaves to the front curb for pickup. By the time he was done, he was ready for a shower.

After he cleaned up, he made a simple meal. He

packaged some truffles, then set them aside to take to Roberto when he saw him next.

When he'd started this hobby in earnest, he'd ordered some small white boxes, and some blue ribbon—correction: the color was sapphire, or so the description read—but he wanted something simple to wrap the treats in. Clean and classy. He set it aside, glad he could at least give a little joy to someone.

Ben missed that about being married, although he hadn't done as well as he might have if he hadn't been so anxious about losing everything and going to prison. He'd wanted his wife to be proud of him, and he had worked hard—only to throw it all away by drowning his fears in booze and the arms of an anonymous woman. He'd killed his marriage as well.

Let it go.

Grace, right? If God forgave him his sin, why couldn't he forgive himself?

Maybe because he owed Jo more than she'd gotten. He longed for her absolution, which he couldn't ever expect. She was collateral damage in his pursuit of wealth. He'd trusted the wrong partner.

She'd never liked Doug. And Ben had made another big mistake in not trusting his wife with the truth. Maybe, if he had, she'd have been his consolation and they'd still be married. Or she might have dumped him anyway. Hard to know unless he spoke with her. But how to do that?

Lord? I can't force myself on her. Please open her heart to listening to my words. Help her come to know You, and I pray I won't be a stumbling block to her faith. Geoff was right. I never stopped loving Jo.

How was he to recover from abandoning her? Sure, she was the one who'd walked out, but she had every right to do so. He'd lost her the day he trusted someone else to do the job he was supposed to do. From there it spiraled out of control. If she'd only let him explain, even if it would have resulted in a terrible fight between them, perhaps they might have salvaged their marriage.

Help me stop second-guessing the past and embrace today. Thank You for loving me when I don't deserve it.

Grace wrapped around him. The future was in God's hands, and God was the One person he trusted more than anyone.

11

GOD DOES NOT REQUIRE THAT WE BE SUCCESSFUL, ONLY THAT WE BE FAITHFUL.

MOTHER TERESA

Another visit to the therapist.

Shirley welcomed her into the comfortable office.

Jo found a comfy spot on the couch and pulled a pillow out to rest her arm on and partly hug. Why she needed that, she had no clue, but baring her heart in this venue produced anxiety in her.

"Anything new happen since our last meeting?"

"God is calling me, but I'm struggling to understand it all."

"There's a reason it's called faith. When we accept the gift of salvation and bow to the King of the universe, the Holy Spirit indwells us, leading, guiding, and praying for us when we can't find the words. He also provides comfort."

"Cool. I didn't know that."

"You don't need to understand everything before taking that step. I've been a Christ-follower for more than thirty years, and I'm still learning new things as I read the Bible, pray, study, and attend worship. I hope to never stop growing in my faith."

"Hmmm. So even after I take that step, I don't have to be perfect? I'll still be growing?"

"You'll never be perfect, before or after salvation, except in the eyes of our Savior, who washes away your sin and presents you to God as flawless and pure."

Jo shook her head. "Pure and flawless?"

"Hard to believe, right?"

"Yeah."

"So tell me more about yourself. You don't need to tell me anything that makes you uncomfortable, but the more you can open up, the more we can work on how to cope with this new life you're leading."

"New life?" Jo stared at Shirley.

"Yes, your life changed when you shot a bad guy. And your life changed when you took steps to seek God. So…new life." Shirley smiled. "Part of the new life, is to let go of things in the past we cannot change. So tell me as much or as little as you want me to know."

Something spoke within Jo. No, not something… Someone. The Voice urged her to open up about her past…the entire past, not just her nightmares over the shooting. She went into her marriage, and how that had turned out, and how she'd reacted a few days before when she'd seen her ex-husband again. "He sent me a letter, wanting to meet to explain what happened and ask my forgiveness. It was the anniversary of the night he proposed."

"Did you go?"

"I debated with myself for so long, the time got

away. I chickened out."

"Why?"

"My heart races when I gaze into his eyes. I think that despite everything, I still love him." She wiped away a tear.

"Why does that make you cry?"

Jo shrugged. "If I had been a good enough wife, he wouldn't have cheated."

"Let me ask you this—are you the same person you were three years ago when you walked away from that marriage?"

"No! I think I'm more confident. I have a career now. I can stand on my own. Back then, I didn't know if I could. I went from sharing a dorm room to being married. Leaving Benjamin was the first time I was ever really alone. I was forced to prove to myself that I could survive."

"That's good. But I want you to consider this. You were married for three years and then divorced for the same amount of time. Your leaving might have also forced Ben to grow in ways you're not aware of. You're afraid of falling in love again with the same man you met in college, but you've both experienced different things in the past three years. He probably didn't remain stuck there in that cafe waiting for you. He needed to forge his own path without you. It's possible that you both grew up in ways you might not have been able to accomplish together."

"So, the divorce was a good thing?"

"The breakup of a marriage is always ugly. It's a crushing of a promise, a covenant, and in almost any situation I've counseled, it leaves wounds. That's true of many hardships people face—death of a child, cancer, abuse…they all change the person experiencing them in a variety of ways. Part of that is how we react to them."

"React?"

"Let me try to explain this in a way you can relate to better. When you drive your patrol car, you cruise along, but then something happens. A car whizzes past you. You have a choice to make in how you respond. Do you chase it and pull it over, or do you let it go?"

"Chase it."

"But chasing a speeding car comes with risks, doesn't it? You might have to weave in and out of traffic without endangering anyone else, while maintaining control of your vehicle and radioing for help, and if you manage to get the car pulled over, you don't know what you'll find when you walk up to that door. Will the person be apologetic, or will they be violent? And regardless of whether you give a ticket or need to arrest someone, you will still have a report to write."

"Yeah, but if I don't act, I'm not doing my job, and I have to face the guilt if that person were to hurt someone else or themselves."

"True. But the biggest personal risk is doing the right thing. And in the case of the shooting you were involved in, the right thing got you and a friend shot."

"And someone's son was killed."

"A person who had already murdered several others, carried drugs on him, and shot at two law-enforcement officials. How many more people might have died if you had not had the courage to give chase and see it through until it was done?"

"We'll never know."

"Right, because you brought it to an end. Those very hard choices have had a profound impact on your life. They have changed you."

"So…Benjamin might be a different person too. I am angry at the person he was three years ago, but he might not be that person anymore."

"Right. Holding on to your anger and resentment, while justified because he wounded you, only hurts you and prevents you from growing."

"But how do I get rid of it?"

"Pray."

"How?"

Shirley smiled. "Ask God to do good things for Benjamin. To bless him and give him peace and love in his life. That his business would prosper."

"Pray? Good things? After what he did?"

"You're praying for the man he is now, not the man he was when you knew him then, remember?"

"But I don't need to meet with him or forgive him."

Shirley sighed. "The longer you hold on to the anger, the more miserable you will be. Listening to his explanation might not be a bad thing. If you don't feel safe doing it alone, bring a friend you trust, or bring him here."

"But I'm not sure I want to have a relationship with him."

"Forgiveness is not reconciliation. Forgiving means you let him off the hook. You don't seek to punish him. You leave justice to God. Perhaps you'll even see him as a broken person in need of grace. It doesn't mean you must be friends. Given the hurt you sustained, he'd have to earn your trust and love, and that could take time, and only if he also wants that. It might be that he needs to forgive you as well."

Jo's mouth dropped open. "What? Why would I need forgiveness?"

"You said if you had been a better wife… I'm not saying that's true, but quite often when a marriage falls apart there is rarely one person who is perfect and never did anything wrong."

"Well, sure. I wasn't perfect, but I didn't destroy our marriage."

"Sometimes we do things without even realizing it."

Jo's heart raced. "You're blaming me for the breakup of my marriage?"

"No, but I think at some level you blame yourself."

The fight drained out of Jo like a balloon with a leak. Deflated, she sat there for a few moments while Shirley waited. "Pray good things for him? That's all I need to do?" She squeezed the pillow tighter.

"And consider meeting with him to clear the air."

"And then I'll be free of this."

"It might be better than that, Jo. You might find that part of your past heals, allowing you to move into your future. It might even help you grow some more into the woman God has called you to be."

Jo swallowed hard.

"Let me pray for you..." Shirley spoke to God softly, while Jo bowed her head, not registering any of the words, as her mind swam with all she'd learned. Her thoughts resembled a traffic jam, with horns honking and no one going anywhere. Stuck. Only she had the power to break the jam and move forward.

It all started with praying for Benjamin. *Whew. I don't know about this, God. You'll have to help me.*

12

WHEN ALL IS SAID AND DONE, THE LIFE OF FAITH IS NOTHING IF NOT AN UNENDING STRUGGLE OF THE SPIRIT WITH EVERY AVAILABLE WEAPON AGAINST THE FLESH.

DIETRICH BONHOEFFER

Ben left the meeting with this new-to-him group. He'd shared his lowest moment and the group had prayed for him. Initially he had worried about joining the group because he hadn't considered himself an alcoholic. It wasn't so much the particular drug but the pull to reach for the mind-numbing aspect of any chemical that made him a perfect fit.

He'd resisted temptation for three years, but he had to admit there had been times when it hadn't felt worth it. He'd flash back to the look on Jo's face when he'd realized she was there, witnessing him at his weakest, and that kept him from taking that first sip. He never wanted to lose control like that again. The consequences were too severe.

His phone beeped.

Call me.

It was his sister, Amalia. He had just walked into the house, so he dialed and waited for her to pick up.

"Benny?"

"Molly, what's up? I haven't heard from you in ages."

"Something's up with you. I can tell."

"You didn't talk to Mum and Dad?" Ben settled into his favorite chair and kicked off his shoes.

"No. I probably should give them a call, though."

"Where are you?"

"I'm in New York right now, but I fly out in the morning for China with a group of parents."

"I keep expecting to hear you've managed to smuggle one of those little ones out of the country for yourself."

"Tempting. Doesn't matter if I go to China, Romania, or even Africa or Haiti…there are so many who need a home. God hasn't called me to adopt yet, only to facilitate the process for others."

"I'm proud of you, sis."

"So, what's up?"

"Why does something need to be up?"

"It's that twin thing. You called me when things went south with Edmund. You knew before anyone else that my heart was broken."

Ben sighed. "I ran into Jo last week."

"How is she?"

"She's a state patrol officer and was injured in a shooting. She looks better than ever in spite of that."

"You never did explain the truth to her, did you?"

"No opportunity. I made a shamble of things, and she was gutted. Not much I could do about it. I tried to meet with her, but she stood me up. I can't say I blame her."

"Rubbish! She should have trusted you."

"Thanks for the vote of confidence."

"How's the church thing going?"

"Well. Mum and Dad weren't too pleased to find out I was still attending. They thought it was a temporary phase I was going through."

"It also means both of us are on the same page with our faith."

"Only appropriate. Hey, wanna join me for Thanksgiving?"

"Love to. I'll be back in time, and I don't have a trip for that week."

"Great! I have plenty of room and would love to be able to spend time with you. It's been too long." All he needed to do was make the bed.

"Yeah, I agree. Even though I'll be out of the country for the next few days, don't hesitate to message me. I'll be praying for Jo."

"Thanks, Molly. I appreciate it."

"Hey, big sisters need to look out for their little brothers."

"Stop it. Three minutes doesn't make you old enough to be trying to take care of me."

"So you say. Love you, Benny."

"Love you too, Moll."

He hung up and sighed. Family could be complicated, but he was grateful for them anyway. He headed off to bed. Tomorrow was another day, and there was plenty to be done. He'd need his rest.

13

IF YOU AREN'T WILLING TO FORGIVE SOMEONE, THEN YOU DON'T TRULY LOVE THEM.

ANONYMOUS

Jo woke in a sweat. Nightmares since the shooting were not unusual, but this time it wasn't Geoffrey who was shot. It was her ex-husband.

She sat, gasping for air, as the sight of Benjamin crumpling to the ground replayed over and over in her imagination. Why? It was Geoff who had gotten shot while on duty. Who'd shoot a computer tech? She hadn't thought of her ex for some time before he showed up at church. She wished she could erase him from her thoughts completely, but she'd be lying. Since seeing him two weeks ago, she'd thought of him often. Watching him with that other woman this past week had ignited old angers and fears.

Benjamin was single. He had no reason to avoid the attentions of a beautiful woman now, and she had no reason to be angry or jealous. She wasn't his wife.

Had he been upset to see her with Geoff? There'd been no indication of jealousy, only appreciation and interest. It was no wonder that he never approached them on Sunday after she stood him up the night before.

That didn't explain why he was in her nightmare. The shooting and seeing him again occurred within days but were unrelated. Geoff was the only link.

~*~

Jo met Geoff for lunch at Culver's, her favorite burger joint.

"You can finally drive, huh?"

"Yup, the doctor cleared me this morning. Feels good to be in control, and able to do something for myself again. Not that I don't appreciate you or Ben and others giving me a lift and helping with stuff." Geoff dipped his french fry in a little container of ketchup.

"I understand. I still can't lift a laundry basket."

"Going stir-crazy at home?"

"It's not like this was a planned vacation with fun things to do."

"Haven't made a trip to visit your parents?"

Jo shook her head. "I should, but Thanksgiving is around the corner and it doesn't look as though I'll be ready to ride a patrol by then. Perhaps I'll go up then."

"How are you liking Orchard Hill?"

"I like it. I'm reading the Bible Pastor Dan gave me, and my therapist challenged me to pray."

"Interesting."

"I have a favor to ask of you, but you can say no."

"I'd do almost anything for you, Jo. You know that."

"I do." She took a deep breath. "The letter you gave me from Benjamin was an invitation to meet at a specific time and clear the air between us. I didn't go for a variety of reasons, but I think it's something I need to do."

"OK…what do you want from me?"

"Can you be there with me when I do see him?"

His eyebrows rose. "Why? Do you see Ben as a danger to you? He's not."

"You can't know that. Oh, I realize he wouldn't physically hurt me, but emotionally, having the support of a friend would be nice."

"I'm not sure about this. Anyone else you can ask?"

"Why?"

"Ben's a friend. I don't want to be seen taking sides."

"My therapist said I could bring him in there."

"So why not do that?"

"This isn't couples' therapy. He wants to explain something from the past. I'm not sure I could handle hearing it on my own."

"I'll come if Ben's OK with it. What is it you want me to do?"

"Just be there. You don't need to say anything."

"A silent observer?"

"Something like that."

"Only with Ben's approval. I get the impression that what he may want to discuss with you is something I'm unaware of about either of you, and as curious as I am about your past relationship, I don't want to get in the middle of anything you both need to work out."

"I don't have Benjamin's phone number. He didn't give it in the letter. I have no way to contact him. Can you give it to me?"

"I can't give you his personal number, but I can give you his work one." Geoff dug in his pocket and pulled out a business card. It was a blue card with white print with Ben's business name, e-mail, web page, and phone number.

Jo picked up the card. "Thank you."

Geoff nodded. "Let me know when you've set something up. I'll call Ben to make sure he's OK with me coming."

"Thanks."

~*~

The buzz of Ben's mobile phone startled him from working out a coding problem. He checked the caller ID.

"Geoff? Hey, buddy. Need anything?"

"Possibly your forgiveness. I don't like being the middleman for you and Jo."

"Why do you need absolution?" Ben asked.

"I met Jo for lunch today. She told me you wanted to meet with her, and asked for your phone number. I gave her your business card."

"Great."

"Maybe not. She wants me to be there when you get together."

"Protection detail? I would never do anything to intentionally hurt her," Ben said.

"Have you hurt her—in the past?"

"Not in the way you think, but yes. I guess you'll hear all my dirty secrets when we meet."

"You're really OK with this?"

"Yeah. I might bring someone along to verify some of what I need to share with her."

"Who?"

"Will."

"OK, but what does he know that I don't?"

"Will helped me out when life fell apart. He was the one who invited me to church. He knows who I was before and who I am now."

"So he knows the down-and-dirty secrets?"

"Yeah. He does. And he knows the truth of things that I need to explain to Jo."

"Why now?"

"I want to ask her forgiveness for the past. I want her free to move on in her life."

"Why would you be the one to free her? It seems you are both intentionally keeping me in the dark about something."

"Nothing that I can think of. Anyway, when Jo contacts me to set up a time, I'm OK with you being there. I appreciate that you don't want to be a middleman, and I never intended to use you that way, except to get that letter to her, since I didn't have her address and didn't want to violate her privacy."

"We're cool, Ben. I admit that I'm nervous about this."

"I am, too. And if it's any consolation, now I'll be confessing my sin to two people I care about—not just one."

"I'll not hold your past against you. It was before you came to Christ."

"Thanks. I appreciate the grace. Something I still struggle to give to myself."

"I do have a suggestion, though."

"What?"

"Bring some of your truffles for Jo. Might sweeten her up."

"I'll consider it."

14

FAITH CONSISTS IN BELIEVING WHAT REASON CANNOT.

VOLTAIRE

Benjamin strode into the church cafe with Will by his side. Jo had called him, and as Geoff had indicated, she'd asked if their friend could join him. She'd had no room to complain when he asked if Will could also join them.

"Why am I here again?" Will asked.

"In case she doesn't believe me about what went down."

"Your word on it should be enough. You're not in court here."

"True. I just want to make sure she understands. Maybe she'll have an easier time forgiving me." They found a table with four chairs—two on each side. Ben pulled a chair out and sat down, with Will next to him.

Geoff and Jo walked in, and after greetings were exchanged, they joined Ben and Will across the table.

"Thanks for coming, Jo. And you too, Geoff and Will."

"Can I suggest praying before we start?" Will asked.

Everyone bowed their heads. "Lord, You understand the truth of our past, our present, and our future. You are a God of grace and forgiveness, and I ask for Your presence here. Thank You for Your faithful love."

"Thanks, Will." Ben took a deep breath and let it out. "Jo, I screwed up big-time three years ago, and my mistakes lost me the best thing I'd ever had in my life, other than God. I didn't know Him then, and I needed to learn some hard lessons." He paused and swallowed hard.

"Before you found me that final night, we'd had about six months of distance between us. You were working a lot and finishing your associate degree, and I was going to school and putting in hours on my business.

"I trusted the wrong person to work with. Doug seemed great at first, but you expressed concerns and I was wrong not to have listened to you. The final night of our marriage was when I hit bottom. Doug had embezzled from a company who'd contracted with us, but the blame turned to me. I'd just discovered I was about to be arrested. Will is a forensic accountant who uncovered the truth of what happened."

Jo narrowed her eyes.

"That night, my world was crashing around me, and you were supposed to be working. I didn't know how to tell you I was a failure and had failed you. I went to the bar and started to drink. I was lost in my misery, and that woman you saw me with was someone I'd never met before. I don't even know her name. She started coming on to me, and my judgment was gone. There was no way you'd stay with a failure like me. That was the only time I'd ever even looked at another woman, and it was only in that bar, at that time. She didn't come home with me, nor did I go with her. And that was the last time I ever drank.

"When I looked up and saw you there, and the pain in your eyes, I realized it was over and there was no redemption for me, even if the courts decided I wasn't guilty. I didn't contest the divorce because I didn't want the stench of my defeat to damage you."

A tear made its way down Jo's cheek.

Shame from the past washed over Ben. His face grew warm and a shiver of fear rippled through him.

"Wait. What? You two were married? Like husband and wife?" Geoff asked.

Ben nodded and turned his focus back to Jo.

"Your leaving me only confirmed what I knew all along. I was never worthy of a woman like you. I'm sorry I failed you. I regret taking that first drink, and I haven't had a drink since then. My life has turned around, but this is the one dark shadow I can't shake.

"I can't go back and erase the past, Jo, but I wanted you to understand that I loved you. That I still love you and always want the best for you. I understood when you left that the best thing I could do was let you go even though it tore my heart out. When I saw you again a few weeks ago, here in church, I could barely hold it together. If you can't find it in your heart to forgive me, I get it. But I wanted you to hear it from me, face to face, just how sorry I was for the hurt I caused you. The failure of our marriage was my fault and no one else's."

Will placed a hand on his shoulder. "I can attest to what he says. It was a messy situation, and it took months to clear Ben's name. He doesn't have a police record, and he started coming to church and turned his life around. I sat with him often as he berated himself for screwing up so badly as to lose you, Jo."

"Wow," Geoff whispered as he leaned back in his chair.

Will rose to grab a box of tissues to place between Ben and Jo.

Ben grabbed a tissue, wiped his face and blew his nose.

Jo bit her lips as she listened, and her eyes glistened with unshed tears. "I'm not sure what to say. It'll take me some time to process this, but I'm glad I know the bigger picture of what was going on that night."

Ben closed his eyes.

"It took courage to say what you did, Ben," Geoff offered.

"I'm not proud of my past, and I've had to start over from scratch without the encouragement and support of my wife. I deserve every lonely night. Every tear shed. Every contract I lost during that time. I'm so sorry, Jo."

"I have a lot to think about." She turned to Geoff. "I'd like to leave now, if that's OK with you."

Geoff frowned, rose, and helped Jo to her feet. He reached out a hand to Ben, who responded with a firm grip. “I’ll be praying.”

15

DO YOU WANT TO BE GOOD OR FEEL GOOD?
TRUTH BEFORE EGO.

T. BLAUER

Benjamin went home and prepared for bed. He opened the drawer in his nightstand and pulled out the one photo he still had of Jo. She'd taken everything else. This was their photo from London on their honeymoon. They'd both looked so happy. And they had been. Would he ever be that happy again? He shoved the photo back in the drawer, crawled under the covers, and rolled onto his side. Tonight, he'd ripped open a huge scab, and internally he was hemorrhaging. He didn't know how Jo was reacting to what he'd shared.

He wanted forgiveness—but it hadn't come.

He wanted to undo the pain he'd caused—but that was impossible.

He wanted more than anything for Jo to love him as he'd never stopped loving her. A hope that he once again needed to destroy, because he didn't know if he could survive losing her affections again.

He could move. His job could be done almost

anywhere. He sometimes traveled to Chicago, New York, and other places around the country. He could set up his home office in almost any location and work. Jo could move on with her life without him reminding her of all that pain, and maybe he'd find someone new to love.

That hadn't worked out too well in the past few years. Women wanted him for his looks, accent, or money.

Jo had wanted him for himself.

~*~

The next day Ben couldn't focus. He finally gave up and went for a run and to pray. He'd hoped for closure after baring his soul last night. He pounded the pavement as snowflakes started to fall. Early November could bring weather like this, and he hadn't checked the forecast before starting out. He slowed down and started home before the sidewalks grew too slippery. After a shower, he settled in front of his computer again and responded to e-mails.

One came from an address he didn't know.

Benjamin,

Thank you for having the courage to tell me the truth last night. It wasn't an easy thing to do. If I have any questions about what you've told me or want to talk further about it, are you open to me writing, texting, or calling?

Jo

Ben quickly typed a response.

Dearest Jo,

I'm glad you found it helpful. Call, text, or write me anytime.

Ben

He sat back in his seat and wondered just what God was up to. Could God heal the wound Ben had left in Jo's heart? Had she really accepted his apology? Was this an opening to healing between them? He sure hoped so.

~*~

Jo heard the notification on her phone and picked it up. Benjamin had responded to her impulsive email and even given her his mobile phone number. He wasn't consigning her to his past. Jo still wasn't sure what she wanted as far as the future. "Dearest?" It'd been a long time since anyone called her that. She wasn't sure how she felt about it.

Could she forgive him? How could he have cared so little for her or their marriage to do all he did by not being honest and sharing his struggle?

She drove to the patrol office in Waukesha to meet with her boss, Captain Jenkins. Time to set thoughts of Ben and their past aside and focus on the here and now—work.

"Sergeant March, glad you could be here. Come in and sit down."

Jo sat as the door closed behind her. A sense of being called into the principal's office in school came over her, which was odd, since she'd never been in trouble before.

"The investigation into the shooting has been concluded, and both you and Sergeant Ross are cleared of any wrongdoing. You did everything according to your training, and are able to return to duty when you're medically cleared."

"I'm going crazy at home."

"How about part-time desk duty as you continue to recover? Ross will be returning in a similar capacity. Might need one of you on dispatch, since others in the department have some vacation time coming with the holidays."

"That would be fine. Any particular shift?"

"To start, you'll be on the day shift, but as you do dispatch that might change. I'll look at putting together a schedule."

Jo sighed. "Thank you. It'll be nice to be back in any capacity."

Captain Jenkins grinned. "We've missed both of you around here. You're a good officer, and don't ever forget it. How are the nightmares?"

"How did you know about those?" Jo asked.

"I've been at this a long time. A nightmare or two are totally normal after that kind of trauma," Captain Jenkins said with a fatherly grin.

"Well, they are better, but weird. I've seen a therapist and expect a few more appointments with her."

"Good. You start next week part-time, but as Thanksgiving gets closer, you'll get more hours."

"Understood."

"Have you been to visit your parents yet?"

Jo shook her head. "No."

"You might want to do that. I can almost guarantee you'll be busy here during the holidays."

"I'll go tomorrow for a few hours."

"Say hello to your father for me."

"I will. Thank you, Captain."

Jo rose and left. Once at her apartment, she pulled out a suitcase and started packing. She stopped to call her mother to let her parents know she was coming for a visit. She sat on the bed next to her suitcase and sighed. She wasn't looking forward to this trip. She loved her parents but never felt as if she had their approval. They had reconciled themselves to her marriage to Benjamin but when that fell apart, she didn't have the heart to share with them all that really happened. And now she understood more of what had went on behind the scenes, but it didn't bring her the peace she would have hoped for.

As she put her clothes in the case with one hand her thoughts went to Benjamin and his revelations the other night. Sure, he had some excuses, but anger still welled up within her. She pulled up the email with his phone number on it. Did she dare call him? Was that the coward's way out? She sighed.

Just call him and get it out, just you and him and no one else.

She picked up the phone, collapsed in her one good chair and punched in the numbers.

"Hello?" he answered.

"Hi, Benjamin. It's Jo. Is this a good time to talk?"

"Yeah, this is fine." His voice was soft and

hesitant. Did he expect her to explode? She never had in their three years of marriage. She wasn't the arguing type. It was part of what made her good at her job. Calm under pressure.

"Good. Listen. I appreciate you sharing what you did the other night but the more I think about it the angrier I become." She stood and paced the small room. "How could you let yourself get into a situation where a stranger would come on to you? Why did you let her continue with that when you knew it was wrong? I don't believe your business was the problem in our marriage although you seem to believe it was. Your lack of communication seems to have been the real issue. How could I have known that you felt we'd grown apart if you hadn't told me? I was working two jobs while going to school for you to achieve your dreams, and you thought so little of my sacrifice that you went into the arms of a complete stranger?" Images of him with that woman flashed in her memory, taunting her. Tears streamed down her cheeks.

"Um, wow. In all the years I've known you, Jo, I don't know that I've ever heard such venom from you. Your questions are all valid. I screwed up big time in all areas of our life together. I was young, stupid, and I don't know why I made such idiotic mistakes. Youth. Arrogance. Pride? I was ashamed to admit what had happened. You being right about my partner was something I couldn't acknowledge. I was a royal fool. I was drinking a lot more than you realized to cope with all the stress I was experiencing. Self-medicating my

ADHD perhaps? That's no excuse.

"I deeply regret how much I hurt you and destroyed our marriage. While I'm grateful I was exonerated from the criminal charges, on that account I wasn't even guilty. Being a horrible husband. A cheater. A drunk. Failing to be honest and honor you as my wife—that's where I failed big time. I would completely understand if you can't forgive me. What I did was unforgivable."

"I hate you." She cried out into the phone. Tears streamed down her cheeks. She grabbed a tissue to wipe them away.

"I can understand that. I'm so terribly sorry." Ben's words were so soft she barely heard them for the blood rushing in her ears.

Silence hung between them as she paced, not sure what to say next.

"Jo, I really am sorry. If there was any way to make it up to you, I would do it. I can't erase the past. It happened and I am ashamed about it, but I've owned my sin and confessed it to Jesus. According to the Bible, my sins are forgiven. That doesn't erase the consequences or the pain it caused you. I don't know what else to say or do. I'm not the same person I was back then… but that's no excuse for what I did to you."

Jo continued to pace and sniff. "I need space to think about this some more. Thanks for listening."

"Anytime, Jo. I am so sorry although I know my apology doesn't take away your pain. I hope you'll learn that God is a loving and forgiving God and my prayer is that you will find Him as faithful and true in ways I never was. He's calling you to Himself, Jo, and I don't want our past, and the hurt I caused, to be a stumbling block for you in knowing Jesus."

"I have much to think about. I need to go." Jo hung up before Benjamin could respond. She went to the bathroom and looked in the mirror. Oh, she was a mess. She washed her face and applied some concealer and makeup. It was time to go face her parents.

On the drive north in weekend travelers traffic, she mulled over Ben's words. She'd been young and stupid too. She knew he was under pressure but didn't understand the business stuff. But did she really need to in order for him to share what he was going through? She never even asked about it. Maybe she'd been a coward back then. She could have stayed and fought for her marriage. But what would that have looked like?

She'd never know.

16

ALL YOU NEED IS LOVE. BUT A LITTLE BIT OF CHOCOLATE NOW AND THEN DOESN'T HURT.

CHARLES M. SCHULZ

The scent of meatloaf, potatoes, and carrots greeted Jo as she entered her parents' Green Bay home.

"Jo! Welcome home!" Her father wheeled toward her. "It's about time."

"Hi, Dad. How are you doing?" She bent over to give him a kiss on the cheek.

"Oh, you know how it is. Everything hurts at some time. Drop your bag. Dinner's on the table and I'm hungry." He turned his wheelchair around and headed down the hallway to the dining room table.

Mom came around the corner. "Jo, about time you got here. Have a seat, dear."

Jo sat, and the food was quickly passed around.

"Can you stay the entire weekend?" Mom asked.

"No. I have plans for Sunday."

"What's is so important?"

"I already told you, Mom. I have plans on Sunday morning. I start back on duty Monday."

"Behind the wheel?" Dad asked.

"No, office duty, possibly some dispatch. I'll be working holidays to fill in for those on vacations."

"Sounds like more of a punishment for the shooting than a reward and opportunity to come back to work," Dad said.

"At least I'll still have a job," she murmured.

"Jo," her mom warned.

"I'm sorry, Dad. I didn't mean that as an insult to you." Jo pushed her half-eaten plate away. "I'm not hungry anymore. It was good, Mom."

"Stay seated, Jo," her dad barked.

Jo obeyed.

"I may not be able to walk, but they refused to let me come back. I was too old for them to consider keeping me on desk duty."

"I understand, Dad, but my injury isn't permanent. I'll be back behind the wheel by Christmas."

"You wish. You're still so naïve. You haven't changed since that mistake of a marriage you made. Why don't you find a nice man, marry, and give us grandchildren?"

"Seriously? I thought I was coming home to visit, not to be attacked," Jo protested. "Benjamin was a great guy, and I don't regret my marriage to him."

"What brought about this change?" her mom asked.

Jo sighed. "I ran into him and found out the truth of what happened three years ago. In case you haven't realized it, I'm a grown adult. I'm free to make my own choices and face the consequences." A weary sadness filled her. She didn't want to discuss this with her parents.

The front door opened and closed. "Jo? Are you here?" a man called.

"Ki?" She jumped to her feet and rushed to the hallway out of sight of her parents.

Her big brother was about to sweep her into a hug until he saw the sling. "Still recovering, I see?"

"Geoff got hurt worse than I did, and the guy who did this is dead."

"I'm glad you killed him, otherwise I'd have had to do it myself."

Jo laughed. Her brother was as big as Geoff and as much of a teddy bear as her partner. He served as a firefighter in Green Bay.

"Come in here and eat," Mom called.

Jo and Ki were in the hallway out of sight.

Jo shook her head.

Ki groaned. "Already ate, Mom. I'm stealing Jo for a while."

"You kids get back here!" Dad yelled as Jo grabbed her coat and ran out the door after her brother.

They hopped into his sport utility vehicle.

Jo giggled.

"Good to hear you laugh again. It's been a while." Ki drove them to a bowling alley, where they found a spot to sit in the bar. "Want a beer?"

She shook her head. "No, thanks, just a cola for me."

Ki went to get the drinks as Jo relaxed. Her life

was so much quieter than this place with the pounding music. Bass vibrated through the soles of her feet.

Ki placed the drink in front of her, and settled into the vacant chair. "So how long was it before Mom and Dad started in on you?" Ki asked.

"A little quicker than I expected. I had hoped to make it through dinner, or maybe dessert?"

Ki laughed. "No wonder you never come to visit. Why would you have been desperate enough to come intending to spend the night? Mom called me right after you told her you were coming."

"My boss asked if I'd seen them, and I thought—"

"That maybe you could handle it? Come on, sis. You can crash at my place tonight. I grabbed your bag on the way out, so you don't need to go back."

"Why can't they see that I'm an adult?"

"They've never appreciated that you're not the fragile flower they wanted you to be."

"You did order some nachos too, right?"

"Of course, I did. With extra jalapenos. Do I know my sister or what?"

"Thanks, bro. So, what's up with your world?"

"Met a girl and I think I'm in love."

"This is what, number five?"

"At least I can move on when my heart is broken."

"Ouch."

"Truth hurts."

"I've seen Benjamin recently. What if he was my one true love?"

"He's back in your life?"

She nodded. "I learned new things this past week

about what happened. He didn't cheat in the way I thought."

"Really?"

"Yeah. I'm having to rethink everything about that night."

"You haven't been able to move on," Ki whispered.

"Maybe I wasn't meant to be married."

"I never saw you happier than when you were with Ben."

"You're the only one who supported my marriage to him, but since the divorce, you've called him names. Whose side are you on?"

"Yours. I really liked Ben, but I support you no matter what, even if you wouldn't share what happened back then. If I remember correctly, his family also adored you."

"I know. I missed them and didn't contact them. Molly tried calling so many times but I never answered." She sighed. "Thanks for rescuing me tonight. So about this girlfriend?"

"Yes, we're pretty serious, but I haven't told her the magic words yet." He flipped to a photo on his phone to show her a pic. "Her name's Michelle." A light she had never seen before shone in Ki's eyes.

"I can't believe you're out with your sister and not with her."

"She's working tonight. She's an ER nurse."

"I'm happy for you."

"Back to Ben. Did he offer you a reason for what he did that night? You never did give me the details and I was too afraid to ask. All I know is you were devastated and angry."

Her brother was an expert at changing the subject when he didn't want to talk about his own life. Jo tucked Ki's relationship away to ponder later. "He did explain, and I am beginning to realize that I had some part in our marriage's demise. Oh, he never said that, but I can see now where I might have failed, too. It wasn't as bad as what he did nor does it excuse his behavior. I left him at the lowest point in his life even before the divorce. I don't want to give the details. He says he didn't fight for me in order to save me from being tainted by what he was going through."

"So are you interested in getting to know the new Ben?"

"I'm not sure. I've changed, and it appears he has as well. We're definitely not the same people anymore."

"Well, maybe you two can be friends with the air cleared."

Jo shook her head. "You always were the hopeless romantic."

"And you were the one watching all the crime shows."

"So, how'd you end up a firefighter?"

"I'm big and fearless. Figured I'd put those strengths to use."

"But you've been getting medical training, right?"

"Yeah, at some point I'll be a certified paramedic, but I'm not sure I'll switch jobs."

"Why?"

"Not enough firefighters. I figure as long as my body can handle the challenge, I'll stick with it and save lives this way."

"Got it. Makes sense."

"You wanna go bowling?"

"With one arm? You'd have to tie my shoes for me."

"We can get you the ramp they give to little kids."

"No. How about darts? I can still do that."

"Bummer for me that it wasn't your dominant arm that was injured, huh?"

"Why? Afraid your little sister will beat you?"

Ki laughed as they went to the dartboard for their competition.

~*~

When they got to Ki's apartment, he hauled her bag to the spare room.

"Thanks, Ki."

"Rest well. I'll take you back to Mom and Dad's tomorrow for lunch, but I'll stay with you."

"They mean well."

"They care."

"They never quite understood me. No pink frilly bows and lace for this tomboy."

Ki raised his eyebrows. "I think you do yourself a disservice, Jo. I saw the men eyeing you tonight. You've turned into a beautiful woman. I promise you pancakes for breakfast."

"You can cook now too?"

"Working in a firehouse, everyone takes turns in the kitchen. I've got some wicked skills."

"I can't wait to be impressed."

"Night, Jo."

"Night, Ki. And thanks."

Jo readied for bed and slid under the covers. Exhaustion didn't quite describe the weariness that melted her into the mattress. Her mind flitted to Benjamin. Why would thinking of him fill her with joy when before it had only brought pain? Maybe she had forgiven him and didn't realize it.

Now to train her heart to not want more. The moon shone in through the curtains. Her time with her parents had agitated her more than she'd expected. Why was that? Was she afraid of going through what her father had experienced? Getting injured on the job and being forced out of work he loved?

Too many officers were being killed in the line of duty now. More than ever before. While she considered herself safer in the area she patrolled, a bullet to her shoulder blew away that myth. Too many others never lived to go home again, much less ride in their patrol car. That was why she wouldn't date anyone else in a higher-risk job. She'd done everything right, and it still ended with injuries to both her and her partner. What if next time it didn't turn out so well? Unlike her father, she didn't have anyone at home to offer comfort and support. At the end of the day, she was just like she was right now—alone.

That hadn't really bothered her before, but she'd seen the joy in her brother's eyes at his love for

Michelle. Now she wondered if love could be possible again for her. To have someone to love like that. A recollection of her time in London with Benjamin after their wedding pained her. She'd thought she had that once. Dreams of a marriage and children and maybe even being a stay-at-home mom had died with the divorce. Or had she killed them? She shook her head. This was not helpful. She had a career now. There was no other option for her.

Or was there?

~*~

The next day, she sat at the kitchen counter as her brother made blueberry pancakes.

"So, Mom and Dad said you're going to church now? What's up with that?"

"After the accident, my partner, who also got shot, asked me to go. I was feeling guilty and had nothing else planned, so I went. I became intrigued."

"That's cool. Michelle and I have been attending one together for the past few months."

"So, what do you think about Jesus?" Jo asked.

"He's become my Savior and my friend. He's changed my life, and taken away my fears about what would happen to me if I died in a fire. I don't want to die, Jo, but knowing where I'm going, gives me peace."

"I'm not there yet, but I'm close."

"I've been praying for you. I struggled too, and to be honest, I worry about you on your job. When you called about the shooting, and later I watched the news, my heart ached for you."

"I've had a lot of thinking to do since that day."

"You can't second-guess your training and your instincts. You do that, and you'll freeze the next time. Don't go there."

"You know this from experience?"

Ki gulped. "I can't save them all, and when we lose someone in a fire, it feels like a failure. It's hard to get past that."

"Sorry. The blessing about being farther away is that I don't hear about all the calls you get."

"I'm sure that between the two of us our parents are constantly worried for our lives."

"I suppose I should have a thicker skin. You're right that they're probably acting out of love for both of us." Jo grinned at him. "Thanks again for the rescue last night."

"You can't avoid lunch. I'll be there, but you'll have to stand on your own."

"I'll try to survive for at least an hour. Then I need to scoot back home."

"Just make sure you're not slinking back."

~*~

Jo walked behind Ki toward their parents' home.

Ki tossed her bag into the car for her. "Ready?"

"Ready as ever."

They walked into the house.

"Mom? Dad?" Ki yelled.

"What? Have our rude kids returned to the scene

of the crime?" Dad asked as he wheeled down the hallway.

"Thought you'd like us together," Jo responded.

"Since neither of our children want to visit more often, why not?" Mom said as she entered the living room.

Jo settled into a comfy chair, and Ki sat next to her.

Mom followed while Dad wheeled in next to her.

"Two of you together. Is this an intervention or a holiday?" Dad asked.

"Neither. However, I do want to say something, and I hope you can both hear me."

"What is it, dear?" Mom asked.

"It must be hard for you to have two children in careers with a higher risk factor, but I would hope you would trust that we are the people you raised us to be—honorable and responsible. Neither Ki nor I take unnecessary risks, and we're both aware of the dangers of our chosen careers. In a way, you should consider our professions as a compliment to the honor and duty you taught us to value." Jo paused to glance at her brother, who nodded for her to continue.

"I know I've not been the daughter you wanted, but I hope you can be proud of who I've become and trust me in all areas of my life. My mistakes are mine to make, and I don't need my parents trying to tell me what to do unless I ask for their advice."

"Well, um, of course, we're proud of you both," Dad said. "But we worry."

"Until an officer comes to your door to tell you the news, I suggest you relax and enjoy your lives," Ki suggested. "Your worry for us doesn't do any good, and we don't want to be second-guessing our training for fear of what you're going to say."

Mom wiped away a tear. "I've always appreciated who you are, Jo."

Jo squinted at her mom. "Really? Then why the criticism of my choices?"

Mom shrugged. "I don't know. I'll try to change. At one time I had hoped for grandkids. You and Ben would have made such beautiful babies. I guess when that ended, I had a hard time seeing the new you. I'm sorry if you believed I didn't still love you."

"I don't want you to change the love—just the constant reminders of my failures."

Her parents held hands and looked at each other. "Fair enough," her dad said.

17

I HAVE ONE DESIRE NOW—TO LIVE A LIFE OF RECKLESS ABANDON FOR THE LORD, PUTTING ALL MY ENERGY AND STRENGTH INTO IT.

ELISABETH ELLIOT

Jo woke up excited about going to church Sunday morning. As she dressed, she remembered her brother's words that she rarely showed her softer side to the world. She pushed through her closet to find a soft pink blouse to add to her blue dress pants and a multicolored asymmetrical jacket to wear over it. It was something she'd picked up on a whim at a thrift store. Normally, she stayed practical with blacks, blues, and neutral tones, but she liked the pink and the vivid colors in the jacket. She went through the trouble to add a little blush to her cheeks and selected a soft pink lipstick. A little mascara, and she was good to go.

Would she turn Benjamin's head as she had in the old days? Did she really want to? Somehow she felt freer than ever from the shackles of the past. It still stung when she thought about what had happened but Benjamin's apology was slowly easing that ache.

Her black sling went on, and she sighed. Her shoulder still ached. Getting dressed was a trial but as she regained her range of motion it became easier. She fluffed her loose hair. At least those waves were more feminine.

Anticipation grew the closer she got to church. She found Geoff talking to Will, who gave her a warm smile.

"Jo, it's good to see you this morning," Will greeted.

"It's nice to see you under different circumstances, Will. Thank you for being there the other night to help clarify things."

He avoided her gaze. "Yeah, well, Ben has been a friend, and I'm glad I could be there in his time of need back, then and again this past week. He's come a long way in three years."

She smiled. "I'm glad to hear it. I wish him only the best."

His snapped his attention back to her. "You've forgiven him, then?"

"That's something I hope to discuss with him. Where is he this morning?"

Geoff cleared his throat. "He had a software installation up in Minneapolis and won't return back to town until later today."

Will grinned. "You can sit with us."

Her spirits sank, but she rallied. "That'd be great."

Sandwiched between the two men, she sat through worship fighting her disappointment. *God, why bring me this far to disappoint me?*

When a song began with words about having compassion, guilt stabbed her that in her stubbornness, she'd withheld forgiveness from Benjamin for so long. It hit her that she also needed to ask for his forgiveness. She wiped a tear away.

The pastor quoted part of Zephaniah 3:17. "The Lord your God is in your midst, a mighty One who will save."

Can You save me, Lord? Am I too late? You've proven how desperately I screwed up, and I need You. Rescue me.

Peace filled her as she settled in to listen to the message with fresh ears. The words on the pages of Scripture came alive, real, and relevant. Wonder suffused her, and she whispered a "thank you" to the heavens.

When the service ended, everyone stood. "Can you men excuse me for a few minutes?"

"Sure. We'll be in the cafe."

"Great. I'll meet you there."

Jo walked to the front of the sanctuary where Pastor Dan had stepped off the stage after leading worship.

"Jo, how are you?" he asked.

"I finally prayed that prayer. Thank you for leading worship today. God used it to break down that last barrier."

"I'm happy to hear that. Renata picked the songs this morning, so I'll pass the word along to her."

Jo's eyes widened. "Renata Blake?"

"You know her? She's Renata DeLuca now."

"Where is she? I'd like to talk to her." Jo scanned the crowd.

"I think she went into the back room. If you go up

these stairs and through that curtain there on the left, you'll get to her."

"Great. Thank you."

"And welcome to the family." Dan grinned.

"I'm glad to finally have a family like this to belong to."

She walked up the steps and found a back room. Renata was there. She held a little girl in her arms. A man next to her held another child. A baby slept in a carrier at Renata's feet.

"Renata?" Jo moved forward.

The stunning woman turned to her with a smile. "Yes?"

"I'm Jo March. Dan told me where to find you."

"Jo, meet my husband and my children. Tony, Rosalinda, Isabella, and this is our son, Liam."

Tony held out a hand. "Nice to meet you, Jo. You're the trooper who got shot, right?"

Jo nodded. "I wasn't as badly injured as my partner. He can hide his wounds better now that he's out of the hospital."

"I'm glad you're recovering. Thank you for your service." Tony turned to his wife and gave her a kiss. "I'll see you at home, sweetheart."

Jo's face grew warm witnessing the genuine affection between them, and she turned away, her heart filled with longing for that kind of love.

Tony set one daughter on the ground, and Renata released the other as he picked up the carrier. "I'll let you two talk. I need to get someone home before he realizes Mom isn't with us." He left, shepherding the little girls.

"You have a beautiful family."

"Thank you." Renata turned her focus to Jo. "I sense you want to talk. Have a seat." She settled into a comfortable chair, and Jo did likewise.

"Thank you for the songs this morning. During one of them, I finally could clearly see my need for Christ."

Renata smiled. "I'm so glad to hear that."

"When I heard your unusual name, I asked Dan if your last name was Blake…"

Renata grew pale, and her back stiffened. "That was my name from my first marriage."

"I'm sorry to bring up something painful, but I wanted to tell you that my father was one of the officers who found your husband. Dad growled like an angry bear when accusations came against you over his death. There are many people who know the truth. The woman he was with sported bruises. He'd been drinking along with his buddies, and he wasn't wearing his orange. Dad agreed with the findings. Your husband was accidentally shot by a hunter."

"Thank you for that. It's a part of my past that I don't like to think about. It's as if God gave me a new lease on life after moving, meeting Tony, and getting help to heal the wounds of my first marriage. Mick's family still doesn't believe I'm innocent."

Jo reached out with her good arm to clasp Renata's hand. "I'm sorry."

Renata sighed. "God is good in that He gave me a godly man, and now three beautiful children."

"I have some good things to look forward to, then."

"You do, but life is hard at times. I was a Christian while still married to Mick. My healing was a long process. I never expected I'd be able to trust a man again, much less fall in love. Then God brought me Tony. He was a safe person, and he respected my boundaries."

"What do you mean by a safe person?"

"Eventually, I could trust him with the truth of my past, and he accepted it. Mick's and my families couldn't. I didn't know things could be so different in a marriage. Tony allowed me to cry without calling me weak. He just loved me right where I was."

Tears welled up in Jo's eyes. "Something I've failed to do when someone needed me."

Renata pulled a tissue box over. "Forgiveness can be hard to ask for, but it's well worth it." Renata grabbed a pen and a piece of paper from a table and wrote down her name and phone number. "Give me a call if you want to talk more. I'm not as flexible to leave the house right now. Still adjusting to having Liam as well as two rambunctious toddlers, but you could come over for coffee or tea sometime and talk more if you want."

"I'd like that. Thank you, Renata. I never expected what God did today, but I'm glad to have met you."

Both women rose as some band members filtered into the room.

"We're preparing to lead the next service." Renata enveloped Jo in a gentle hug. "Please do call."

"I will." Jo left and found her way to the café where Geoff and Will waited for her even though the crowds had thinned.

"Where did you disappear to?" Geoff asked.

"I just saw someone I needed to talk to. Made a new friend."

"Cool." Will shifted his feet. "Jo, I'm wondering if I could take you to lunch today?"

Geoff frowned.

Jo shook her head. "I think I'll pass. I have a lot of things to think about and laundry to get done, as I'm back on duty part time tomorrow. Perhaps another time."

"Can I have your phone number?" Will asked as he handed her his phone, which was open to a contact where her name was already typed.

"Sure." She punched in the numbers. "This is my personal cell phone. I usually have it turned off when I'm at work."

"Got it. But if I text you, you'll eventually get the message?"

"Right. Why don't you text me now, so I can put your name in my contact list?"

Will blushed. "Fine." He sent her a text with his full name, Will Dalton.

"Got it." She shoved her phone back in her bag. "Guys, it's been an interesting morning and a crazy weekend. I'm heading home."

"Are you sure you're OK, Jo?" Geoff asked.

"Yeah. Probably even better than OK." She gave him a grin and headed to her car, stopping to grab her jacket from the coatroom first. She had so much to share with Benjamin when she had a chance.

~*~

At home, Jo reheated leftovers for lunch. She snuggled into a chair in the living room and ate. The quiet was nice after her crazy weekend. The traffic in her head was able to clear as she took stock of where she'd come in the past few days.

All because of Benjamin's courage in confessing to her.

That's really where it had all stemmed. Her courage with her parents, emerging a victor instead of a victim; her connection to her brother; meeting Renata and finding hope at the cross.

God offered me compassion.

She hadn't given Benjamin that when they'd met. Guilt suffused her. She longed to clear the air between them. Perhaps both would be freer to pursue whatever God had in store for each of their lives.

She really wished she could talk to Ben, but Will had said he was out of town. She opened her laptop and logged into her e-mail account. She e-mailed him a note. Would he even respond? Did she have the courage to go through with this and meet him alone?

It wasn't that she was afraid of Benjamin. She was, however, afraid that she still loved him too much to walk away again, yet she had no claim on him. He was no longer hers. It was only now that she realized she'd put nails in the coffin of a love that wasn't dead.

When had she become so macabre? Skeletons escaping her closet, and now caskets? She shook her head and hit send with a short prayer that Benjamin would have mercy on her and be willing to meet. She longed to relieve herself of her burden of guilt.

18

CHOCOLATE CRAVES YOUR LIPS, MELTS AT YOUR TOUCH, AND SAVORS THE MOMENT.

ANONYMOUS

Benjamin dragged his bags into the house. Home. Always good to be home. He unpacked his suitcase. Once that was done, he tossed a load in the washer and unpacked his laptop bag. Once everything was where he liked it, he turned on the computer and typed in his password. He opened up his e-mail and scanned through them.

There was an e-mail from Jo.

He swallowed hard as his cursor hovered over the line to open it. He jumped up and paced. He'd been thinking about her and praying for her so much, and now she'd e-mailed him?

Oh, this couldn't be good, could it?

He strode to the kitchen and got a glass of water. He took a few sips and set it down. He really could use a good run. Ben ran his fingers through his hair as he paced. *Suck it up, big boy. Just read it already.*

While walking back to his computer, he took a deep breath. He clicked the message.

Dearest Benjamin,

Why did it please him so much when she used his full name and "dearest"? He could almost hear her say it.

I had hoped to touch base with you at church this morning. Some wonderful things have happened and, for some reason, you're the only friend I feel comfortable sharing them with.

His heart warmed. Friend? He'd take being her friend.

I want to confess some things to you that God has revealed, and I'm wondering if we could meet. Will told me you were traveling, but if it's not too late, could you call me? I start back to work part time tomorrow and don't have my new schedule yet, but I'm eager to clear the air between us and do better than I did the other night. I don't plan on bringing anyone with me. Just you and me. Dinner? Coffee? Whatever you're comfortable with.

Oh, and most importantly—I forgive you.

All my love,

Jo

Ben leaned back in his chair. She forgave him. His shoulders relaxed, and a soft smile crept across his face. He would give her the honor of a response and meet with her whenever and wherever she wanted. He picked up his cell phone and dialed the number she had listed after her name.

"Benjamin?"

"Yes, Jo. I just read your e-mail. Thank you. I would love to connect. Dinner is fine. My treat. It's been a long day, and I'm hungry. Would you like to meet at the diner downtown?"

They set the time, and Ben ran to check his appearance. He combed his hair and brushed his teeth. He glanced at his phone for the time and headed out to his car. Deep breath. *I can do this. It's not a date. Just friends.*

Right. Easy as pie.

Not.

~*~

Butterflies flitted around in Jo's stomach as she drove up to the restaurant.

Benjamin was waiting outside in the cold.

As Jo walked toward him, his face broke into a grin. How would she get through this?

He kissed her cheek and shepherded her inside the restaurant where they were quickly seated in a booth. They placed their orders.

What was she doing here? Nervousness overtook her. "Thanks for meeting me," she said.

"It's the least I could do, Jo. You gave me the honor of hearing me out last week. Thank you for the gift of your forgiveness."

"I hope you'll be more generous than I was when we met."

His brows knit together. "Why?"

"Because I realized I have some things to confess too."

Benjamin's eyes grew wide. "I'm sure your sins are nothing compared to mine."

"Is it a competition?"

"No." The waitress returned with their food and drinks.

"Thank you," Benjamin said to the waitress as she walked away. He turned to Jo. "Can I pray for us?"

"Sure."

He reached a hand across the table.

She complied and extended hers, reveling in the warmth of that tiny embrace.

"Lord, thank You for this food and drink and for the opportunity to mend the hurt of the past for both Jo and me. You are a God of love and forgiveness, and we thank You for Your grace and mercy to us. Use this food to strengthen our bodies, and let our speech bring honor to Your name." He released her hand.

"That was a pretty tall order."

"Hmm?" Benjamin cut into his steak.

"You asked God for a lot."

"He's a big God. Never in a million years would I have imagined running into you in church or being able to sit down and tell you the truth of what happened before and after you left. Only God could enable me to do that."

"Perhaps so. Only God could soften my heart toward you. I apologize for not offering you my words of forgiveness that night. I was confused and struggling to grasp all that it meant. You totally rewrote the story I'd been reciting to myself about our marriage."

"I hope it was rewritten in a way that gives you peace about the past."

Jo shook her head. "I've found peace in Jesus, but

as for the past—I realized that all along I was blaming you and thought that…well, what I thought was irrelevant, because it didn't change that part of the story."

He frowned.

"I always thought that if I'd been a better wife, you'd never have done that."

"Not true. You were a wonderful wife. I adored you."

"Liar. If I had been a better wife, you would have confided in me, knowing that I would have loved and supported you through that difficult time. Instead, I played the victim and left without giving you a chance to explain what was going on."

"I might not have," Benjamin protested.

"Why? You couldn't trust me with the truth?"

"I was filled with shame and self-condemnation for failing you and failing my parents."

"Benjamin. I always believed you would do great things. I never said you were perfect and that you couldn't make mistakes—or that I'd stop loving you if something bad happened. When I spoke my vows to you, I meant them. In poverty and wealth. I would have walked through that with you."

"I'm sorry. I should have trusted you more. You're stronger than most people I know. I was weak. Broken. Lost." He sighed. "Looks as if I have more to apologize for than I thought."

"I didn't come here to convict you of wrongdoing but to admit my own. I should have held on and fought for you. I thought I wasn't worth fighting for because you let me go so easily."

"There was nothing easy in letting you go, Jo. Ask Will. He'll tell you how broken I was. He even threatened to call the police one night because he feared I'd kill myself."

"Would you have done that?"

"I considered it several times. I had nothing left. You were gone. I was broke. My name was being slandered. What was left for me to live for? Molly came and gave me a good swift kick and a lot of hugs and helped me through."

"I'm sure she hates me for what I did to you."

"It wasn't your fault."

"Why do I feel as if it was? I took half our money. You needed that."

"All I had was yours, Jo. If you had cleared out all our accounts, I wouldn't have blamed you."

"It was cruel."

Benjamin leaned back and grinned. "Are we fighting over who was the worst sinner in our marriage?"

Jo chuckled. "Yeah, we are. Silly, huh? It's over and done with. I forgive you for mistakes real and perceived. Will you forgive me, too?"

"I could never have hated you or held anything against you, Jo. I fully deserved your censure. Of course, I forgive you."

"You lied about not holding anything against me."

His eyes narrowed. "Why do you say that?"

"Because when you saw me again, I caught you biting your tongue from saying something mean."

"I—you're right. I wanted to hurt you as you had hurt me. I couldn't do it."

"Why?" Jo asked.

"Because I saw you as God saw you—precious, lost, searching. I couldn't do anything that would get in the way of you coming into a relationship with Him."

"You really have changed from the past."

"Yeah. I remember those last few months, how I used my anger and frustration to keep you at a distance. It was almost a knee-jerk reaction to want to return to that." Ben frowned.

"I too easily played the victim and retreated instead of fighting for our marriage."

"Forgiven?"

"Yes, Benjamin. Forgiven?" Jo asked.

"Yes."

"Good."

Ben grinned and leaned forward. "Now, how was church?"

~*~

Jo floated home after Benjamin walked her to her car, kissed her cheek, and told her to have a good week. All the years and pain had fallen away, and they could now be friends in spite of their past.

She'd never asked him how he'd feel if she dated Will. Was she even ready to move on to a new relationship?

The last thing she'd want to do was to hurt

Benjamin, but there was nothing else between them now. No animosity. No romance or wedding vows. Only friendship.

But the thought of him dating someone else was hard for her to swallow. She had no reason to be jealous. He wasn't hers anymore, and she wasn't his and never would be. At least the skeletons of the past could rest in peace now.

~*~

Benjamin returned home with a bounce in his step. He entered his house. His empty, lonely house. His spirits sank. Sure, he and Jo were at peace now. The past was out in the open and a new understanding forged between them, but what did that mean? Could they be friends? Acquaintances? Friendly exes?

Maybe it meant they could both move on in their lives. Start over fresh with someone else, without the past rising to haunt them.

The phone rang.

"Hey, little brother." Molly's voice rang over the line.

"Aren't you on a trip?"

"Yeah, but somehow you've been on my heart and I thought I should check in with my womb-mate."

"Gross. I hate it when you use those words."

"At least you were a gentleman and let the lady go first."

Benjamin laughed. "Stop it. What's up?"

"We're waiting for the allotted time before a judge

will grant parental rights, and then we'll be off to the embassy. More appointments, some family bonding and sightseeing."

"Tough job you have."

"It's hard when things don't work out. We had a teen being adopted who at the last minute decided not to go through with it."

"They have a choice?"

"After a certain age, they do."

"Ouch. So all that money raised and time taken off was wasted?"

"Nah, heartbreaking, but they found another child. Not sure we can make the process go quickly, though. They'll likely have to return in the future for that one."

"How do you help them?"

"Love them, listen. Wipe tears and give them options."

"Doesn't it tear your heart out?"

"It does. But so does watching a family meet their new child for the first time. I shed buckets of tears as I take video and snap pictures for them."

"You'll be a great mom someday."

"I gotta find an awesome guy first."

"I'm sure you will."

"Maybe I'll find him when I come to visit."

"You planning to stay for a while?"

"Possibly longer than that. I got an offer to head up the office in Milwaukee."

"Seriously? You're moving here?"

"Considering it. You open to a houseguest while I

get my life set up there?"

"I have plenty of room. How could I turn down my womb-mate?"

"Oh, yeah, I can see why you don't like that term. Fine. I'll be flying in about the third week of November. I'll email you the details."

"I'm happy for you, sis. I look forward to spending time with you."

"Why, you need me to be your wingman?"

"I don't want a wingman—sometimes I do need protection."

"Are the ladies still chasing you down?"

"Yup."

"I'll be praying for you, Benny."

"I look forward to having you close, Amalia."

"Molly. You know I've never liked Amalia."

"I just like to give you a hard time. Payback for all the ways you tortured me through the years. Have you legally changed it yet?"

"No, but maybe that should be the first thing I do after I get settled. I need to go. Someone is calling for me. Love you, bro."

"Love you too, sis. Take care."

"You, too."

Ben hung up. Well, life wouldn't be so quiet or lonely once Molly got here. He shook his head, realizing the craziness his life was in for.

He checked more email and finally crawled into bed. His heart was full, but his dreams kept straying to Jo and the fun times they'd had. He wondered if she still had pictures of them from back then, and if he could get copies. They wouldn't be so painful to look at, except to remind him of something precious he'd lost. That wasn't necessarily a bad thing. Melancholy could be good sometimes.

19

CHOCOLATE BRINGS A SMILE TO THE LIPS ON CONTACT, LEAVING A DARK KISS BEHIND.

ANONYMOUS

Jo awoke the next morning with a lighter heart. She was at peace with Benjamin after three years of heartbreak and distance. While nothing could undo the past choices they'd both made, they could be friends. Too bad she couldn't hope for more. She dressed in her uniform and drove to the State Patrol office.

"Jo! Welcome back," Captain Jenkins said. "Here's your desk."

The desk was stacked high with file folders. "What's my task?"

"We're behind in getting some of this data into the computer—so that's your job."

"Data entry?"

"Yes." He handed her a piece of paper. "Here's your schedule for the next two weeks as we head into Thanksgiving." He gave her a pat on her good shoulder as he went back to his office.

Jo looked at the page. She had some days that were almost full days. Part-time didn't mean twenty hours. While she couldn't complain about that, it was an odd schedule that had her on dispatch during some of the busiest times, and almost full-time over the holiday weekend. *Suck it up, buttercup.* It was better than sitting alone at home twiddling her thumbs, and she was able to go to church on Sunday mornings, not starting in the office until noon on those days. She needed to get over it and not whine.

She was a State Patrol Officer, not some toddler who should be having a temper tantrum because things weren't fair. Her father was wrong. While it wasn't ideal, it wasn't punishment. She was part of a team, and with her injury, she should be glad there was work she could still do.

~*~

Jo went home in the afternoon and changed out of her uniform. She collapsed into her favorite chair and soaked in the silence. Her phone rang.

"Hi, Will."

"Hey, would you be up for a date on Friday night? I forgot to even ask if you've been to our adult ministries group on Thursdays. We sometimes have really good discussions."

"I have a shift that night. My schedule is all over the place the next few weeks. Friday night works, though." Did she really want to do this?

"Great! Have you been to DeLuca's Cucina?"

"I know where it is, but I've never eaten there."

"Great. I'll make reservations. Can I pick you up at six?"

"Sure." She gave him her address and then wandered to her closet to see if she had anything nice to wear. She frowned. She might need to do a little shopping.

~*~

On Wednesday, Ben stopped work early since he had started before the crack of dawn. He went for a run outside in the sunshine. Soon he'd abandon his outdoor runs for the gym, but for now, he appreciated not having to talk to anyone or look at a computer.

He and Jo were at peace. His sister was due to be here soon. It had been a long time since he'd shared a living space with another person—much less his sister. But they'd always gotten along well, so he gladly anticipated her arrival.

He finished his run, showered, and prepared to go to meet with Roberto and the guys for his support group.

Alex and Tim had arrived before him and Robbie walked in a few minutes later. They sat around a square table.

"Hey, Ben. How are things going?" Robbie asked.

Ben explained the conversations with Jo, the clearing up his past mistakes, and the sense of freedom it had brought. "I wanted her forgiveness for her sake, but when she didn't give it, I was heartbroken. Why? My goal was for her to be free from carrying resentment. I didn't think I needed her forgiveness for myself. When we met the second time, she confessed her mistakes to me and we even argued about it, there was a comfortable familiarity to it that surprised me. No more animosity. No more tension.

"The fact is, I always loved her, and while I'm sad our relationship is over, I'm almost sadder about that than I was back when she left me. With the air cleared between us, there's nothing. I even gave Will permission to date her. Like he needed that? I have no claim on Jo, but my heart doesn't seem to get the message."

Tim placed a hand on his shoulder. "You love her. Mistakes of youth and miscommunication tore you apart, but those obstacles are gone. It's not as though you can pick up where you left off. Too much time has passed, and you've both grown a lot, but there's no law that says you can't re-establish some kind of relationship with her."

Ben frowned. "I don't know. I don't think I could reconnect right now. I've not really dated much over the years due to self-condemnation over my sins. Now I'm free from those. I don't want to grasp on to Jo because she's my first and only love so far, and because of that, she's a known quantity."

"How did you feel when Will asked you about dating her?"

"Jealous. Angry. If he weren't a good friend who'd been with me through my darkest hours, I might have even slugged him," Ben confessed. "Besides, even if I were interested, I don't think she would be."

"Did you ask her?" Alex inquired.

Ben shook his head. "No. I think we both need

some space to process what we know and explore other relationships. My sister is coming to town and will be living with me for a while as she gets settled into a new job and finds her own home. I'm really not in the market for a wife right now."

"They can be a wonderful gift." Roberto shared. "but I'll admit, marriage can be hard."

"Enough about me. How are things with you, Alex?" Ben asked.

The men took turns talking and encouraged and prayed for each other. When Ben arrived home later, his mind was filled with unanswered questions. *Jo. Lord, bless her, please? Give her the happiness she deserves, even if it isn't with me.*

~*~

Jo didn't work until later in the afternoon on Thursday, so she could keep her counseling appointment in the morning. She walked into Shirley's office and took a seat, propping her slinged arm on a pillow on her lap. Was it because she needed the physical support, or was the pillow a buffer from the painful reality of what she wanted to share?

"How are you, Jo?" Shirley asked.

"I'm healing well and am back on duty. And I've forgiven Benjamin." Jo went on to explain the two meetings with him and her time with her brother and parents.

"Sounds as though you've been busy. Any more nightmares?"

Jo shook her head. "Not about the shooting. I do have some strange dreams about Benjamin that leave me really sad."

"Why?"

"If I had acted differently that night, we might have weathered the storm and still be married."

"You still love him?"

"Yeah."

"So, what's the problem?"

"Will asked me out on a date. You were right, three years have passed since Benjamin and I had a relationship with each other. There's nothing to indicate that things would be better if we pursued something now. He's got his life and I have mine. I've seen him with women at church and I'm going out with Will tomorrow night. Benjamin has obviously moved past 'us' so I need to as well."

"How do you know he's over you?"

"He said he wanted to give me freedom from resenting him. He wanted me to forgive him for my sake."

"A noble reason. Do you think he was lying about that?"

"Benjamin is a straight arrow. A little hyper, but not intentionally deceitful."

"Yet you held a belief for three years that he had cheated on you."

"I wanted to be the victim. My brother pointed it out. I can't be that little girl anymore. I'm a survivor. I hope I've grown up. Matured. Become responsible for my own choices and their consequences. The fact is—I realized I screwed up our marriage by running away. I never gave him a chance to explain. I sensed something was wrong but was too afraid to ask. If I had, I could have been there for him when he needed me most."

"A lovely thought, but not the reality of what happened," Shirley pointed out.

"Yeah. So now that I've forgiven him, how do I forgive myself? My brain is hurling tons of accusations at me and it's as if I'm stuck in a traffic jam with horns honking, unable to move."

"Let's take your metaphor a step further. How does a traffic jam disappear?"

"The obstacle blocking traffic is removed and the cars slowly move forward, eventually able to gain speed."

"So, what's the obstacle?"

"Forgiving myself."

"You told me you'd accepted Christ."

"Yes."

"So He has forgiven you of all your sins—past, present, and future."

"I hadn't thought of it that way."

"If God tells you He has forgiven you for your mistakes, whether intentional sins or not, why do you think you have a right to hold on to them?"

Jo let her shoulders droop. "I don't, but I still don't understand how I can stop the thoughts that shame me."

"Benjamin forgave you when you confessed to him."

"Right."

"And you believe he speaks the truth."

Jo nodded.

"Accept it. Embrace it. Step into your future with freedom."

"Easier said than done."

"True. Listen, I can't tell you who to date or marry. You'll have to lean on God for guidance with those choices and decisions, but you are free to move into your future unburdened by the shame of the past. Consequences don't go away. You are still divorced. But I've known divorced people to grow, repent, and remarry. You'll just have to determine what it is you really want in your life and realize that Benjamin also has those same choices before him."

"And Will?"

"Go out and enjoy yourself. Maybe he'll be a good friend, if nothing more. We can never have too many of those."

"He's been a friend to Benjamin."

"That could make things tricky."

"Yeah."

"But don't shut him out because of that. Don't deny yourself the opportunity to explore and learn in the process. One date doesn't mean you have to keep going out with him."

"True. I've got a lot to think about."

"Part of dealing with the complexities of life. Let me pray for you before you go." Shirley bowed her head. "Lord, You've begun a good work in Jo's heart and in her life, cleansing her from her past mistakes and freeing her to move into the future You have for her. Walk with her, continue to heal her, and protect her as she goes back to work. We love You, Jesus."

"Thank you." Jo stood and walked to the door.

"Jo."

She turned to face the therapist.

"It's not a sin to be happy." The therapist winked.

Jo gave her a smile and left for home to change for her shift at work.

~*~

Benjamin arrived at the Adult Ministries group on Thursday night with a headache. Programming on a new network hadn't gone well and his first tests had failed. Something was wrong in his code, but he finally set it aside to get out of the house. He walked into church to meet with the group.

Pastor Dan was leading the study tonight, and Ben found a seat near Will.

"Ben, hey, just wanted to tell you—Jo said yes."

Heart racing, Benjamin turned to Will. "Yes?"

"To a date." Will elbowed him. "You didn't think I'd ask her to marry me that fast, did you?"

"No." Benjamin stared straight ahead. How would he survive seeing his friend dating his ex-wife? What if Will married her? Could Benjamin spend the rest of his life seeing her at gatherings, longing for her, and not able to have her?

After the study, people mingled over coffee, usually decaffeinated, and some treats others had brought.

Ben walked over to Geoff. “Hey, how are you?”

“Getting better. Still not ready for full duty, but I’ll be starting desk duty and dispatch next week. Part-time and just in time for the holidays.”

“I’m not sure whether I should be happy or sad for you,” Benjamin said.

“It’s part of the job. If I weren’t on desk duty, I’d be patrolling during the holiday traffic. It gets crazy out there. I figure it’s more important for the officers with families to get some of those holidays off. My turn will come someday.”

“That’s gracious of you,” the woman standing next to him said. She focused on Benjamin. “I’m Candace Macy.”

“Oh, sorry, I should have introduced you,” Geoff sputtered. “Candace, this is Benjamin Elliot. Benjamin, Candace moved here about a month ago, but this is her first night at group.”

“It’s a pleasure to meet you, Candace.”

“I need to go chat with Will.” Geoff excused himself, leaving Candace and Benjamin alone.

“Have we been set up?” Benjamin asked with a grin. Not that he minded a whole lot. Candace was pretty.

“I’m not sure. It’s nice to meet you, though. Geoff mentioned you.”

“Really? What did he say?”

“Only that you’re a computer software developer who owns his own business and makes truffles on the side.”

Benjamin chuckled. “Geoff loves my truffles.”

"Why make chocolate?"

"It started as a way to unplug and slow down. I have ADHD, which is great for helping me focus, but I can get too preoccupied and can be impulsive. Making truffles slows me down."

"Interesting. So, you have multiple tabs open in your mind and you hop from one to another? Kind of like having various websites open on a browser?"

"An apt description."

"I'd like to try one of your truffles sometime. Do you sell them?"

Benjamin shook his head. "No. Selling would mean business and needing to have my kitchen certified by the State and special licenses, etc…not worth going there, and it would take all the fun out of the process."

"You consider it fun?"

"In a way. I get to be creative, and I know it brings people joy. It's nice to do something that doesn't have a price tag attached to it."

"So, what does a girl have to do to get a taste?"

His eyebrows rose. "I could bring some for you on Sunday."

She frowned. "I work Sunday morning this week."

"What do you do?"

"I'm on a temporary assignment as a manager for an airline at General Mitchell International Airport."

"Do you travel a lot?"

Candace shrugged. "Our company is based out of Atlanta, so that's home base for me, but I travel as needed and get to stay in one place usually for a few short months."

"Over the holidays, though? That's tough."

"Not really. I can fly home whenever I need to, and I had a week off before settling in here. I get to see new places and meet new people. I like being the fill-in person."

"I suspect you're more than that."

"Astute observation. I do assessments while I'm in town on the functional operations, and customer service on the ground and in the air for those based here."

"A covert operation?"

"Not really. Most realize I'm there to check out things. Corporate spy is what they call me behind my back. But it's what I enjoy."

Benjamin chuckled. "I'd love to show you around a little while you're here in town. When would you be free?"

"I have Saturday off."

"Sounds good." He pulled out a business card. "Email, text, or call and we'll set something up when you're ready."

"You're not pushing for a commitment right now?"

He shrugged. "You might go home and change your mind. No pressure. Just an opportunity to get to know each other and enjoy some of what Milwaukee has to offer. If you think of something you've heard about and want to check out, let me know and I'll see if I can make it happen."

"Color me intrigued." She took the business card

and stuck it in her purse. "I look forward to getting better acquainted, but only if you promise to bring some truffles."

"Sure. If chocolate tilts the scales in my favor, I can promise you truffles."

Candace grinned. "I'm glad I got to meet you, Benjamin."

"It's OK to call me Ben."

"I'm thinking that those who care most about you don't."

"My sister calls me Benny, but she's the only one I'll allow to do that."

"I've been warned. I'll be in touch, Ben."

"Night, Candace." He walked away to get his coat, as the group was clearing out and it had gotten late. He hoped she contacted him. It gave him something to anticipate on the weekend, and it had been a long time since he'd experienced that.

20

CHOCOLATE IS THAT DARK AND BEAUTIFUL KNIGHT WHO CHARGES IN ON HIS GALLANT STEED READY TO SLAY DRAGONS WHEN NEEDED.

ANONYMOUS

Jo had found a cute dress and some dress boots to wear for her dinner with Will. It had been so long since she'd been on a date, and the last one had been with Benjamin. They had moved into a relationship without the tension of dates. They'd gotten to know each other at the bar and become friends, and it had grown from there. She'd hang out with him when her shift was done, and he'd walk her home so she'd be safe.

She'd always felt safe with Benjamin.

Will? "Anxious" was a better way to describe her state of mind. And it was all her, not him. He was Benjamin's friend. Was it a betrayal to Benjamin to go out with Will?

I'm a free agent. I can date anyone I want. I don't need Benjamin's permission.

Maybe so, but she'd never want to hurt him.

The bell rang to her apartment. She grabbed her purse and went to the outside door. "Hi, Will."

He wasn't unattractive by any means, but his

darker hair was cut too short for her taste and he was taller than…Benjamin. She really needed to stop comparing men to her ex-husband.

"You're ready?" Will asked.

"This was the time you told me you'd come. Why wouldn't I be?"

"No reason, just that not all women take that to be a firm time. I'm honored that you do. Gives me hope that you like me."

"I have no reason not to like you. Benjamin trusted you years ago, and enough to bring you to that meeting. He's generally a good judge of character."

"Except for the jerk who embezzled and tried to get him jailed."

"One exception I hope he's learned from." She slipped into the car after he opened the door. He closed it behind her and went around to the driver's side.

Sliding in, he said, "Ben learned his lesson in a painful way. Makes me wonder if he'll really ever trust most people again."

"Why do you say that?"

Will shrugged as he pulled out to the highway. "He's not had any relationships since you left."

"Perhaps this is a topic we should steer away from."

"You're correct. I'm sorry."

"No, it's natural that we would talk about our common ground in Benjamin. I just don't want to have a relationship with you to gain information on him. If we are to be friends, we'll need to find other topics to discuss."

"A wise woman," Will said as he drove into the parking lot at DeLuca's.

"Not so very wise," Jo mumbled. *If I'd been wiser, I'd still be married to Benjamin.*

"What?"

Jo shook her head. "Nothing, just talking to myself." She gave him a smile.

"I've done that at times, but usually when I'm nervous. I hope I don't make you that way?"

"I'm fine," Jo assured him. She needed to be. Will deserved her best effort to be a friend. She didn't want to leave a bevy of wounded men in her wake.

The image of Geoff laying sprawled on the concrete flashed across her memory and she flinched. The door opened, and Will helped her out of the car. She shivered.

"It's cold out here. Let's get inside. Maybe we'll get a spot near the fireplace."

Grateful that he'd mistaken her reaction, she shoved the memory aside and allowed him to put an arm around her as they hustled out of the cold November wind to the doors of DeLuca's Cucina.

"Oh, it smells wonderful in here," Jo exclaimed as Will helped her take her coat off.

"Hi, Will," a gorgeous blonde greeted them.

"Stephanie, this is Jo March. Stephanie is married to Roberto Rodriguez, the lawyer who helped out Ben."

"Wow, small world." Would everything come back to Benjamin?

Stephanie escorted them to a table close to the

fireplace.

Will sat opposite Jo, and a young waitress came to bring them fresh water and bread.

Jo opened the menu and quickly decided on her meal. "It's not often I find pesto on the menu. Most Italian restaurants stick to the more traditional marinara, spaghetti, or cheese sauces."

"I'm not fond of basil. I'm going for the lasagna. It's what I always order here."

"Never try anything new?"

"Rarely. When I find something I like, I stay loyal to it."

"So, what happens when a restaurant stops carrying that item on their menu?"

"I'm a traditionalist. There's no way a restaurant like this will ever stop serving lasagna."

Jo grinned. "Probably a safe choice, then."

After the waitress collected their orders, silence hung between them.

"This feels weird," Will confessed.

"Why?" She understood why it was that way for her, but him?

"Ben has been a friend, and I was there when life looked hopeless. I never thought in a million years I would meet the woman who had brought him to tears like that."

"Wait—"

"I'm not blaming you, Jo. He told me why you left and what you thought. I'm glad he had the opportunity to tell you the truth. And yet…"

"What?"

"I wonder how you could have ever thought that of him? I've never seen anything in Ben that would indicate someone who would be any less than faithful, honest, and responsible for his actions. I don't understand how someone who had known and loved him for years could have ever questioned his integrity."

"I confessed my failures to Benjamin when I met with him privately. There's much I struggle to forgive myself for. God says I'm forgiven, and so does Benjamin. Do I have to beg your forgiveness as well?" Jo asked.

Will shook his head. "No. Not when you explain it like that. You're a beautiful woman, Jo. I still don't get why Ben wouldn't pursue you now and left the field wide open."

"Excuse me?"

"I asked him if it was OK if I asked you out."

"Why did you need his permission?"

"Because he's my friend and I didn't want to hurt him."

"That was kind of you. But you realize we are divorced. There is no relationship between Benjamin Elliot and me and there hasn't been for three years."

"Maybe so, it's just…"

"What?" Would they ever get past Benjamin?

"I've seen the way he looks at you."

"That's his problem. Not yours. Not mine."

"Maybe so, but he's my friend. While he may not pursue a relationship with you, I think he still loves you."

"Nonsense."

"Is it?"

"Does it matter? I thought we were on a date…can we try not to bring Benjamin into this again?"

"Maybe this was a mistake."

"Listen. I get that you're friends. I'm grateful you were there for him when things were hard. But we've all grown through our experiences, and we're not the same people we were back then. If all you can ever see is who I was three years ago, when you only knew me through Benjamin's eyes, then there is no hope of even a friendship between us. With all these doubts, why did you even invite me out?"

"I thought I could get past it. I'm sorry to ruin our evening like this."

"I'm sorry. I don't go out much. Maybe we can change the subject?" Jo offered.

The food arrived.

"Why did you decide to join the State Patrol?" he asked.

"My dad was in the patrol until he was injured in an automobile crash during a high-speed chase. Benjamin and I had talked about the possibility of me joining the State Patrol but we planned to wait until his business was up and running. But when things fell apart, I had already finished my two-year degree with an emphasis on criminal justice. I was quickly accepted into the training program. Probably more to escape my own heartache over the divorce, but also to establish a career for myself without a man."

"You worked hard so he could focus on school

and get the business going."

"Yeah, it was a sacrifice I don't regret making. You do things like that for someone you love."

"Do you enjoy your job?"

"Yes, I do. Maybe because it was how I was raised with the understanding coming from my father. Or the honor that comes from serving the public."

"What about the danger with what's going on around the country?"

"I doubt someone who works at a bank walks to the building every day worried they'll be robbed and shot in the process. Nor does a pilot get behind the cockpit of a plane anxious about crashing. You go in and you do the job you were trained for. Not that I don't remain on the alert when I pull someone over. Thankfully, Wisconsin has a lower incidence of those kinds of crimes, but obviously my own bullet wound proves that bad things do happen, even here."

"You're not wearing the sling tonight."

"I'm allowed to have some time with it off. I generally wear it, but I need to also start moving the arm around more. I figured this was a relatively safe venue for me to go without it."

"There have been police here in the past."

"Yeah, I read about that."

"Stephanie, the gal you met when we came in. She's the one who was attacked and held hostage."

"I'm sure she doesn't want to be reminded of that." Jo sipped her water.

"Probably not. Life moved on for her. Marriage, a family, and now part owner here."

"I don't know that we were meant to be defined by those kinds of moments. The more important ones are the relatively mundane ones."

"I don't understand."

"How we live our life, day to day, when no one is watching. How we treat others when we don't think it matters. Little acts of kindness that become a habit. Our ability to show compassion to those who are hurting. We all struggle with something. I would hope my ability to do those kinds of things would define me more than killing a kid who got mixed up in the wrong crowd and made a bad choice on the day I was on duty."

"Our character."

"Right, and as I read Scripture, the more our character reflects who Jesus was, the more we will be defined by our faith put into action. It's not the big things that make someone a hero. Those moments are only when people notice, but they should only be a small portion of the reality we live."

"Wow. That's a bit too profound for a first date. Sorry I asked."

"I don't know if this qualifies as a date, Will. I hope we can be friends, but with our ties to Benjamin, maybe being friends is the best we can hope for."

Will sighed as he pushed his empty plate away. He sipped some water. "I'm sorry."

"For what?"

"For ruining what I hoped would be a romantic evening."

"Instead, we had a nice conversation. There's

nothing wrong with that. We enjoyed a meal together, and perhaps we will be good friends to each other, and to Benjamin, moving forward."

"Sounds good." Will paid the bill. Once in the car, he turned to her. "I am beginning to think Ben was a fool for letting you go without a fight. Just my opinion, Jo."

"Thank you. I agree." She winked at him.

He chuckled and drove her home.

He walked her to the front door, and she turned to him, extending her hand. "Thank you, Will. Despite a rough beginning, it ended up being a nice evening."

He shook her hand and nodded. "Yeah. Good night, Jo."

"Drive home safely."

He gave her a salute as she opened the door. "Aye, aye, Trooper March."

Jo entered her apartment. Even on her first date in three years, Benjamin had haunted her. *Lord, when can I move past him?*

~*~

Will e-mailed him a cryptic message.

Jo and I will only ever be friends. We had a nice time last night, but I won't be asking her out again. She's a great girl, Ben. You, however, are an idiot. Will

Ben chuckled. He wasn't sure what warranted the insult, but part of him was relieved Will wouldn't be dating Jo. He was too afraid to ask himself why.

Ben finished his morning run at the gym and hit

the showers before heading home. He'd work on a little bit of code before meeting Candace for lunch. He wasn't sure yet where they'd go from there. She wanted separate vehicles because she was on call for any emergencies at the airport. He could respect that.

When he finished work, he grabbed his coat and keys and a small box of truffles he'd made the night before.

Arriving a few minutes early to the restaurant, Ben found the line of people going out the door. He pushed through to put his name on the waiting list in hopes that Candace would be there by the time his name was called. He wandered back outside to wait.

What was he doing? Candace was only here for a short time. Was she safe? Is that why he'd suggested they connect? In a few months, she'd be gone, and he'd be free of any emotional entanglements.

You, however, are an idiot.

Those words stung. He wondered what had happened between Will and Jo. Of all people, he thought perhaps they'd hit it off. Will was a great guy and had been a wonderful friend. In spite of that, he experienced relief in knowing they wouldn't be dating. But what about the next man, perhaps one he didn't know, who approached her and asked her out?

She's a big girl and can take care of herself.

True. She even carried a gun now.

"Hey, daydreamer." Candace stood before him, blocking the sun.

"Oh, yeah. The bane of ADHD, daydreaming."

"Anything good?" She wiggled her eyebrows.

He shook his head. "Nothing worth sharing." He handed her the small box. "Your truffles, as requested."

"I'm tempted to try one right now."

"That's fine. We could have another fifteen minutes before we get a seat."

She popped one in her mouth and groaned in delight. "Wow. These are good, Ben. Really good. You could be making a fortune."

"I do it for fun. If I did it for money, it would suck the joy out of it."

Candace motioned to the restaurant. "I've heard so much about this place."

"I thought maybe when we were done we could go check out the Mitchell Park Conservatory."

"The Domes? That would be awesome."

Soon Ben's name was called, they sat, and ordered, and Ben listened to Candace rattle on about the recent struggles she'd had with her staff. Ben found himself tuning out. *Stop it. Give her the gift of your attention.*

"Sounds like you enjoy solving the problems."

She smiled. "It's what I'm good at."

"What's the hardest part of the job?"

"Terrorist threats. When we need to increase security. I have to supervise more closely. The staff isn't being paid so much that a bribe would be unheard of."

"Seriously?"

She nodded. "I work in conjunction with TSA, Homeland Security, and sometimes even the FBI when necessary. It's not a common occurrence here in

Milwaukee, but in other areas of the country, the threat is higher and more serious. Some of those places have someone like me permanently in place."

"Do you ever get called to those places?"

"Sometimes during a heightened alert I might, but usually no. Maybe someday I'll earn the right to have a position like that. By then I expect I'll be tired of traveling and temporary relationships."

"Do you always seek out a church wherever you go?"

"Yes. My faith is important, and it's easy to become unhinged and deviate from God's path without good instruction and relationships."

"Smart woman."

"I'd like to think so."

The bill came, and he pulled out his card to pay.

Candace's phone rang. "Excuse me a minute. I'll take this outside. It's too loud in here." She rose to leave.

Ben got his card back and followed her outdoors, arriving as she ended the call.

"Bad news?" he asked.

"Yeah, I need to go in. I'm sorry. Hopefully, I can take a rain check on the Domes."

"Sure. I understand." He leaned forward and gave her a kiss on the cheek. "Have a good afternoon."

"You, too, Ben. Thank you for lunch."

She ran to the car and drove away.

Ben wandered to his own vehicle and traveled home as well. Part of him wondered if she really had to go to work or if it had been a failsafe in case she wanted out of the date. His internal battle raged.

Stop being so suspicious.

But I'm nothing special.

***Jo used to think so**.*

And then she left.

With a sigh, he entered the house and went back to his office. Once he buried his head in work, he could block out the negative thoughts.

21

TRUE FAITH MANIFESTS ITSELF THROUGH OUR ACTIONS.

FRANCIS CHAN

The doorbell rang around six o'clock that evening, and Ben wearily dragged himself from his office. Peeking through the window, he spied Molly. He unlocked, opened the door, and wrapped her in his arms. "Molly! Why didn't you tell me when you were flying in? I'd have come to get you at the airport." He stepped back.

"Nonsense. I needed to rent a car anyway. Maybe Monday you can help me buy a new one, so I can return this rental."

"I'd love to. Come on in." He grabbed her bags. "That's it?"

"I've had to live lightly for many years. Mum and Dad have some boxes of mine that I've instructed them to ship to you. Might take a while for it all to get here."

"I can't believe you're here. You could have texted or called to let me know you were on the way, at least. What if I'd been out?" He closed the door.

"Like where? On a date? Are you dating again?" Molly shrugged off her coat.

"Well, I did have lunch with someone today. I doubt it'll go anywhere."

"How's Jo?"

Benjamin sat in a chair and motioned for her to join him. "Jo is healing well. She's been coming to church. We've talked about the past and cleared the air. We're good."

"Then why are you dating someone else?"

"Excuse me?"

"Take Jo out."

Benjamin shook his head. "You're nuts. Even if she has forgiven me, that doesn't mean she could ever trust me again."

"You can't trust her." Molly's voice was soft. "Yet you still love her."

"It doesn't matter."

"I beg to differ. But big sister is here to take care of you, Benny." She hopped to her feet. "Where's my room, and how soon can we get dinner?"

Benjamin reluctantly rose and took her to the spare room that would be hers. "I made sure you had a desk in here, so you could work from home if you wanted to. My internet is great."

"Still no big-screen TV?"

"I tried to cut out distractions. Just a little one in the kitchen to catch the news is all I need. Sometimes I'll watch a show on my laptop. Since it's just me, it's not as if I require a huge monitor on the wall for that."

"Now that I'm here, that might change."

He chuckled. "I expect a lot of things will change with you around."

"I'm like a whirlwind."

"True. What are you in the mood for?"

"Chinese. I heard there's a great place on Appleton Avenue. I checked the reviews online."

"You heard right. How much time do you need?"

"Fifteen minutes?"

"I'll be ready. And Molly?"

"Yeah?"

"I'm glad you're here."

"Don't get too excited. Mum and Dad said either we both come home for Christmas or they'll come here."

Ben dropped his jaw but recovered quickly. "Oh, no. Really?"

"They aren't that bad." She winked. "I'll be out in a few."

The door closed, and Ben went to clean up and shut down his computer until Monday. It would be great having his sister in town.

~*~

Jo finished her night shift and scooted home to shower and change before church. There would be time enough to sleep after the worship service. It was hard to believe this coming Thursday was Thanksgiving already. She'd be working, relieved to have a good excuse not to go to Green Bay to be with her parents. Her brother would stop for a meal at their parents' home after his shift. He joked in his last phone call that he'd be mailing her a piece of pumpkin pie.

She hated pumpkin—pumpkin pie, pumpkin-spice lattes—all of it. Ugh. He knew that about her and did it to bug her. She wouldn't put it past him to send it in the mail. It would be just like him. She grinned. She was sending him a drumstick she'd burnt and saved just for this occasion. It was in her freezer right now. Siblings could be so much fun.

She arrived at church and scanned the crowd in the lobby. Someone else spotted her first.

"Jo!" Molly Elliot came rushing toward her, weaving through the crowd.

"Molly?"

A close replica of her brother, Molly had hair longer than her brother's, and her eyes twinkled. She enveloped Jo in a gentle hug. "Oh, dear sister, it is a dream to be able to see you again."

"I'm not your sister anymore, Molly."

"Nonsense. Come sit with me and Benny."

"That might be awkward."

"I'll protect you from my little brother. I want to hear all about what's going on in your life."

Geoff approached. "Good morning, Jo. Sorry to interrupt, but do you want to sit with me?"

Molly's eyes grew wide. "Well, tall, dark, and handsome. Who are you?"

A smile crept across Geoff's face as his eyebrows raised. "Geoff Ross. I'm Jo's partner at the State Patrol."

"You're the other officer who got shot. Are you OK?"

"Getting better, and you are—?" Now a soft

redness colored his cheeks.

Jo shook herself. "I'm sorry. Geoff, I'd like you to meet Molly Elliot, Benjamin's sister."

"I didn't know he had a sister."

"A twin, no less," Jo offered.

"He doesn't like it that I brag that I'm a prettier version of him." Molly winked at Geoff. "The benefits of being born first. Why don't you join us?"

"O-OK." His voice had a softness to it that Jo had never heard before, and his gaze stayed glued to Molly.

Jo stood aside, astonished at her partner. He'd been attracted to her, but he was captivated by Molly. And Jo couldn't blame him. Molly was a force to be reckoned with. Like a puppy on an invisible leash, he trailed after Molly as she headed toward the auditorium. Shaking her head in amazement, Jo followed. This would be fun to watch.

~*~

Jo sat on one side of Molly as she inserted Geoff on the other side by Benjamin. An "ex" sandwich, in a way. Too bad it wasn't a double-stuffed cookie—although there was a lot of sweetness between the two in the middle, who kept whispering to each other during the service.

When worship was over, Jo made her way out of the aisle, followed by Molly, Geoff, and Benjamin. Molly hooked an arm through Jo's good one. "You'll join us for lunch."

"Sorry, Molly. I would love to reconnect, but I only got off work this morning at seven and I'm exhausted. How long are you in town for?"

They entered the cafe. "I got transferred here. I'm staying with Benny for the moment until I find a place of my own. I'll still have some traveling to do but I plan to make this area my home." She dropped her voice to a whisper. "Someone has to keep an eye on Benny."

"He hates it that you call him that."

Molly grinned. "Yup. Why do you think I do it? Before you go, let me get your phone number. I'm not working this week, so it would be great if we could get together for lunch."

"My schedule is a bit odd right now, but I probably can do that on Tuesday."

"Great." Molly punched her number into Jo's phone as Jo did the same for Molly. "I've missed you, sis. Rest well and call me anytime. It's no longer an overseas call."

"I'll call or text to confirm Tuesday after I sleep and double-check my schedule. Then we can decide where to go."

"Sounds great!" Molly enthused. "Now I need to go stake out that big guy. He's not taken, is he?"

Jo shook her head. "Nope. He's not dating anyone. And he's a wonderful guy. Any girl would be fortunate to snag him."

"That girl wouldn't be you, would it?"

"No. I won't date anyone in law-enforcement."

"So I have your blessing?"

"Why would you require my blessing? He's not mine."

"He's your partner."

"Fine. Go with my blessing, but don't mess with him, Molly," Jo warned.

"Furthest thing from my mind. Sleep well, Jo."

"I'll do my best." Jo walked out. She'd not seen Will and had only given Benjamin a brief wave of acknowledgment.

In her apartment, she closed all the shades and collapsed into bed. Her stomach would be her alarm clock. She didn't have to work until tomorrow morning. This new schedule would be brutal.

~*~

Benjamin frowned as Jo left without talking with him. His attention was soon riveted to his dynamic sister.

She threw her arms around Will, who hesitantly returned the embrace. "Willy. Am I right? You're the one who saved Benny three years ago. Thank you!"

"Will. No 'e' about it." Will answered. "And you're welcome. I think."

Just as quickly as Molly had hugged Will, she turned her full attention to Geoff, who was standing there, mouth agape.

Molly gave the big guy a mock punch on the shoulder. "Now, don't get all stuffy on me, Geoff. You're the one I like."

Geoff cleared his throat. "Will, this is Molly Elliot."

"An immovable object meets an indomitable force, huh?" Will joked.

"I don't understand," Geoff protested.

"I think you do. Seems Cupid has been busy, but not on my behalf."

"Geoff, I see you've met my twisted sister, Molly." Ben nudged her.

"Twisted?"

"Didn't you just get sucked into her whirlwind?" Ben joked, as Molly hooked her arm through Geoff's free one.

"Yeah." Geoff glanced down at the woman as if mesmerized.

Molly scowled at her brother. "He likes to tease me. Just because he can be the Tasmanian Devil himself with tons of energy, he likes to make me seem worse."

"Your parents survived the both of you?" Geoff asked.

Molly laughed. "Endured might be a better word."

Ben nodded. "Shall we head home?"

"No. I'm going to lunch with this man right here."

"Really?" Ben tried not to grin. Geoff sure seemed smitten.

"Yeah, lunch," Geoff muttered.

Molly hugged Geoff close. "Thank you. I promise you won't regret it. Oh, and it's my treat since I coerced you into it."

"I was open to the idea before you asked," Geoff offered.

"Have fun, kids." Ben gave a wave and walked

away. Looked as if he was alone for lunch, but he couldn't help but chuckle at how his sister had bowled over the big State Trooper with just a smile.

~*~

Benjamin paced until his sister came home from lunch. "Molly, what are you up to?"

"Have you ever had a moment when the stars align, and a rope tugs you into another person's life so forcefully you believe it's God speaking to you?"

"Sure, when I saw Jo in a bar the first time, weeks before I ever even spoke to her. You're talking about Geoff Ross?"

"Yes. There's something about him that clicked the minute I gazed into his eyes."

"Does he feel the same way?"

"I think I knocked him off his game, but he'll rally. I'm counting on it."

"Are you chasing him?"

"Today I did, but now the ball is in his court. I have high hopes for him."

"Mere infatuation."

"Benny. I've never experienced anything like this. I've met a lot of men over the years. None of them ignited something inside me like Geoff did. They've tried. He didn't have to do anything for that spark to catch. I'm not a teenager anymore. You don't have to protect me from evil boys. Jo said Geoff was a good man. I trust her opinion. After all, she married you, didn't she? Obviously, the girl has excellent taste."

"And then she left me."

"Without you doing anything to get her back. A mix-up that could be remedied if you wanted."

"Leave my love life alone, will you?"

"We're twins. Don't we do most things in tandem?"

"You didn't fall in love and marry when I did."

"True. But I was still in England. Maybe I needed to meet a Wisconsinite like you?"

"Just stop it, OK?"

"Fine. I'll let it go for now, but that doesn't mean I can't pray for you and Jo."

Ben covered his ears. "Lalalalala, I can't hear you."

"I'm going to go dream of Geoff."

"Molly—"

She scampered out of the room and closed her bedroom door before he could finish the sentence. He sighed and slumped into a chair.

The phone rang.

"Yes, Mum?"

"Did Molly make it safely?"

"Yes, she's landed in Milwaukee like a category-four hurricane—slaying all before her."

"Benjamin Wentworth Elliot, your sister is not that bad."

"You're right. She's here, she's safe, she's currently taking a nap."

"I'm glad to hear it. I wanted to give you the dates for our arrival in Milwaukee."

"I thought Molly was joking."

"No. She wasn't. She told us you weren't coming

here, so *voila*! We shall come to you."

Benjamin groaned and wrote down the dates. His house would be full, and he'd likely be bald by New Year's Eve. Heaven help him.

22

WHEN LIFE HANDS YOU LEMONS, THROW THEM BACK AND ASK FOR CHOCOLATE.

ANONYMOUS

Jo crawled out of bed. She'd only allowed herself a few hours, and now her stomach growled. She pulled out a frozen dinner and heated it up in the microwave. She stood in the kitchen to eat it. Jogging was off-limits so far, but she needed to move. She walked into her spare bedroom, where she kept a recumbent bike. She pulled up a television show and sat down to ride.

She worked up a good sweat and then hopped into the shower. After getting dressed in jeans and a zippered sweatshirt, she reluctantly put the sling back on and grabbed her coat. Might as well go and pick up some Christmas lights for her little tree, since her lights never made it from year to year. She'd be working during the best sales at the stores and hated to go when there were big crowds anyway.

Jo strode into the large retail store and one-handedly pushed her cart to the Christmas area. She turned the corner for the lights, and her cart ran right into another one.

"Oh, I'm sorry, I should have been more careful."

Jo apologized and bit her lip.

Benjamin grinned. "Well, if I bump into anyone, might as well be you."

Molly peered around her brother. "Jo! I'm glad to see you. Hey, we're getting a bite to eat when we're done here. Would you like to come with us?"

"Where?"

"Thought we'd do that noodle place," Molly gushed. "I've been craving noodles. Comfort food."

Benjamin turned to his sister. "You're in need of comfort?"

Molly shrugged. "I'm in love, what can I say?" She winked at Jo.

"Really? With whom?" Jo inquired.

"Your handsome partner. Please say you'll join us."

Jo chuckled. "Sure. I'll join you if Benjamin is OK with that."

"Why wouldn't I be? We are friends now, right?"

"Sure. I only came to get a new string of lights for my little tree. I'll be on duty over the holidays, so I figured I better get them now."

"Are you working on Thanksgiving?" Molly asked.

"Yeah. Wednesday night and Thursday night. Twelve-hour shifts. Seven to seven. I think Geoff got stuck with the alternating ones."

"Wow, that's rotten. You'll come join us for Thanksgiving, won't you?"

Jo's eyebrows rose as she searched Benjamin's impassive face. A grin stole over her at Molly's running roughshod over her brother. "I'll want to get some sleep but could come in the afternoon."

"Oh, that'll be lovely!" Molly exclaimed. "I just need to select some more lights for Benny here, and some unique ornaments, garlands, and a tree topper." Molly started tossing stuff into the cart as Jo moved around to find her lights. "Now, Ben isn't happy about this, but we're decorating before Thanksgiving. It will be so much more festive."

"Has it been a while since you've been in the States for a celebration?"

"It has. For the last few years I've been in other countries over the holidays as families have picked up their kiddos. While it's fun to watch from a distance, I've missed this fun. Benny is indulging me."

Jo looked at Benjamin. "I doubt he had much of a choice."

Benjamin pursed his lips. "Life with my sister is never dull."

"I'm going to browse. Let me know when you're done."

"Will do!" Molly exclaimed.

"You're having way too much fun with this, Moll," Benjamin said.

Jo chuckled at the twins' banter as she moved to another aisle.

Once out of sight, she took a deep breath. Dinner with Benjamin and Molly? And Thanksgiving? *God, what are You up to?*

~*~

Molly shoved Ben in next to Jo on the booth seat, not that he minded sitting close to his ex. When their food arrived, his sister asked Ben to pray for them.

"Lord, thank You for this food and for bringing my sister to town, and this opportunity to be with Jo. Bless our conversation; may it glorify You."

Molly leaned forward. "So, what can you tell me about Geoff?"

"Me?" Jo put a hand to her chest.

"Yes, you, silly. You're his partner, right?"

"We partnered up for my orientation, and we are often on shift together, but in separate cars. So 'partner' is a loose description."

"Dish, girl."

"He's a great guy. I don't know what else you want to know. I'm not sharing his secrets. He's not dated much, from what I've observed. You went to lunch with him today, right?"

Molly's smile grew wide. "Oh, yes, we did. And we're having dinner tomorrow night, so I guess I didn't scare him off."

"He is a State Trooper. I suspect it would take a lot to terrify him," Ben said between mouthfuls.

"I thought maybe I'd messed it up big-time, Benny. I gushed about the orphans and how I wanted to adopt a lot of them. How's that for finding a way to a man's heart?"

"He didn't run screaming from the restaurant?" Ben raised his eyebrows.

"No. He didn't. I left it up to him whether we went out again, and he texted me this afternoon. Obviously, he's enchanted with me."

Ben was about to speak, but Jo put her hand on his arm and gave him a warning glance. He sighed and withheld comment.

"What was that about?" Molly asked.

"What?" Ben asked.

"That silent communication between you two. Were you lying in telling me you weren't back together? Because that was such a couplish thing to do. It was charming to behold. Mum and Dad will be thrilled to hear about this."

Jo's mouth dropped open. "No—"

"We're not dating. We're..." He glanced at Jo. "Just friends. Don't push it, Molly." The warning in his voice was clear, and Molly backed down.

"Fine, it's just—"

"Let it go," Ben said firmly.

They ate in silence for a few minutes before Molly started to talk about things that had happened on her last trip. She finally rose to go to the bathroom, leaving Ben and Jo alone.

"I'm sorry about that. She's a bit—"

"Excitable?" Jo grinned. "I get it. When I left you, I hurt more people than you, and I lost a family I cared about very much. It was one of my regrets."

"Mum and Dad are coming for the holidays. I'm sure they'd love to see you. They've been calling to check up on how you are doing."

"That's sweet of them. So, you'll have a a full and busy home. Did you buy a big enough house?"

"Why do you think I bought a house?"

"Just figured it would be one of the things you would do. You always used to mention homes and what kind you would like someday. Did you get it?"

"Yeah, I did. There's enough room, but them being here will cramp my style," Ben conceded. "I love my family, but—"

"They can be a bit overwhelming."

"Exactly."

Molly returned, and they finally rose to leave.

Ben tossed the car keys to Molly. "Start the car, please. I'll walk Jo to hers."

Molly's eyebrows wiggled in the lamp-lit parking lot.

Ben strode silently by Jo's side to the car and held on to the top of the door after it opened. "Jo—"

"Listen. I know you didn't want any of this. If you don't want me around for Thanksgiving, I'm fine with that."

"That's not it at all. I'd love it if you came. I just wanted to apologize if I sounded harsh in stopping Molly with her matchmaking."

"It's OK. I understand that when I left you, it was a permanent thing. I closed and locked a door with my actions. Friendship is the most I can hope for between us."

His gaze softened. "That's not it at all, Jo. I meant it when I said I've always loved you. I also realize that apologies don't wipe away the sins of the past. If you were ever to consider me as a suitor again, I'd have a lot to prove to you that I've changed."

"Suitor? Come on, Benjamin." She frowned. "You

didn't come after me then. Why would you pursue me now? I'm not seeking a husband. I would have accepted you when you were broke, but you didn't trust me enough to give me the chance."

He sighed. "Another sin to chalk to my account."

"Benjamin—"

"Good night, Jo." He turned to walk to his own car.

~*~

Jo settled behind the wheel and started her vehicle. Why had she shut him down? Was she again that younger version of herself, afraid to be rejected, so she had to do it first? She might have killed any opportunity to see if there was any chance for them. And she'd hurt him in the process.

Stupid, foolish woman.

She drove home and cried herself to sleep.

23

CHOCOLATE WARMS, COMFORTS, AND SYMPATHIZES

ANONYMOUS

Molly dragged Ben from one auto dealership to another.

"What exactly are you looking for?" Ben finally asked.

"I'll know it when I see it."

"Really? Because we've test-driven several cars and you've not picked one."

"Maybe that's the problem. Maybe I don't want a car."

Ben turned to her, puzzled. "You want a sport utility vehicle like mine? Can you afford that?"

"No, not that. I want a minivan."

"What? Why?"

"Because I want to get married and start adopting children, or fostering, or maybe even having my own."

Ben shook his head. "Let me understand this. You just moved. You're changing jobs. You're not married or dating anyone, and you're already planning for kids?"

"I'm dating Geoff Ross."

"Even after you told him your dream of having a litter of children?"

Molly grinned. "Yup. He's taking me out again tonight, remember?"

Ben shook his head. "You're crazy."

"I'm quite serious. I don't know why I feel this urge, but I do. I want kids. I've waited long enough, and I've been continually frustrated every time I leave a country with all those sweet babies stuck unwanted, unloved, in orphanages."

"You want Geoff to be their father?"

"Maybe?" She shrugged and walked down the lot to the minivans, with Ben trudging along behind. "There. That one." She pointed to a dark cherry minivan. "And just so you know, I've lived frugally and I've saved up enough money to pay cash for this."

"You're not buying a house right away too?"

"Nah, I'll wait until after I get hitched to get that, and then my hubby and I can purchase it together."

"Heaven help him," Ben murmured.

Molly patted him on the shoulder. "Now, now, little brother, just because you can't make your love life work doesn't mean I'll fail too."

"Ouch."

"What did you say to Jo last night anyway?"

"I'm not going there with you."

"You shot her down, didn't you? Destroyed any possibility of reuniting with her."

Ben pursed his lips and shook his head as he crossed his arms. "I'm not discussing it."

She shook her head. "You don't have to. I'm your

twin. I already know." She slapped him on the back of the head.

"Hey!"

"You deserved it. Now let's go buy me a car." She led the way back to the salesman as her sullen brother followed behind.

~*~

Walking into a restaurant to meet a friend was something Jo hadn't done in a long time. She spied Molly at a booth and slipped in. The waitress came and took their order.

"I'm glad you could make it. How's work been going?"

"Holidays bring out the speeders, drinkers, and crazies. It also adds more cars to the highways as people head over the river and through the woods to Grandma's house. And when it's not busy, it's dead and boring."

"You must be tired."

"I got some rest after my shift. Geoff is on duty now, and I relieve him at seven. I'm glad he had off…said something about a date?" Jo winked at Molly.

"Yes, he took me out and it was wonderful." Molly grinned.

Jo reached a hand to her friend. "He's a great guy. Please don't break his heart."

"I'm staying and ready to put down roots. There's something special about Geoff that gets my insides all gooey."

"You've probably turned Geoff inside out, and Benjamin—you're probably driving him bonkers."

Molly laughed. "You know him too well." The food arrived.

"Mind if I pray for us?" Molly asked.

"Go ahead."

"Lord, thank You for this food, and for reuniting me with my sister. You know our hearts and our future, and I pray You would lead and guide us."

"Thank you. I've not become comfortable talking to God out loud yet."

"Just remember it's only really between you and God. It can be hard not to worry about what other people think of our prayers, though."

"OK. Praying itself seems hard."

"Again, Jo, it's a conversation. You can sit and listen to God, read the Bible, and then tell Him whatever's on your heart."

"Even the bad stuff?"

"Now, what kind of bad stuff could be on Jo March's heart?" Molly probed.

Jo set down her fork. "I desire things I shouldn't, and it confuses me."

"What things? Material things, or perhaps a man?"

"I was married before, and there are things I miss from that time in my life. Going places with someone who loves the same things you do, always someone to talk to, sharing food and fun. Never being lonely."

"Understandable. What other things do you miss?"

"Someone to greet at the end of the day. Someone

in my corner. Hugs. The comfort of rolling over in bed to be snuggled by someone who loves me." Jo wiped a tear away.

"You never desired that with Geoff or Will?"

"How do you know about Will?"

Molly waved her away. "Just answer the question."

"No. Geoff is one of the sweetest men I know, but he's more like a big brother to me. I also adore my brother and enjoy being with him, but it's not the same."

"And Will?"

"Will is great friends with Benjamin and was there for the hard times when I wasn't. Benjamin is what comes between us. I like him just fine, but he knows things about me…and I'm jealous that he was a faithful friend when I failed Benjamin."

"How come you always call Benny by his full first name?" Molly asked. "I'd hate it if someone called me Amalia all the time." She shuddered.

Jo smiled. "I don't know. He's always been Benjamin to me. I've respected that it's his full name and I always wanted to honor him by using it. Maybe I'm a little jealous. Jo sounds like a nickname, but it's my full name."

"No middle?"

"No. My brother Ki doesn't have a middle either. Our parents thought it was superfluous."

"Wow. My full name is Amalia Seraphina Elliot."

"I remember. Benjamin didn't get off too easy either."

Molly laughed. "I almost feel sorry for him. Benjamin Wentworth Elliot."

"Kind of appropriate, though. I loved *Persuasion*, and Captain Wentworth did marry Anne Elliot," Jo said.

"True, and it was a lovely expression of my mother's love of everything Jane Austen, but it's a mouthful."

Jo sighed and took another bite of her meal.

"Dish, girlfriend. What's going on with you and my brother?" Molly probed.

"For three years, I blamed Benjamin, when in reality I was the one who left him at his lowest."

"He understood why you left, Jo. He screwed up. I won't defend him on that score. I screamed at him not to let you go, and we didn't talk for months after that because he wouldn't take my calls."

Wiping a tear, Jo stared down at her food. "It's in the past."

"Is it? Those tears look pretty here-and-now from where I sit. Are you finding it easier now to blame yourself for the divorce than to be angry for what he did that he let you go?"

"I understand why he did it," Jo said.

"Doesn't make it right or hurt less."

"Does it matter? It's just…"

"What, Jo?"

"I can tell he's changed. And I still—"

"Love him?"

Jo nodded. "How pathetic is that?"

"Not pathetic at all, sweet sister. You both have

come to know Christ, and He specializes in miracles and restoration."

"Divorce is final."

"Death is final. How would you feel if—?"

"Devastated."

"So, what will you do about it?"

"Nothing. Benjamin still needs to choose me. It doesn't matter what I want when he's moved on."

Molly shook her head. "You two have to be the most foolish people I know and love. Here." She placed a small white box wrapped in sapphire blue ribbon on the table. "These are from Ben."

Jo frowned. She touched the box and caressed the ribbon. "But why?"

"Because this is what he does now to unwind. You don't realize just how much he's changed, Jo. He doesn't work on Sundays unless it's an emergency. He tries to turn off the computer at five if he can. He only has a little TV in the kitchen. I forced him to buy a big one so I could watch it. He unwinds by jogging and biking, and to slow his thoughts down he makes these. Open it."

Jo slowly undid the ribbon, and it fell to the side. She lifted the top part of the box to reveal beautiful round balls of chocolate. She looked up at Molly. "Are these what I think they are?"

"Truffles."

Jo sniffed. "Those were always my favorite."

"Try one. I bet they taste better than any you've had before."

Picking one up, Jo popped it into her mouth,

closed her eyes, and moaned. When she finally swallowed, she opened her eyes. "You're right. These are divine..."

"Given the look of ecstasy on your face as you ate, I surmised it. That's good theater." She set down her phone.

"You did not record that, did you?"

Molly nodded.

"Never show that to anyone."

Shrugging, Molly looked at her phone. "Oops, seems I accidentally emailed it to my brother."

"Molly!" Jo couldn't believe how unapologetic her former sister-in-law was. "Why do you keep trying to push us together?"

"Because I love you both, and you were better together. You both still love each other."

"We don't even know each other anymore."

"Easily rectified."

"Just stop it." Jo looked at her watch. "I should get going. I want to catch a nap before I clock in tonight."

"Can you join us for Thanksgiving?"

"You already asked, but I really shouldn't."

"You have to work that night, right? You're not spending it elsewhere?"

"Correct."

"Then come around noon. Enjoy a meal on us, and you can rest before you work."

"Fine. I've missed you, Molly. Thanks for meeting me for lunch, and tell Benjamin I loved the truffles."

"I will."

Jo went home and placed the box of chocolates on

the kitchen counter. She glanced around her apartment and thought how empty it was of life and love. *Not now.* She needed to sleep so she could work that night. She changed for bed, shut the blinds, and crawled under the covers, remembering the wonder of the chocolate…and other things she'd left behind three years ago.

~*~

A text caught Ben's attention. Molly. *Check your email.*

He sighed and did as she requested. She hadn't returned from lunch yet and had promised to bring him something to eat. His stomach growled.

It was only Tuesday, and his sister hadn't been there for more than four days, yet everything was turned upside down. The tree was up in the living room, and yesterday he'd not been able to work at all. Molly had forced him outside to help her hang the icicle lights around the front of the house. She had them on a timer, and he admitted they looked pretty. Still, it was hard to focus with her energy and interruptions.

He rose to fill his coffee cup, returned to his desk, and flipped open the email. A video file was attached, so he clicked on it. Jo enjoying a truffle.

He'd shoved to the back of his mind Jo's love of chocolate. He closed his eyes against the image of her delight. He hadn't realized Molly had taken some of his truffles. *Dash it all.* He loved his sister, but she was meddling way too much.

It took all he could not to say anything last night when he came upon Molly in a passionate embrace with Sergeant Ross. He admired Geoff, and if anyone was man enough to handle his sister, it was the State Patrol officer. Was it wrong that Ben prayed for a quick courtship, so Molly would be off his hands? At this rate, she wasn't planning on moving out anytime soon. Granted, she'd not been here long enough to start apartment-hunting, but still… He'd have a reprieve when she started her job on Monday.

At least until their parents arrived. He groaned. He loved his family, but he had finally achieved a somewhat functional life, and to do his work he needed structure and quiet. Sometimes music could help block out distractions, but he hadn't done that in a long time. He might need to revisit it. He'd discovered many artists and enjoyed their music. He'd have to dig out his headphones to block out the sounds of the people in his house… Now, where had he put those? He rose to go to the closet and rummage through until he found them.

The door to his office crashed open.

"Ta-da! I've come bearing lunch! Did you get my email?"

Benjamin dropped the headphones onto his desk and grabbed the bag of food from his sister. His mouth watered from the scent escaping the bag. He pushed her out of his office, closing the door behind him. "Yes. I got your email."

"And?"

"What did you tell her?"

"Only that you made the truffles for her."

Ben closed his eyes. "Those are her favorite chocolates. Why would you do that?"

Molly placed her hands on her hips. "Why haven't you given her some before this?"

"I don't want her to think I'm trying to curry her favor."

"A girl likes to be wooed. I'd say those chocolates could get you to the altar pretty fast."

He frowned. "Altar?"

"Yeah, as in marriage?"

"Why are you pushing? Been there. Done that. Total loser in that department. Just leave it alone, Molly."

"You still love her."

"Which means nothing."

"It's everything, Benny. She still loves you. You didn't pursue her back then. So do it now. Don't make the same mistake twice in letting her get away from you."

"She's not mine. It's over. She divorced me, if you remember."

"You didn't fight for her."

"Well, forgive me for being too busy at the time trying to stay out of jail." Ben plopped the bag down at the table and pulled out the packaging inside. He poured himself a glass of water and sat to eat.

"I'm sorry you had to go through that. How did you feel when you heard Jo'd been shot?"

Ben bit into his sandwich and chewed. He

swallowed before answering. "Scared."

"Why?"

"She used to be my wife. I care very much about what happens to her. I wasn't the husband she deserved."

"Nonsense. I told her when we'd eat our big meal on Thursday. We'll have leftovers later when Geoff gets off duty and stops by."

He rolled his eyes. "Fine. By the way, that was some kiss last night."

Molly's face turned a shade of pink. "Geoff's a great guy."

"A love connection for you?"

She shrugged. "Maybe."

"Good. Maybe he'll take you off my hands."

"Hey!" Molly gave him a shove. "You should be happy for me."

"I am. It's just weird watching my sister and a friend kissing on my front porch."

"You didn't need to come to the door."

"What kind of brother would I be if I didn't? Hmmm?" He grinned. Finally, he could turn the tables on his sister. "Do I need to have a talk with him?"

"About what?"

"I don't know. Tell him all your dirty secrets so he doesn't waste time."

"Benny," she warned.

"Just kidding. Your relationship is your own business. Which also means, I might add, that my relationship is mine."

"What relationship?"

"Touché." He finished his meal, crumpled up the bag and napkin, and dumped them in the trash. "I need to get back to my office. Please try to avoid doing a new paint job in my living room. I like the color as it is."

"You're not helping me decorate?"

Ben shook his head. "I gave you Monday, and now I'm behind on some projects. I need to get back to work. I seem to have some added expenses since you moved in."

Molly grinned. "I promise you'll love what I do. Do you mind if I play Christmas music?"

"Go right ahead. I'll be putting on my noise-blocking headphones."

"You're such a nerd."

He shrugged. "But I'm your nerd. Later, sis." He strode to his office and closed the door. Would he even recognize his home when he came out later?

24

THERE'S NOTHING BETTER THAN A GOOD FRIEND, EXCEPT A GOOD FRIEND WITH CHOCOLATE.

ANONYMOUS

Benjamin promised his sister he would get the turkey in the oven. The internet had been helpful to both of them as Molly had researched all the traditional trimmings for Thanksgiving. They'd moved to England when they were so young she had no recollection of just how American's celebrated. Her mother never carried the American celebration with her to England. Molly'd baked pumpkin pie the day before and was planning the side dishes.

The house looked like something out of a magazine, until one walked into her bedroom, which looked as if a tornado had swept through. He could only shake his head at her shenanigans. She still slept.

He basted the turkey and placed it in the oven. After lacing up his running shoes, he tossed on his jacket and gloves and headed out for a jog. It was cold, but the sidewalks were dry. He really liked the quiet of this time of day.

As he traveled down the road, he wondered how Jo really was. What had happened between her and

Will to make his friend send such a cryptic email telling him he was an idiot? Will was sharp, and he had no doubt that his friend's assessment of him was correct. He turned the corner to continue his route.

Thanksgiving morning was even quieter than most days. Most likely the only people working were medical professionals, law-enforcement, and first responders. He wouldn't need to go into his office unless an emergency arose, but since he didn't typically deal with retail customers, he was likely safe.

The wind bit into him through his clothes, and his cheeks grew raw. He turned the corner to head for home. Would he ever dare to ask Jo those deeper questions? Was he ready to hear the answers? What if she really had liked Will and somehow Ben had unintentionally messed it up for her? He couldn't figure out what he could have done wrong.

He let himself back into the quiet house, enjoying the warmth. After shedding his clothes, he shaved, showered, and dressed in casual clothing for the day. He normally wore business casual even when home, because he didn't know when or if he'd need to leave to meet a customer, but today? Today he tossed on jeans and a long-sleeved t-shirt.

Benjamin stared in the mirror. Had he changed much in the past three years? He thought maybe he'd filled out more with muscle, since he'd been exercising, especially running. He wasn't beautiful like his sister, although they shared similar features. Funny how they were opposite in so many ways and yet sensed when something was wrong with the other person—even while she was overseas.

There had been an excitement about her since Sunday. It vibrated around her, and he worried she might be setting herself up for a fall. Maybe he'd need to have a chat with Geoff? *Nah*. His sister was an adult and could handle her own relationship. He only hoped she would slow the train down.

Benjamin grinned as he walked into the kitchen to pour a cup of coffee and grab a bite to eat. Geoff and Molly's courtship would be fun to watch.

He grabbed his journal and Bible and headed to his favorite chair in the family room. He had to admit the Christmas tree added a warm ambiance to the space, something that had been missing in his life for far too long. Jo had always done a great job with decorating and making even the humblest living space feel like home.

Why did it always come back to Jo?

~*~

Molly bustled around, setting a beautiful table, as Ben tried not to get in the way. "Just sit, Benny. Watch the Thanksgiving parade on the television." The television was on, but the sound was low and he'd been avoiding it.

"Fine." He plopped down into his favorite chair and stared at the television.

He wasn't sure how much time had passed when the doorbell rang. He jumped up. "I'll get it."

"You'd better!" Molly called from the kitchen.

Benjamin rushed to the door and opened it. He sucked in a breath at the vision before him. Her loose springy waves of hair captivated him all over again. "Jo. Come in."

She stepped inside, and Ben helped her off with her coat. Molly must have told her the dinner was casual, as she wore jeans and a soft, long-sleeved top that flattered her figure.

She gave him a shy smile. "So, this is your house?"

"Yeah. When my business turned around, it did so in a big way. I've been here about a year now."

"I'm really happy for you, Benjamin."

"Jo? Is that you?" Molly bustled out of the kitchen and enveloped Jo in a hug. Jo grinned.

"How many people did you invite over?" Jo asked.

"Only you for now. Geoff will come when he gets off work," Molly enthused. "Benjamin, go show her your house, and hopefully by the time you get done with the tour we'll be ready to eat." Molly bustled away.

"You don't have to if you don't want to," Jo offered.

"Molly has gone to a lot of trouble to decorate, so I had better do as she says." Benjamin shepherded her down the hallway to the bedrooms, and then to the back room where his office was.

"So this is where you spend most of your days?"

"Yes. I love the windows in here."

"Perfect for daydreaming?"

"You know me too well. Sometimes I watch the

birds at the feeder or the squirrels scampering across the yard. If I'm struggling with something in a program, that view will usually help me get to a solution."

"It looks peaceful."

"It is." They walked out, and he shut the door. "Let me show you downstairs. It's finished off, but I have to confess the space goes largely unused." He showed her the space, decorated with comfortable furniture and a gas fireplace.

"It looks as if it could be something cozy, but right now it feels empty," Jo said.

"Only because Molly hasn't decorated here yet. Give her time."

Jo grinned and gave him a side hug. "You have a beautiful home, Benjamin. I'm happy for you."

Her touch made his stomach flip.

She backed away.

"Let's head back upstairs, and I'll show you the front room before we eat the Thanksgiving meal Molly slaved over."

"Sounds good."

Benjamin didn't know whether Jo was being polite or really liked his home. When they got to the living room at the front of the house, he came to stand beside her as they took in the Christmas tree. "I'm sorry I was never able to give you all of this. I had always hoped that I would someday."

She turned to face him. "We both made choices we have to live with. I don't resent your success. It came with a high price tag."

"You."

"What?" Jo asked.

"You were the price tag. I'm sorry." He watched her closely. Even after all they'd been through, he still loved and admired her.

"We've been over this before, Benjamin. You don't need to keep apologizing." She stepped closer.

"I'm not sure you want to do that," he warned her. His pulse beat double time.

"Why not?" Those beautiful eyes and plump lips were so close.

Benjamin bent over, and their lips met. It was the sweetest thing he'd ever experienced. He stepped back and pointed up.

Mistletoe.

Jo blushed and ducked her head.

"I won't apologize for that, Jo." He took a chance and wouldn't regret it. There had been a spark in that kiss. Had she experienced it too?

"I hope not," she whispered, her cheeks pink.

"Dinner is ready. Come and eat," Molly called.

"After you," Ben said as he followed Jo out of the room.

~*~

Jo's entire body tingled from that kiss. Something about Benjamin still stirred desire deep inside. How would she get through a meal with him and his matchmaking sister?

Benjamin pulled out her chair and helped her sit.

He did the same for Molly before he took his own place at the head of the table.

"You'll pray for us, right, Benny?" Molly asked.

"Sure. Dear Lord, thank You for the bounty of this food You've blessed us with, and thank You that Jo could join us. We love You and appreciate all You've provided for us."

"Amen!" Molly said as she started passing around the food. "Save room for pumpkin pie, Jo."

Benjamin turned to Jo. "I tried to warn her, but she wouldn't believe me."

"It's OK, Benjamin."

"You really don't like pumpkin?" Molly asked. "I thought he was making that up to stifle me, since I've kind of gone a little overboard since arriving here."

"Benjamin doesn't lie," Jo asserted.

"No. His lips always speak the truth." Molly focused on her food.

Jo's eyes met Benjamin's as her face warmed. Did his kiss tell the truth?

Molly talked about a variety of topics while Jo and Benjamin listened. When they were sufficiently stuffed, Jo spoke. "I can help you with the dishes."

"No way. You and Benjamin go sit down in the living room and visit. I have a method to my madness for getting this cleaned up. Relax. I know you have to work later."

Jo followed Benjamin to the living room. He motioned for her to join him on the sofa and turned to face her as he sat.

"I'm sorry for my sister's match-making."

"She loves you and wants you to be happy," Jo assured him. "I get that." Did his apology mean he wasn't interested in her that way? Why would she even wish for that? She glanced at her fingers. A secret part of her wanted Ben to make it all right—as if they'd never divorced. What foolishness was that?

"Do you understand she believes I can only be happy with you?"

"Is that what you think?" Jo hoped.

"That I could only be happy with you?"

"Yeah."

"I was only ever really happy when I was with you, Jo. If I had to go back six years, I'd marry you again. Hopefully, I wouldn't lose you. There's been no one else since you. I've dated, but…none of them were you."

Jo stared at her lap. "I think I spent the past few years hiding behind being a victim of your bad choices. Now that I understand the truth, I wish I could have a do-over too. But there are no do-overs in life, and we are no longer who we were then." Oh, but a do-over would be great wouldn't it?

"Right." His voice sounded sad. "Can I ask a personal question?"

"I suppose."

"What happened with you and Will?"

She sighed and slumped back into the comfortable couch. "He took me out to dinner and was very sweet. But it seems that he can't date me because he believes you and I still love each other. And it would be hard for me, because he was there for you when I wasn't. It was awkward."

"No kiss goodnight?"

"There haven't been any of those for three years or more, Benjamin."

He leaned forward, and his hand came up to touch her face, forcing her to look at him. His lips met hers with a gentle touch. She longed for more. He sat back, but one hand fingered a lock of hair by her ear, sending shivers through her. He smiled that secret smile that spoke of delights.

Footsteps were headed their way.

Benjamin dropped his arm and averted his gaze.

Moment lost. Why did that make Jo so sad? They weren't a couple. Hadn't been for a long time. Part of her wished Molly's dreams could be reality and Benjamin could love her again.

"All done. What's on television?" Molly said as she flipped the channel.

Jo's eyelids drooped.

~*~

The movie ended, and it was already dark outside. Molly motioned to her brother. "You should wake her up. She has to work at seven."

Ben nudged Jo.

"What? No sleeping beauty action here? Come on, Benny. Be the prince for once."

As though he would kiss her with his sister watching? "Jo? Wake up," Ben said.

Molly groaned.

He glared back. Sisters could be a real pain.

"Huh?" Jo stretched as her eyes fluttered open.

He'd been watching her for some time now, instead of the movie, reaching over to touch her hair once or twice. "Time to get up, Jo."

She jerked up, leaping to her feet as she checked her watch. "Oh! I need to leave. Thank you for a wonderful meal. Benjamin, I almost forgot, thank you for the truffles the other day. You know they're my favorite."

Ben's face warmed at the compliment. Maybe it wasn't such a bad thing that Molly had taken some to her. He walked her to the door out of Molly's sight. "Night, Jo. I'm glad you were able to come."

Jo yawned. "Thank you for inviting me."

He moved forward, but she put a hand up. He halted.

"I'm confused." She turned and walked to her car.

Yeah, as if he wasn't? Ben entered the house and stood by the front window to watch Jo leave. He turned back to Molly.

"It's all good?" she asked.

"As good as it can be." Benjamin strode down the hallway. Sometimes a man just needed to be alone. He'd be dreaming of Jo tonight for sure. He closed the door to his bedroom and knelt by the bed.

Thank You, Lord for bringing Jo back into my life and wiping the slate clean between us. Although a friendship is nice is it too much to ask You for more? My deepest wish would be to be with my wife again—so I can spend the rest of my life loving her…

25

CHOCOLATE IS A TRUE FRIEND, A TRUSTED CONFIDANT, AND FAITHFUL LOVER.

ANONYMOUS

Ben stood in the lobby at church.

Candace approached him.

"Morning, Candace," Ben said, as Will and Geoff approached. "Have you met Will? You already know Geoff. This is Candace."

"Morning," Will said.

"Nice to see you again." Geoff shook her hand before turning to Ben. "Jo here?"

"No." Ben frowned. "Jo texted Molly to say she was really sick and had a hard time getting through her shift. She said she had a bad cold, but I know Jo. She doesn't do colds."

Candace frowned. "Joe? She?"

"Jo is a friend, and yes, a woman," Ben said.

"Just how well do you know this woman?" Candace asked, arms crossed and a frown marring her pretty face.

Geoff and Will's eyes grew wide.

Ben shook his head. "It's really none of your business, Candace. Gentlemen, I'm going in to sit down." Ben strode into the sanctuary, where music played and the countdown for the service already appeared on the big screens. He found a seat and settled in.

Molly sat next to him. "You look angry," she said, elbowing him.

"It's nothing. Someone just irritated me, and I'm worried about Jo."

"Did she get sick like that when you were married?"

"Only once, and I had to drag her to the doctor."

"So, you're really concerned."

"Yes, Moll, I am. I never stopped loving her. It's not like a faucet you can turn on and off."

"What if I told you I had her address?"

Hope surged within. Tamping down his eagerness, Ben turned to her. "Do I even want to know how you got that?"

"I asked her for it for Christmas cards. Did you forget we are doing them this year?"

He rolled his eyes as Geoff came to sit on the other side of his sister.

Geoff leaned over. "You OK, Ben?"

"I'm fine," he lied.

After the service, he made a quick stop at a store before he arrived home. Molly was out with Geoff. He strode to the kitchen to cook.

~*~

Jo checked her phone after she woke from her nap.

Her last shift had been miserable, with her headache and sniffling. Now that she was home, she was getting even sicker. She'd texted Molly earlier to let her know she wouldn't be at church. She found a text from her former sister-in-law.

I think Benny was looking for you. Nice way to play hard to get.

I'm not playing. Jo texted back.

Get well, sis.

Thanks.

Jo set the phone aside. She really wanted to go back to bed, but that would mess up her sleep later. She needed to do something to help her stay up, so she turned on her laptop to check any emails. Nothing urgent there. She opened her search engine, typed in "Benjamin Elliot", and began reading about his thriving business, but also found articles referring to his legal troubles. It had been a case for the FBI to handle? She hadn't known that. It sounded far more serious than Ben or Will had let on. Will had never told her who he worked for. Was it the FBI? Benjamin's partner had gone to jail. Jo had never liked him. By her calculations, he'd be getting out right around Christmas. She hoped Ben was aware and the man didn't have any plans for revenge.

She grabbed her notebook and began to write a prayer asking for God to protect Benjamin. Why his safety meant so much to her was not something she wanted to look at too closely, but she understood God was up to the task of taking care of her ex-husband.

The doorbell rang. Jo cinched her robe tighter and

headed for the door. She peeked out and saw her ex-husband there. She opened the door. "Benjamin?"

"I brought you something."

Sure enough, his hands were full with a big box. She let him in and put a tissue up to her mouth, as if she could hide her bone-shattering cough.

Ben strode to the kitchen and started unpacking the box. He set aside a small white box with a blue bow.

Truffles? Yum!

He pulled out some flowers and glanced at her. "Got a vase?"

"Sure." She went to grab one, and he took it, filled it with water, and arranged the colorful flowers he'd purchased. He set those on the table. "Did you eat yet?"

Jo shook her head. "What are you doing here?"

"Taking care of you. Come, sit down. Homemade turkey noodle soup, just the way you like it." He placed a steaming bowl on the table with a spoon and a glass of water and some homemade bread, making her stomach growl.

Jo did as he asked and sat down. She flashbacked to how he had cared for her when she'd been sick, and even gotten her to the doctor years ago when it was something they really couldn't afford. That sacrifice probably saved her life. How could she have forgotten something like that?

"Wait. Before you eat, let's take your temperature." He studied the digital thermometer and groaned. "Oh, Jo. Get back to bed. You might be needing a doctor."

"How bad is it?"

"One hundred two."

"No wonder I feel so miserable. Can I eat now?"

"See what you can manage." He sat down and watched her.

"You're not joining me?"

"Already ate. Had to give it the old taste test, right?" He winked at her.

Jo's heart did a weary flip. She finished her soup and shivered.

"Come on. Back to bed, sweetheart."

She allowed herself to be led there, and he tucked her in.

"Rest, Jo. Get well."

"Thank you, Benjamin." Her eyes drifted shut, and in spite of the pounding in her head, she rested, grateful that someone cared. It had been a long time…

~*~

Ben went to clean up the kitchen. He picked up around the small apartment. When that was done, he checked on Jo again. She was still burning up. His heart ached for her.

A coughing jag had him rushing to her side. "Hey, sweetie." He helped her up to drink some water. "I'm thinking you need to see a doctor."

Jo groaned. "Whatever."

"Can you get dressed? I'll drive you to the emergency clinic."

"Sure." She rolled out of bed, and Ben swallowed. Even sick, she was beautiful to him. The sleeveless pajama top revealed her shoulder. He reached out to touch the puckered skin where she'd been shot.

"That must have hurt."

"Yeah. Can you give me a minute?"

"Right. I'll be in the living room. Call if you require assistance."

"I think I can manage."

He left the room, closing the door behind him. He sighed. Jo's face was flushed red, and she wasn't steady on her feet. She stumbled out of the bedroom and went to the bathroom. Her bone-rattling coughs sent a shiver of fear up his spine.

When she finally made her way to the living room, she collapsed on the couch.

"Need help?"

"Shoes?"

"Sure." Ben grabbed a pair of shoes and helped her get them on. He reached for her scarf and coat and escorted her out of the house to his car. Once she was buckled, he got in and started it up. Thankfully, it heated quickly.

Jo shivered and coughed next to him.

When they got to the clinic, he helped her out of the car and inside, putting a mask over her face while they waited.

After the doctor had seen her and sent her for X-rays, Ben escorted her back into the small examining room. The doctor bustled in. "Well, Jo, you have pneumonia. I have a prescription here. Since you're not dehydrated, I'll send you home. Do you have someone to help out and watch over you?"

"I can do it. I also think she'll require an excuse for work."

The doctor nodded and wrote one out.

Jo shook her head. "You have a job too."

"I can do that almost anywhere. You're more important." Ben turned to the doctor. "Thank you." He took the note for Jo's boss and shepherded her out to the waiting area to assist her with her coat. "Come on. We'll drop this off at the pharmacy, and I'll return to pick it up when it's filled so you can rest."

"I might want some more of that soup," Jo whispered.

"I made a big batch anticipating that."

~*~

Once Jo had been fed and tucked back into bed, Ben drove out for the medicine, returned, and gave her a dose. He settled back to relax and pray. Sure, he could work, but this was still his Sabbath. He'd read and rest. Jo might be in for a rough night, and he wanted to be there for her.

~*~

A thump awoke Benjamin from where he dozed on the sofa. He jumped up and ran to the bedroom to find Jo trying to pull herself up off the floor.

"Jo? Are you OK?"

"Dizzy." She coughed.

He raised her to the edge of the bed and kept an arm around her as she coughed to clear her lungs.

"Did you need the bathroom?"

She nodded.

"I'll help you there and wait until you're done."

"Thanks," she rasped.

Jo slumped heavily against him. Her arm around his waist reminded him of all he'd lost when she left.

She went into the bathroom and closed the door.

He leaned against the wall and waited.

"Done," a soft voice called.

He opened the door to find her resting against the vanity.

"I look like crap," she mumbled.

"Probably feel like it too. Are you hungry or thirsty?"

She shook her head, and he helped her back to bed.

"We need to prop your head up higher so you can breathe easier. Pillows?"

"All I have are these two, but there are some on the sofa."

Ben rushed to get them and pushed them under the mattress at the head of the bed. He piled up the other two.

"Drink some water and take your medicine."

Jo did as he asked, and he helped her into the bed. "I'm going to slide down."

"I'll come check on you."

"Just stay and hold me up."

"I don't think that's a good idea, sweetheart. Rest."

"I don't deserve you," she gasped, as her glassy eyes closed.

"That's why it's called grace, Jo. None of us deserve to be loved." Her breathing slowed. "And I never stopped loving you," he whispered, before he left the room.

He glanced at the clock. 4:00 AM. Monday morning. He hadn't had much sleep. He'd have to get Jo to call work in a few hours. She'd left a message for her captain last night.

Ben flipped open his laptop, which Molly had delivered. He logged on and tried to focus on his own work. Coffee did little to revive him. He gave up and went back to a chair, now that the sofa was bare of even the slightest comfort. He grabbed an afghan to cover up, and while not totally comfortable, he dozed.

Dreams of happier days comforted him. He was grateful that God had brought him into Jo's life and established peace between them, so he could be there for her. Who else would care for her?

At seven, his phone rang. "Hello?"

"Benny? How is Jo?" Molly asked.

"She's still really sick, if not sicker. She had a rough night."

"At least you had sense enough to get her to the doctor right away."

"Yeah. Hey, first day of work, right?"

"Yup. Anything you want me to drop off before I go in?"

"I had hoped to run home to shower, but she's too weak to even get up on her own. A change of clothes?"

"*Eww.* You want me to go through your underwear drawer?" Molly joked.

"Just forget it. Enjoy your first day, Moll."

"I'll be over in twenty. Shaving kit as well, I assume?"

"Whatever you think is necessary. I missed No-Shave November, but there's still a few days left, right?"

"We don't want you scaring Jo now, do we?"

"Thanks, Moll. You're the best."

"But of course I am. I was born first."

"Cheeky dame," Ben muttered, as she laughed and hung up the phone.

Ben shuffled to the bathroom, then went to Jo's room. He put a hand on her forehead. She was still burning up. Her eyes flickered open.

"Benjamin?" she whispered.

"Yeah, hey, I think you should call the station." He handed her the cell phone by her bed.

Jo dialed the office. "Captain Jenkins? Did you get my message? Yeah, pneumonia. The doctor insisted on at least a week. He emailed you the excuse, but I have a paper copy if you need it for your files. I'm sorry. The good news is my arm will be good as new by then." She nodded at something that was being said. "Thanks, Captain." She handed the phone back to Ben.

"No problem?"

"I'm sure it's a huge problem, but what can I do?" She coughed.

He sat next to her to hold her and rub her back. When she finished, he leaned her back on the pile of pillows.

"Just call if you need me. I'm not going anywhere."

"Don't you have to work?"

"I brought my laptop. I can work in between making sure you get better."

A tear ran down her cheek.

His heart ached for what she was going through. "Hey," Benjamin said, as he pushed a curl off her cheek to catch the tear. "It'll be OK. Don't worry about it. Rest and get well."

She nodded and closed her eyes.

What more did he expect?

He walked to the kitchen to brew some coffee. He'd require a good dose of that. A soft knock on the door drew him there. He opened it, and Molly slipped inside with a bag.

"Good morning, Benny. You look like crap. You aren't getting sick too, are you?" She handed him the bag. "I packed more than what you probably needed, but hopefully it's enough to tide you over." She tugged a plastic bag from behind her. "I brought your pillow too. Sounded like you weren't sleeping too well on that sofa. What'd she do? Pick out the ugliest thing she could find from Goodwill?"

"Moll—"

"I know. Be kind. I love Jo to bits. Just feels like you both lost something when she left you. You lost someone whom you adored, and she lost out on what you have now."

"And what do I have now?"

"Money. Success."

"Pretty worthless, considering the cost."

"Pursuing your dreams didn't cost you your marriage. That idiot who embezzled did."

"And my own pride and foolishness. As for him, Jo tried warned me. She never liked him."

"And now you're older, wiser, and even more attractive, if I must stay so." Molly winked. "Gotta go. Call me if you need anything. I'm off at 5:00 PM and can drop by on the way home if you want me to."

"Thanks, Molly. Have a great first day at work."

She grinned. "I'll try my best. Should be interesting." With a wave, she was gone.

Ben tossed the pillow on the sofa. He might catch a nap later. He made a quick check on Jo before he slipped into the bathroom to freshen up. When he emerged, he peeked in on his patient again. She'd slid down further on the pillows, so he went in to ease her back up.

"Benjamin," she murmured, as she dragged an arm around him and turned her head into his shoulder before going limp. He wrapped the arm under her around to pull her up and closer, and settled against the headboard to enjoy this unasked-for affection from his ex-wife. She'd probably be horrified when she woke up. He couldn't help it. Exhaustion overtook him, and his head rested against hers as he drifted to sleep.

26

CHOCOLATE HOLDS POWER OVER DEPRESSION VICTORY OVER DISAPPOINTMENT.

ANONYMOUS

How could Jo experience such warmth and security when she ached all over and every breath hurt? She fluttered her eyes open to see Ben's chest. Her arm hugged solid muscle, yet it was a comfortable pillow. He smelled wonderful. Benjamin. Over three years had passed since she'd experienced the warmth of a man's embrace, care, and compassion. Who else would sit with her when she was so ill? She'd never asked him to do it. A melancholy washed over her. This too would pass, and she'd be alone again.

She stank. She hated to wake him, but she needed to use the bathroom and maybe take a shower. She patted his chest. "Benjamin?"

"Hmmm?" He hugged her tighter and sighed.

"Wake up. I need to use the bathroom."

"What?" His eyes opened, and the arm pulled away as he tried to disentangle himself from her. "Sorry. I got stuck and didn't want to disturb you." He rolled his shoulder, which had probably stiffened in that position. "I'll help you up."

She yanked the covers back to place her legs off the edge of the bed. “Let me get some things first. I need to shower.”

He stood and helped her up, supporting her as she gathered fresh undergarments and pajamas.

“Where do you keep extra sheets? I can change the bed. You’ll feel better with that.”

He’d remembered how much she loved fresh sheets? “In the hall closet. Thanks.”

Once he’d helped her to the bathroom, he gave her a soft, sleepy smile. “Call if you need me.”

“I will.”

Jo struggled to remain upright long enough for a shower, and was extra careful getting out of the bathtub. She dried off, dressed, combed, and conditioned her hair. Maybe she’d be able to stay awake long enough for it to dry. She gathered up her dirty clothes and opened the door.

Benjamin was waiting in the hallway for her. “Here.” He took her bundle, tossed it in the laundry basket, and then returned to her. “Want some soup?”

“Yeah, that’d be nice.” She leaned on him as he helped her to the kitchen. A cup of hot apple-cinnamon tea was already steeping for her. She lifted the bag and inhaled the comforting scent. “Stevia?”

“Already added, just as you used to like it. If that changed, I’m sorry.”

“It hasn’t changed.” She dipped the spoon into the warmed soup and took a sip. “Not sure how you got it just right, so I don’t burn my tongue.”

Ben grinned as he sat with a cup of coffee in front

of him. "I'm talented."

Jo ate her soup, surprised at just how thirsty she was. "What time is it?"

"Almost noon."

"Seriously? I had you trapped for that long? No wonder your shoulder was sore."

"Don't worry about that. I'll be fine. It was kind of nice. Will you be OK for a few minutes here? I can get a load of laundry started."

"I'm fine, but you don't need to—"

He was up and to the door. "I don't mind running to the basement with a basket, since it will be hard for you. I'll be back in a few minutes."

Jo ate her soup and sipped her tea. A glass of water was sitting close by with her pill bottle. Was it time for another dose?

He returned.

"Is it time for my medicine?"

Ben checked his watch. "Yeah." He opened the bottle and shook out the pill into her waiting palm.

She swallowed it with the water and then chased the bitter taste with her tea. "Are you going to eat?"

"Not yet. I'll get something eventually. I think Molly packed me some Thanksgiving leftovers. Probably a turkey sandwich."

"Sounds yummy."

"Want some?"

"No. Not sure I'm up for a full sandwich. I think I'd like to stay up for a little while, though. Anything good on television?"

"No clue."

"Right. Molly said you didn't even watch much television and she foisted one on you."

"I've watched shows I like on my computer through subscription services, but only after I've managed to get my tasks accomplished."

"Are you managing to get any work done?"

"No. I'm afraid to even listen to my business voice mail."

"You have two phone numbers?"

"Yeah. Just easier to keep business separate from personal life."

"You didn't use to do it that way."

"Hard lessons learned." Ben helped her to sit in the recliner. "I'll get you more tea."

"Sure, that'd be nice." She grabbed the remote and started flipping through channels until she found a movie she wanted to watch.

Ben cleaned up the dishes and brought her more tea. He poured himself another coffee, sat at the table, and flipped open his computer.

Why was Benjamin doing this? She enjoyed being pampered, but it brought back the memories of happier days. She wished he'd come and snuggle with her, perhaps on the couch. She spied a pillow on the couch, which was the most awful piece of furniture she owned. Guess that wasn't an option. Poor man.

~*~

The door's shutting woke her from her doze, and the television was now showing some movie she had no desire to watch. She turned it off.

Ben carried the laundry basket down the hallway.

"Hey."

He started. "I didn't realize you were awake. I was trying to be quiet."

"It's all right. Think it's time for a visit to the bathroom."

Benjamin rushed forward to help her get the footrest to her recliner down, and she clutched her chest at the pain there.

"You OK?"

"It hurts to breathe."

"It'll get better as the meds kick in." He helped her down the hallway, and she slipped into the bathroom. After she finished, she went to her bedroom. The covers on the freshly made bed were turned back. Ben hovered close, and she was glad she wasn't so dizzy she couldn't walk on her own. He rushed ahead to make sure the pillows were stacked so she'd be on an incline.

"Thanks." She climbed in and pulled the blanket up. She patted the side of the bed for him to sit.

He did, and faced her. Dark shadows highlighted his eyes, and a few hairs had fallen onto his forehead.

"Why are you doing this?" Jo asked.

"I remembered how sick you got that one time, and I was worried another bout of pneumonia would be worse for you."

"I appreciate your care. If you need to leave, I think I'm doing better now."

Benjamin shook his head. "I'm staying at least one

more night, in case that dizziness comes back, and until that fever has broken."

"Thank you. I like having you here." Except it made her long for more…

A soft smile played on his lips. "I'm glad I could do this for you." He kissed her cheek. "Get some sleep, and then maybe I'll fix something different for dinner."

"It wouldn't involve leftover turkey, would it?" she asked.

"And mashed potatoes. Another of your favorites."

"Sounds wonderful."

"Get some rest."

Jo closed her eyes, thanking God for providing for her and orchestrating things so Benjamin would be back in her life for something like this. She'd never have been comfortable with Molly or Geoff functioning in this capacity. Benjamin had an intrinsic understanding of just what she needed and when.

27

YOUR FAITH WILL NOT FAIL WHILE GOD SUSTAINS IT; YOU ARE NOT STRONG ENOUGH TO FALL AWAY WHILE GOD IS RESOLVED TO HOLD YOU.

J. I. PACKER

A few days later, after Jo had recovered sufficiently, Ben was back home working. A knock on the door disturbed him in the middle of a code.

"Benny?" The door cracked open, and his sister's voice grew louder. "Benny?"

He jerked his attention to her. "Huh?"

"No dinner?"

He glanced at the clock. "Sorry." He rose and followed her to the kitchen, flipping on the lights. "No date with Geoff tonight?"

"No. He works at seven. We've kind of been on an opposite schedule. He's off on the weekend, since Jo will be back."

"When do you get to talk to him?"

"We send each other emails when we're off, and I already called him on the way home to wake him up so he can eat and get ready to go in."

"You really like him a lot."

Molly sighed as she leaned against the counter.

"More than a lot."

"Love?" Ben asked.

"I think so."

"Is it mutual?"

"Yeah, as far as I can tell."

"I've not known Geoff long, but I can say I've never seen him so besotted before."

"Mother would be proud to hear you using such an old English term."

"I suppose I should be ready for them. They are due to arrive in two days."

Molly shook her head. "You're worried about them being here for nothing. It'll be wonderful to be together again for Christmas."

Ben frowned. "If you say so."

"I do."

"Miss Pollyanna."

"I'm not. I've seen so many lost and hurting children over the years it would break your heart, Benny. God at least gave us a wonderful father, who didn't just 'step' in, but adopted us and gave us his name. While I'll never forget our real father, we were both so young…"

"I don't recall much of him. I do remember when he died. Mostly how sad everyone was." Ben continued to bustle by the stove.

"Yeah. I'm glad I had you."

"Ditto. Aren't you worried they might cramp your romance with Geoff?" Ben asked.

"Ohhh, romance. I love that word," Molly said. "No."

Ben frowned. "Dinner's ready."

"What are we having?"

"Tacos."

"Yum." Molly helped him get the taco shells, salsa, and other taco elements to the table, and they sat and enjoyed their simple meal.

"How was your first week of work?" Ben asked.

Molly shrugged. "I'm used to doing paperwork and making phone calls, but today I had to wave a group off to China to bring their children home. That was hard."

"You miss the traveling?"

"I do and I don't. I just wish it was me going to get my own child."

"Someday, Moll. You'll be a great mom. Is Geoff on board with that dream?"

"He hasn't run from it. For such a big guy, he's really a sweetie, and would be a wonderful dad."

"I'm sure he would."

"Don't you want kids, Ben?"

"Kind of need a wife first. I don't want to be a single dad." He put up a hand. "Do not pitch Jo's attributes to me. When God determines it's time, I'm sure He'll bring the right woman into my path."

"It's not Candace?"

"No. She's a temporary distraction. A beautiful woman, but she's not someone who will be staying around."

"Maybe she requires a reason to stay."

"Molly?"

"Hmmm?"

"First you tell me to marry Jo and now you're pushing me to Candace? Why?"

"Well, things are moving fast with Geoff, and it would be cool for us to have a double wedding."

Ben groaned, rose from the table, and returned to his office, shutting the door firmly behind him and leaving Molly to clean up the kitchen.

~*~

Jo walked into her therapist's office. "I think this will be my last time here," she announced.

"Why would you say that?" Shirley asked.

"I just think we've covered everything we need to. You will clear me for duty, right?"

"I think you are ready emotionally to get back to work. Are you sure there isn't more you want to explore? How are things with your parents?"

"Our relationship is better. I think my career has been a stumbling block for them, but they've come to accept it."

"Have you come to accept it?" Shirley asked.

"Excuse me?" Jo stiffened her spine.

"From some of the things you've shared, I catch an undercurrent of uncertainty about your career choice."

Jo relaxed into the overstuffed chair. "Maybe so. I don't really have any other choices, though, do I? I've trained hard for this. I'm good at what I do."

"I understand you've worked hard. Many people go to college, start one career, and end up in an entirely different one. It's not unusual to find that something isn't as good a fit as you initially might have thought—even if you are good at it. You always have a choice."

"What else would I do? At one time I had thought that maybe…"

"Maybe what?"

"I'd kind of hoped to be a stay-at-home mom with my kids. Kind of silly, though, to be expecting a man to be taking care of me when I'm perfectly capable of bringing in a decent income."

"So the dream died along with the marriage."

"Yeah."

"I wonder if you've fully grieved that loss. Of course, it's not an option, and I'm glad you're not out looking for a man to take care of you so you can have that dream. Relationships are so much more complex and not quite so…transactional."

"Transactional?"

Shirley grinned. "A marriage, for example, isn't a matter of one person doing something to get something from the other and vice versa. A woman doesn't promise to keep the house clean and raise kids if the husband can support them financially. Raising children ideally takes two parents. Same with keeping a house. Both people help out, hopefully doing the tasks that they are best at. Not every man is great at balancing a checkbook, and sometimes a wife takes on the role of paying the bills. Some couples do it together because it's an act of the mutual respect they have. You don't have transactions. A marriage is more fluid than that and works best when both give everything to the relationship instead of being stingy about it. Does that make sense?"

"I think so. You're saying that it's not like we each have our own bank account, figuratively speaking, to deposit or withdraw from; we all put in, and we both would withdraw, but hopefully there'd be far more deposits so the relationship can be healthy."

"That's a fair way to describe it."

"It still doesn't help me."

"You can go back to work, Jo. If you ever want to return to see me to process more of this kind of stuff, I'd be glad to see you. Let me pray for you before you go."

Jo walked out of the office in a daze. There really wasn't a "you scratch my back, I'll scratch yours" method to marriage. Not that she really had considered what she had with Ben. In some ways, though, she felt as if she'd been giving more when they were younger so he could get his business going. Then it all fell apart. She had taken a loss in so many more ways than she'd realized. The past was the past, though. She was back to work as a State Trooper. Destiny or not, this was what she needed to do right now.

A few days passed. As happy as Jo was to be back behind the wheel of her squad car, writing speeding tickets wasn't a lot of fun. For some reason, everyone seemed to be in a hurry today. She flipped on her lights to pull over another car. As it eased onto the edge of the road, Jo took a deep breath. She checked online, and found that the temporary plate indicated the owner was…Amalia Elliot? Oh, boy. Stepping out of her squad, she made her way to the minivan. When she got to the window, she groaned. It really was Molly. Mrs. Elliot was in the passenger seat. Mr. Elliot was in the second row.

The window was already rolled down. "Hi, Molly, Mrs. Elliot, Mr. Elliot."

Hellos were given, but all the occupants seemed stunned, with wide eyes and mouths agape. None of them had ever seen her in her role as a State Trooper.

"You're not really giving me a ticket, are you?" Molly asked.

Jo shrugged. "I can't play favorites. You were twenty miles over the speed limit. Driving too fast when the road is still slippery is dangerous for you and the cars around you. You know better than that, Molly. License, registration, and insurance card, please."

Molly complied with a frown. "Wait 'til my brother hears about this."

Jo chose to remain silent. She went back to the patrol car, ran the information through the database, and wrote out the ticket. She headed back and handed them all to Molly. "Welcome back to the United States, Mr. and Mrs. Elliot. I hope your visit is a good one. See ya, Molly. Please understand, I'm just doing my job. Drive safely."

Molly didn't say anything else but rolled up the window.

Jo walked back to her squad and took a deep breath. Would Geoff have let her off? And what did it matter? She pulled back into traffic as reports of a stranded vehicle three miles ahead were phoned in. She radioed her response and headed out to help the motorist, providing a warm place for them to sit while waiting for the tow truck to come.

~*~

Shouts pulled Benjamin from his office.

"Benny! You won't believe what Jo just did!" Molly wailed.

"She gave your sister a speeding ticket, of all things," Mom said.

"No mercy, but she really looks great in her uniform." Dad winked at Ben.

Benjamin wanted to dig a hole and hide. "Sit down and start from the beginning."

They settled at the table, and Ben zipped his lip to indicate they were to stay quiet. He poured cups of Earl Grey tea for his parents and Molly, and when he finally had his coffee, he joined them. "It's nice to see you, Mum and Dad. How was your flight?"

"Don't go changing the subject," Molly protested.

"Take a breather, sis. The ticket isn't going anywhere, and you need to cool off," Ben said.

Mom nodded. "He's right, Molly."

"Fine." Molly stood up and went to her room, slamming the door shut.

"Keep that up and you can check into a hotel," Ben yelled after her.

Mr. Elliot chuckled. "Sounds like something I probably said to her when she was a teenager."

Mrs. Elliot chuckled. "True. And Molly *was* speeding. She was eager to bring us to see your beautiful home."

"It was a surprise to see Jo in uniform, but I give her props for sticking to her guns and doing her job in spite of Molly's attempt to intimidate her," his father said.

"Funny that Molly would stir the pot like this, since she's been trying to get Jo and me back together."

"Back together? As in married?" his mom asked.

Benjamin shrugged. "Jo and I are friendly, but our marriage is in the past."

Mom's shoulders drooped. "I'm sorry to hear that."

"Why don't I show you to your room, so you can get settled in? I would suggest you don't sleep, though. Jet lag and all. You'll do better if you stay up until after dinner."

"We know the drill, son. Show us the way."

Everyone rose from the table, and Benjamin gave them a tour of the house before leaving them at their room.

Molly had still not made an appearance, but she'd likely be stewing for a while. She used to get speeding tickets when she was younger. He'd insisted cruise control be a feature on her car, and she'd agreed. If the roads were wet, though, it was contraindicated, but she should have been more careful. Poor Jo. Probably not a high point in her day and would make future interactions awkward. But maybe putting space between Jo and Molly would be good, and get his sister off his case. He returned to his office to finish working on some code.

An email caught his attention.

Dear Ben,

My employer wanted to thank you for your assistance in helping us with that embezzlement case. The software you designed was an asset. I suspect we might have further need of your help in the future. As always, it was great to work with you again.

Will

Closing his email program, he settled into another program he'd been requested to hack into and find bugs. He preferred designing software, but blowing holes in someone else's programs made him good money. If it helped improve national security, all the better. A knock came on his locked door. He logged out and shut his system down before answering. He opened the door, and Molly pushed her way in.

"Did you cool down? Are there any holes in my wall I need to repair?"

"I haven't punched a wall since I was seventeen." Molly pouted.

"Good to know." Ben settled into his chair and motioned for her to sit in another one.

"I'm sorry I blew up at you. Even Jo didn't deserve my attitude. Getting a ticket is bad enough, and I was speeding, so I deserved it, but getting it in front of Mum and Dad?"

Ben nodded.

"You were always the good one, the best student, top of the class. Emotionally stable. And me? The screw-up. I want Mum and Dad to be proud of me like they are of you."

"Me? The guy who blew up his marriage and almost landed in jail?"

"You have a degree, a good career, a beautiful home..."

"And you have traveled the world giving orphans homes with people who desperately want them. You made that possible, Molly. Don't try to compare us side by side. We share similar features and a birth date, but there's nothing wrong with you being exactly who God created you to be. I'm proud of you, if that means anything. I admire your courage to step out and experience the world as you do. Try new foods. Visit new places. Make new friends. None of that is who I am. My circle of friends is small, and other than flying back and forth to London, I rarely go very far from home."

"You could still get Jo back, you know."

"It's too late for that."

"How do you know if you don't try?"

"Why is it so important to you that Jo and I reconnect?"

"Because I want to believe that if you can stay in love, the future isn't hopeless for a gadabout like me."

"Hey...you have a great guy in Geoff. He's solid in his faith, and he'll treat you well. What are you concerned with?"

"That I'll screw it up. That I'll start to settle down and get the itch to travel again."

"I thought you wanted lots of kids."

"I do."

"Who will take care of them?"

"Well, me, of course."

"And you don't think that'll be enough of an adventure to keep you on your toes? Look at what Mum and Dad had to go through with us."

"You mean with me."

"No. Us. I wasn't always an angel. Your antics just got more attention than mine."

Molly sighed. "So I'm not hopeless?"

"Nope. Not in the least. But if you slam doors, we seriously need to look at you moving into your own place."

She raised her right hand. "I solemnly swear to never slam my bedroom door again."

"Oh, but the front door, back door, and any other doors are fair game?" Ben joked.

Molly snapped her fingers. "Bummer, you saw through that one."

"I always was smarter than you, big sister."

Molly reached forward to punch his shoulder. "And I was always stronger."

"Bet I could beat you in a mile run, though."

"Probably true. I hate running. More of a dance exercise girl myself, which reminds me, I should join the gym."

"I'll remind you on Monday."

"Thanks, bro."

"Anytime. Now, any plans for how we can still do our jobs, and occupy Mum and Dad?"

"Not a clue, but they can do things on their own, right?"

"Yeah, but I'm thinking it might be good for me to

go work in an office this week, just to be safe," Ben said.

"Contract job?"

He nodded.

"That means they'll probably want my car. Will you be able to drop me off at work? Would that be on your way?"

"I can do that."

"What are you making for dinner?" Molly asked.

"I'm planning to take us all out to eat. Is Geoff available?"

"Not sure I'm ready to foist them on the poor guy."

"They aren't bad."

"They'd have him running for the hills in no time."

"I don't think he'll be scared off that easily," Ben assured her.

"I'll ask him. But will you ask Jo?"

"Like she'll want to come face to face with you and Mum and Dad after today's ticket?"

"I don't think she scares that easily."

"We'll see."

"You'll at least contact her?"

"If she's on duty, she won't be answering her phone. I'll shoot her a text, though, if that'll make you happy."

Molly stood and ruffled his hair. "That'll suffice." She left the room, shutting the door behind her so slowly he could barely hear the click.

Ben leaned back and texted Jo.

Molly regrets her words. Wondering if you're available for dinner tonight with the family. We're eating out. My treat.

He got no immediate response, but then he hadn't expected it.

28

FAITH IS WHAT MAKES LIFE BEARABLE, WITH ALL ITS TRAGEDIES AND AMBIGUITIES AND SUDDEN, STARTLING JOYS.

MADELEINE L'ENGLE

When her shift was over, Jo came home and collapsed. A message was left on her phone. Geoff.

Did you really give Molly a ticket?

Yes. I had to. 20 mph over. What would you have done?

My job.

Thanks.

Jo yawned. That might put a damper on Molly's matchmaking attempts. Who would want a sister-in-law who could arrest you? She discovered a missed text from Benjamin. She responded.

Exhausted. Going to pass. Thanks for the invite.

She turned off the lights and headed to bed.

~*~

Jo reluctantly attended church the next morning. She didn't relish running into Molly. When Jo had left Benjamin, it was Molly who'd harassed her with phone calls. She'd been in Europe at the time—Romania? The distance did not stop her from saying: "Jo, it's wrong for you to leave Benny. You need to be together. Ben would never cheat! You shouldn't run away from such a wonderful man."

But Molly hadn't been there and didn't know everything. To this day, she wondered if Molly knew the heartache both of them had endured. Not that Jo had considered Benjamin's pain back then.

It made her treasure their tentative friendship all the more now. She only hoped Molly's outrage hadn't driven a wedge between them.

She found a spot and sat alone, praying as she listened to the recorded worship music playing in the sanctuary before the service started. She sighed when a presence settled in next to her. Slowly opening her eyes, she turned to the intruder in her space. Benjamin.

"Good morning," he said with a smile.

"Back atcha, Benjamin."

"You are still one of the only people who uses my full name. That makes it special when I hear my name on your lips."

A shiver traveled up her spine. She wasn't sure how to respond, so she changed the subject. "How's Molly?"

"She's over her little temper tantrum and regrets the way she acted toward you."

"I've suffered worse."

"I'm sure you have. Are you ever afraid to walk up to a car, not knowing what you'll experience?"

"I try not to think about it. Always be on the alert, but try to be as non-threatening as possible, given the fact that I wear a uniform and carry a gun. Bulletproof vest gives me some security, although it's beastly hot in the summer."

"I'm glad you have that protection."

"It doesn't protect against every bullet. Only those aimed at my core. Thankfully most criminals aren't marksmen."

"You are?"

She nodded.

The worship band stepped onto the stage.

Molly slipped in next to Benjamin. When it came time to greet those next to her, Molly shoved past her brother to give Jo a hug. "I'm so sorry."

Benjamin inserted himself to put an arm around Jo for a side hug. The look in his eyes gave her a tremor of excitement. Had he wanted to kiss her? In church? She turned away as the band started up again, trying to refocus her thoughts. It was inappropriate to desire her ex-husband. Especially during worship. *Lord, help me!*

By the time the service ended, she had built a wall up around herself. She stood and followed Molly and Benjamin into the aisle, moving to the cafe.

"How are your parents liking their visit so far?"

"You mean beyond the shock of seeing you in your uniform? Dad said you looked great, by the way. Too early to tell. We couldn't get them up to come to church."

Molly interrupted. "Why don't you come to the house for lunch to visit? I'd like a chance to redeem myself."

"I'll pass, but thank you for the invitation."

Molly pouted.

"I understand how embarrassing and stressful it can be to see those lights and get pulled over. I was just doing my job. It wasn't personal. I had no clue what kind of car you drove or that you'd even bought one."

"Benny helped me."

"He's a great guy." Jo winked at Benjamin, who turned slightly pink. "It was nice seeing you both this morning. I think I'd better go. I'm on duty in a few hours."

"It was nice seeing you again, Jo," Ben said.

"Be safe out there," Molly added.

Jo nodded and went to get her coat to leave. Memories of lazy Sundays spent with Benjamin as a young bride flashed through her mind. Good thing he couldn't see her now, because she was certain her own cheeks had turned pink. *Laundry. Think about laundry.*

Right. As if that would help.

~*~

"Where you going, son?" Mr. Elliot asked.

Ben set his laptop bag in his office, locking the room as he left.

"I have my men's group tonight." Ben opted not to try to explain how alcohol contributed to the demise of his marriage. His parents likely wouldn't understand. And accountability for spiritual and emotional growth would be totally foreign to his father.

"Maybe I should come with you?"

Benjamin shook his head. "Closed group. No visitors."

"What kind of group is that? Is this part of your church?"

The church his parents refused to join them at on Sunday, opting to sleep in and make pancakes, leaving his kitchen a mess. Maybe this was payback for when he was a sloppy teenager?

"They're friends from church. We share the same faith, but we also share some of the same struggles. Can we leave it at that? I'm not sixteen anymore. I don't need to tell you everything I do."

"As if you ever did that. I don't understand. We came to visit you, and instead we keep seeing you and Molly leave. I thought you worked from home?"

"I normally do, Dad, but since my parents keep interrupting my labors, which right now is a highly-classified government job, I have gone into the office instead."

"Government?"

"Not saying any more." Ben tossed his keys in the air and caught them. "I'll be back later. Feel free to mess up my kitchen."

"Where's Molly?"

"I don't know. Maybe she's meeting Geoff for dinner? She told me I didn't need to pick her up tonight."

His father groaned. "If I wanted to spend this much time with your mother I could have stayed in England."

"Later, Dad." Ben shut the door to the garage behind him and left.

~*~

Ben reached the restaurant, grabbed a booth, and ordered coffee and some soup. He wasn't very hungry. The results of his software hacks had helped Will today in uncovering data in an ongoing federal investigation. It was beyond disturbing, and Ben didn't know if he had the stomach for the danger that could come with that kind of work.

Robbie soon arrived, followed by Alex and Tim.

"Hey guys, how are you doing?" Ben asked. "Sorry, I ordered first—been a long day, and I missed lunch."

"Not a problem." Tim waved for the waitress to come, and the rest of the men gave their orders.

"How's life treating you, Ben?" Alex asked.

"My sister is wreaking havoc in my home, and my parents arrived. My ex-wife is attending church here, and we've been getting along well. My sister is trying to reunite us."

"You've mentioned this before. Do you love her?" Roberto asked.

"Never stopped."

"Then why not pursue her? Just because you got divorced doesn't mean you can't remarry her. Neither of you knew Christ back then, and you've both grown up in the past few years. Don't let a past mistake force you to make another one now." Robbie sipped his coffee.

"Are you serious?" Benjamin asked.

Robbie nodded. "Marriage is hard no matter what,

but if you've always loved her, why would you walk away from that?"

"Just because I love her doesn't mean she'll come running back into my arms. I've been trying to prove to her that I've changed my ways, but not to win her back. Just to earn her respect after how I screwed up."

"How?" Tim asked.

"I begged her forgiveness and confessed what I'd done wrong. I took care of her when she had pneumonia and something else I'll keep secret."

"If she doesn't know, then how can she see you're different?" Alex asked.

"I didn't do it to win her back. I did it because she deserved at least that much from me. She doesn't need to know it was me. I don't want credit or for her to think I'm trying to manipulate her."

"Anything else?" Tim inquired.

"I tried to treat her with the kindness and respect I would give any friend."

"So, no touching or kissing."

"We kissed at Thanksgiving." Ben rolled his eyes. "Mistletoe. My sister hung mistletoe, and I used it as an excuse."

"And?" Robbie asked with a grin.

"She didn't slap me," Ben said.

"Have you asked her if she'd be interested in pursuing a relationship with you again? Beyond friendship?" Alex asked.

"No."

"Then do it and stop hiding from your feelings. No alcohol?" Tim asked.

"Not a drop. I've not even been tempted. But I have struggled with working too much, now that my parents and sister have taken over my home. Still a struggle not to get lost in the code as an escape from the reality—the questions—and my loneliness."

"Even with a full house?" Robbie asked.

Benjamin nodded. "So, enough about me. How's your pain been? It's been some time since your back surgery. Still doing physical therapy?"

The discussion moved on, much to Ben's relief. Pursue Jo? Would she even be open to that? Could he handle her rejecting him a second time?

~*~

He wandered into the house after the meeting. His parents were watching a movie by the light of the Christmas tree. "Good night, Mum. Dad."

"How was your secret meeting?" Dad asked, putting the movie on pause.

"It was good. Sorry I couldn't take you with me. I'd love to have you join me for church on Sunday, though."

"We'll see," Mom answered. "You look tired, son. Maybe you should get some rest?"

"Yeah, I have an early morning." They gave him a wave, and he walked to his office to make sure everything was secure. The software hack wasn't even with him. He'd left the thumb drives at the FBI offices. He'd admitted to Will that he was a little paranoid that the people they were after would find out he was the one behind this. Will had assured him he was safe.

When he entered his office, he discovered it had been tossed. File drawers were opened, and the contents lay in a pile on the floor. The closet door had been taken off the rail and had dented the drywall, where it rested at an angle. His laptop was gone, along with the power cord. He checked the windows. One was left slightly open. He strode to his bedroom and found nothing amiss.

Will had obviously downplayed the importance of this. He grabbed his phone and called Will.

"Ben?"

"Yeah, hey, remember how you said I was safe? Well, someone was in my office and stole my computer while I was out. My parents were here, but I doubt they'd do anything like this."

"Did you touch anything?"

"No. But if you send someone, can you do it quietly? It's late, and I don't want the neighbors asking questions."

"Got it. I'll phone it in. Don't touch anything."

"Fine. Are you sure the drives are safe at your office?"

"I'll go check. Be careful, Ben."

"I'm trying."

He left his office without shutting the door. He checked the other bedrooms. Everything was in order. No one was there. *Whew.* He walked back to the kitchen and began doing the dishes that had piled up. It was better than pacing the floor. His mother walked in.

"I thought you were going to bed?"

"Someone is stopping by in a few minutes."

"Who?"

"FBI. My office was broken into."

"What!" Mom exclaimed, holding a hand to her chest. "While we were here?"

"Apparently."

"Why?"

"Not sure. Looking for a thumb drive that isn't here, I suspect."

Her eyes narrowed. "What kind of work are you doing? Nothing illegal, I hope?"

"Nothing of the kind. I'm sorry. I had no idea that anything like this could possibly happen. We are in no danger right now. I'm waiting for the FBI to arrive."

"Are you safe?"

"As safe as I can be. I'm a software designer. I don't carry a gun."

"But you have friends who do."

"True, but I'm not calling off-duty State Patrol officers here to protect me. Not their job."

"I bet Jo would come."

Molly walked into the house, followed by Geoff. "Hey, is there a party going on? I see cars pulling up outside."

"Someone broke into the house!" Mom blurted out.

"What?" Molly asked, eyes wide as she grabbed Geoff's arm.

"Geoff, do you have your gun?" Dad gushed.

"I don't make a practice of going on my dates

armed with a weapon when I'm off-duty. I have a concealed-carry permit and a handgun in my car. Do I need it?"

"Probably not," Ben stated. "Want to join me in checking out the basement? I hadn't gotten that far. Molly, let the FBI in when they arrive."

His entire family gaped at him, not saying a word.

Geoff went outside to get his weapon and returned with two FBI agents.

Great. Looked as though it would be some time before Ben could sleep tonight. Weariness weighed his shoulders down.

29

I HAVE BEEN DRIVEN MANY TIMES UPON MY KNEES BY THE OVERWHELMING CONVICTION THAT I HAD NOWHERE ELSE TO GO.

ABRAHAM LINCOLN

The tech shook his head. "No prints. Check to make sure they didn't take anything besides the laptop, and let us know."

"I didn't have the software here."

"Just be careful. You might want to get a security system installed," one of the agents said to Ben.

"Good idea." Ben escorted the men out of the house and locked the doors.

Geoff sat with Ben in the kitchen. "You OK?"

"Just never imagined someone would come after me."

"Can you tell me about why they would?"

"Sorry. No."

Geoff nodded. "Do you need anything?"

Ben shook his head. "Other than rest and time to clean up this mess? I'm good. Just tired. I won't be able to sleep until it's all set to rights, and they gave me freedom to do so. No crime other than breaking and entering."

"It is upsetting, though."

"Yes."

"Want me to hang around tonight? I don't work tomorrow. I can sleep on the couch," Geoff offered.

"I don't want to put you out, but it'd probably make my parents and Molly feel safer." Ben rose. "I need to go straighten up."

~*~

Jo had the day off. She had received a cryptic text from Molly the night before, but she waited until 8:00 AM to call Benjamin.

"Hello?"

"Benjamin? Molly said something was going on but didn't say what."

Mumbling came over the line.

"Benjamin?"

"We had a break-in last night. Nothing was taken. FBI was here, and Geoff spent the night to help Mum, Dad, and Molly feel safer. Nothing else happened. We're fine."

"FBI? Why would the FBI investigate a breaking-and-entering call?"

He sighed. "Because they tossed my office, probably looking for some work I'm doing for Will at the FBI as an outside contractor. What they were looking for wasn't here."

"I'm glad you're OK. Do they think you're in any danger?"

"No, they don't."

"Benjamin. Don't act all tough to me. That had to

be upsetting."

"Ticked me off. I spent hours trying to get things in order just so I could sleep."

"Wanna do breakfast or lunch?"

Silence.

"As friends, Benjamin. Having someone invade your space can be traumatic. I just want to be your friend."

"Fine. Can you meet in an hour?"

"Sure."

He gave her a location and hung up.

Jo stared at her phone. Benjamin didn't want to admit he was rattled by what happened, but she knew him better than that. Having a houseful of people probably wasn't comfortable either. She finished dressing and drove to the sit-down restaurant he'd recommended for breakfast.

Ben pulled in.

She got out of her sedan.

"Hey, Jo."

They walked into the restaurant together. His hand at her back warmed her, even through her coat.

They sat at a booth and ordered food.

Benjamin wasn't meeting her eyes.

"What is it?" she asked.

"I love you," he blurted out. "I would like it if we could date."

"Excuse me? Did I hear you correctly? But why? What's the point? Been there—done that—bought the wedding rings." Jo's soft smile took the sting out of the words. Her heart raced at the thought of dating him, but that was foolish, wasn't it?"

He sighed. "We both made our mistakes, but we're older and wiser. Can you honestly say you feel nothing for me anymore? Haven't I proven to you that I've changed? Matured? That you could trust me again?"

The waitress came to set the food down.

"I'll pray." Benjamin bowed his head but reached for her hand.

She placed it in his, and he squeezed, sending a zing all the way to her heart.

"Lord, bless this food. Thank You for keeping us safe in this scary world. Thank You for Jo, and our friendship. Amen."

He let her go, and she reached for her coffee to warm herself up after the chill that followed. An emptiness that threatened her if she didn't treat this man with care. She weighed her words carefully.

"Benjamin. You are the best man I know. You have grown and changed beyond my wildest imaginings. I love you and your family. I just don't know that I can erase all the past, even having forgiven you and understanding the *why*—I'm not even sure you can trust me again."

"Could we date and explore this further?"

She swallowed hard. "I suppose that would be OK. But no pressure."

"Did I do that the first time around?"

Jo shook her head. "You were sweet and patient. I was the one eager for more."

He smiled. "You had me wrapped around your

little finger."

"And your accent charmed me."

"Does it still?"

"No one sends a thrill through me like you do, Benjamin."

"I like the sound of that." He grinned and dug into his omelet. "So, when are you off work so I can take you out again?"

"I'm off today but need to rest. Perhaps tomorrow?"

"It's a date."

When they were done eating, Benjamin walked her to her car.

"It's cold out," she said.

"Let me warm you for a minute." Benjamin kissed her gently, and true to his word, she warmed up. Until he pulled away. She groaned.

"Not fair."

"Not married."

"You said you wouldn't pressure me."

"I didn't. I only spoke the truth." He opened her door, shut it, and then waved good-bye as he headed to his own vehicle.

She planned to date her ex-husband, who might want to marry her—again? Was she nuts?

Certifiably so. She texted him when she got home.

Please don't tell Molly or your parents we're dating.

He responded.

Fine, but they'll figure it out.

How true was that? This could be messy. The last time they'd dated, neither of their families were involved in any way. This was a new wrinkle in any chance for a happily-ever-after-again.

Why did she hesitate to hope it could happen? God didn't let dreams like that come true, did He?

~*~

Ben walked into the office he used at the FBI and sat to meet with Will and his boss, Special Agent Mertz. She was a no-nonsense agent with straight dark hair pulled back in a braid.

"Are you OK, Ben?" Will asked as they were seated in a conference room.

"A little shook up. Never expected someone to come looking for that. My laptop was gone, but thankfully everything was saved to a cloud, and nothing was stored on the laptop. I ordered a new one last night, and it should be here tomorrow. I have an old one to do basics on for now, and I wasn't even using mine to do this work."

"You were smart not to have the thumb drive in the house," Mertz said.

"Is there any other threat to me or my family?"

"I'm surprised they came after you. How would they even know?" Will asked.

"I did have my laptop open here yesterday. If they were tracking my IP address…and then discovered it at my home?"

"Possible, but why, if you didn't program from there?"

"Emails? It doesn't matter now. I have nothing at

my house, in my car, or on my person for them to retrieve."

"Unfortunately, that's not true," Mertz said.

"Why?" Benjamin asked.

"You still know the code and hack in your mind," Will answered.

"So, what, they'll be coming after me now?"

"I highly doubt it. We're on the verge of being able to make arrests, thanks to your work. Agents are out taking care of that right now. You'll likely be asked to testify in court, but that shouldn't be a dangerous thing."

"Fine. Whatever you want. Just glad to help. I know what it's like to be falsely accused, so I'm glad we were able to save this person from the same fate."

"We'll call you if we need more of your help," Mertz said as she stood.

The men rose.

Ben grabbed his jacket. "Time for some Christmas shopping. I can't do much else until my new computer arrives and I get it set up."

"I'm sure that will take some time. I'm sorry about all that," Will responded.

"Cost of justice, I guess," Benjamin said. "See you Sunday, Will."

"Stay safe."

Ben drove to Mayfair Mall and wandered around looking for gifts for his parents and Molly. He found a few items and had them gift-wrapped while there. He'd be giving Jo truffles. Those were always her favorite. That obviously hadn't changed, if that video

Molly took was any indication. Some others on his gift list would get those too. He might not be able to work in his office, but he did have something to keep him busy in the meantime. He drove home to find the house peacefully empty.

He stashed the gifts under the tree. While he hadn't liked Molly turning his life upside down, he had to admit she'd warmed up his home considerably with her decorating. He was beginning not to mind the television either, although he rarely watched it, and made her pay the cable bill.

He walked back to his office. Everything was in tidy piles, but far from being organized. He decided to make the chocolate instead of working in there. That would be something to do when he needed to escape his family. It sounded sad to say that, but he really wasn't used to them all being around.

The phone rang. He turned off the Christmas music he'd been playing.

"Hello? Molly?"

"Yeah, calling from work. Mum and Dad took my car. Said they were driving up to Green Bay to do some shopping and visit Lambeau Field. Remember how fascinated Dad has been with American football? He insisted on visiting the home of the Green Bay Packers. Just thought you'd like to know."

"You'll need me to pick you up from work?"

"Geoff will get me and take me out to dinner. You have a rare few hours with the house to yourself."

"Wonderful. I already have some gifts under the tree and was in the process of making chocolates."

"Can you make extras? I'll pay you for them. They'll be great gifts for my staff."

"I can do that. How many?"

She gave him a number and then hung up. He set the phone down and turned the music back up. He'd finished his regular chocolate truffles and was now ready to work on some dark chocolate ones with peppermint.

Time flew, and small white boxes of chocolates had piled up, awaiting their blue-ribbon wraps. Some were single-flavor, some were multiple, and all were labeled.

He slumped into his favorite chair in the dark house lit only by the lights Molly had put on a timer.

Alone…again.

30

FAIR? YOU WANT FAIR? LISTEN, A FAIR IS A PLACE WHERE YOU GO TO RIDE ON RIDES, EAT COTTON CANDY AND CORN DOGS, AND STEP IN MONKEY POOP.

BENNY URQUIDEZ

Jo had been first on the scene of a horrific car accident. She phoned it in and started helping. By the time everyone was taken away by ambulance and she had worked with fellow officers to write up the accident report with all the data, she was struggling to hold it together.

A young family had lost half their members. Jo had done all she could to keep the husband alive with CPR in the icy-cold snow, but her efforts hadn't been enough, given the extent of his injuries. The mother had been blessedly unconscious through that, and the little boy who survived had been in shock. A baby died in spite of her car seat. First responders were on the scene quickly, but never fast enough. Not that anything faster could have saved any who had died.

She rolled into the station at the end of her shift to report in.

Captain Jenkins took her aside. "Jo. You did your

job, and you did it well. How are you holding up?"

She fought back tears. "I just keep thinking how hard Christmas will be for those families. The empty spots at the table. That wife'll wake up to find she's a widow and lost a child as well. How does one live through that kind of pain?"

"That little boy might have been an orphan, had you not done all you could for them and others. You had someone covering up that mother and called out to others who pitched in to help. You went above and beyond the call of duty, and I'm proud of you. You can visit any of the survivors in the hospital if you wish or attend the funerals. But even more than that, you can pray for them."

Jo nodded. "Thanks, Captain." She hung up her hat, grabbed her winter coat, and headed home. It was later than normal, but it seemed that the worst things she experienced on the job always happened at the end of her shift. She supposed she should be grateful for that. It would be hard to patrol and do her job as shaken as she was.

Once home, she got out of her car, went inside, and changed into her comfy clothes. Her phone rang.

"Yeah?"

"Jo."

"Good morning, Geoff. What are you doing up so early?"

"I work today. Heading in soon to take Josh's spot—he's come down with the flu. Heard about the accident. You OK?"

"Yeah. I look forward to when we get to work

together again. It was hard not having you there."

"Try not to think about it."

"Easier said than done."

"Should I call you later?"

"No. Thanks. I'll see you at church tomorrow. I have a date tonight."

"Really? Anyone I know?"

"Benjamin."

"About time. I'm happy for you both."

"Thanks. See you tomorrow, Geoff. Stay safe out there."

"Vest is on. The only thing I'm missing is my sure-shot partner. Get some sleep, Jo. You did well today."

Jo hung up, grateful that Geoff had given her other things to think about. Her own father had been injured in a car accident on the job. He'd done dispatch until they determined his disability to be permanent. She'd always admired him and wanted to be as heroic as he was. She was finding out the hard way that it wasn't as good a feeling as she'd hoped for. She began to wonder if she was really cut out for this line of work after all.

Enough maudlin thinking. What she needed was sleep. Shutting the blinds, she crawled into bed, recalling how Benjamin had so lovingly cared for her when she was sick with pneumonia. Thoughts of Benjamin were happier ones, so she imagined she was holding him as she hugged her pillow. Why was she being tortured with thoughts of what-could-have-been now?

~*~

Jo woke, dressed, and waited for Benjamin to come. She'd called the hospital to check on the families that had been rescued last night. Perhaps she'd visit them later, unless Benjamin would take her now. That would probably be a little much to ask.

A knock on the door alerted her to Benjamin's arrival.

He stepped inside and looked around. "Still no Christmas here?"

"I haven't had the time or energy."

"You're not the Grinch?"

"No. Not at all. But hey, I got a favor to ask. Can we stop at the hospital before we eat?"

"Sure. Not a problem." He held out her coat. "Anyone in particular you aiming to see?"

"Survivors of an accident I helped with."

Benjamin nodded and escorted her to his car. "Bad night, huh?"

Jo groaned as she settled into her seat. After Ben buckled up, she spoke. "Occasionally, I question if I'm really cut out for this line of work. I don't want to end up like my father, but sometimes it seems as though the emotional toll could be far worse."

"I wish I had an answer for you. Seems too long ago when we had some different dreams."

Subdued, she whispered, "Yeah, but a lot died back then. More than we realized at the time."

Benjamin didn't respond, but his gulp told her he heard and understood her meaning. When they arrived at the hospital, he came in with her and motioned to the gift shop.

"Any kids?"

"Yeah, one little boy."

Benjamin grabbed a teddy bear, went to the register, and paid for it. He handed the bear to her. "Let's go see him first."

They got room information and went to the pediatric ward. The little boy had undergone surgery on his leg. They entered the room, and Jo walked to the bed where the little boy reclined. His brown eyes followed her. "Who are you?"

"I'm Trooper March. I helped your family after your accident this morning. I brought you something." She handed him the teddy bear. "I'm sorry you have to go through this."

"I haven't been able to see Mom, Dad, or my sister. No one will tell me anything."

"Maybe they don't know everything yet and don't want to tell you until they do. It was a messy accident." Jo bit back tears. If they hadn't told him, she wasn't about to. "You're a brave boy, and you're really cute. I expect the nurses will be happy to help you with anything you need. I'm glad you're getting well."

"Thank you." His eyes told her he suspected the worst.

"I have to go. I'm praying for you and your family."

He nodded and hugged the teddy bear close.

Jo backed away and headed to the door. Once in the hallway, she turned into Benjamin's arms and let him hold her. When she had her wits together, she pulled back. "Thank you," she whispered. "Let's go see his mom."

Benjamin nodded and walked silently by her side until she stopped at the mother's room.

The nurse by her bed spoke. "She's resting after her surgery earlier, but she should recover." The nurse bustled out.

Jo went to the bed and clasped the hand that wasn't attached to anything. She squeezed it gently. "I'm so sorry I couldn't do more. You are in my prayers."

The young mom didn't stir or open her eyes. Jo offered a quick prayer for her recovery. She let the woman's hand go, left the room, and grabbed Benjamin's hand. He held it tight and walked beside her as they left the building.

"There were others, right?"

She nodded. "This was the car with the worst damage and injuries. The only fatalities. The rest were probably released from the emergency room after treatment."

"I'm sorry you had to be there." He opened the door to her car.

"It's my job." She slipped in, and he closed it.

Once he got in on his side, he started the engine. "If you'd rather not go out to eat—"

She leaned forward and kissed him. Her gloved hand caressed his face. She ended the kiss and discovered Benjamin was as breathless as she was. "Dinner would be fine. I want to be with you."

He gave her a soft smile and a nod. "Dinner it is, then."

~*~

When they arrived at the steak house, they were seated at a table. Ben sat adjacent to Jo after placing a kiss on her hair.

"One of the things I always appreciated about you was that you don't ever try to talk away my feelings. You understand when quiet is the best response."

"Not always. But thank you. I could tell you were sad about what happened. That little boy lost his father and baby sister, right?"

Jo nodded. "And the mom hasn't awakened yet to learn the truth."

"That'll be harsh."

"Yeah."

They ordered their food, and a wine list was brought. "Care for a glass of wine, Benjamin?"

"No. Water is fine. I gave up alcohol after I lost you, but I won't stop you from enjoying some if you want."

Jo shook her head. "No. Water is fine. Can I get a lemon slice in there?"

The waitress nodded and left.

"I'm sorry I forgot that you believed your drinking contributed to our problems."

Ben shrugged. "Not sure how much it contributed, but it was my way of coping instead of telling you how bad things were. The alcohol didn't help, that's for sure. Especially that last night when I got so drunk. I didn't leave the bar until closing and had to call a cab. I couldn't even walk home. By then you were gone, but I was too inebriated to even care. I sure cared when I woke up the next morning, though."

Jo sighed. "Did you even fully grasp what happened?"

"Not right away. I was told the next night, and it wasn't until then that I realized how bad things were. It was as though there was a window of time to win you back, and it had closed before I even recognized it was there. I was too proud then to come to you and confess how badly I'd screwed up. I hope I've proven to you that I really have changed. I'm not the same man I was back then. I won't be making those same mistakes."

"My perception of you has changed."

"For the better?"

"Definitely for the better." She grabbed his hand, and he prayed over the meal.

~*~

When Benjamin dropped her off later, she unlocked the door and invited him in.

"Not a wise idea, Jo."

"Why? You stayed with me for several days while I was sick," she pouted.

"True. But you're not sick anymore."

She pouted. "I thought we were dating. Don't we get to make out?" Jo winked.

"A kiss good night. I don't want to go further than that unless we're married."

"Sounds as if you're pressuring me." Now her

hackles were raised. Did he want her or not?

"No pressure—just a boundary."

"Then I suggest you kiss me."

Benjamin obliged, much to her satisfaction. She pulled back. "Thank you for dinner—and for just being there for me."

"Anytime, Jo."

She slipped into her apartment, locked the door, and wondered how Benjamin would respond if she told him she loved him. How did she ever get past all that hurt and pain to trust him again? But did she really trust him? Love demanded trust, didn't it?

~*~

Jo worked Sunday morning and came home ready to do laundry and pay bills. She sat down at her laptop and went to balance her checking account. An automatic payment hadn't gone through. She checked with the company online who held her student loan.

Her balance was zero.

There was no way. She checked the payment history, and sure enough, there was a payoff of the loan two weeks ago. To the penny. She found the lost email that confirmed the payoff. But who? How? She messaged the company to make sure it wasn't an error. They responded quickly. No error. Strange.

She took care of the rest of her bills, and after ironing her uniform, she went to bed. Tomorrow was Monday, and she and Geoff would be patrolling together. It had been a long time.

As she went to sleep that night, she had visions of the accident from the other night. Her heart raced when she realized the man she was trying to revive was Benjamin. Panic seized her, and she awoke with a jerk. Everything within her wanted to call him and make sure he was OK. Ridiculous. But she couldn't shake the terror, so she dialed his phone.

A sleepy voice answered, "Jo? Is everything all right? It's two in the morning."

"I had a horrible nightmare, and I had to call to make sure you were well."

"I'd always hoped to be in your dreams, but not as part of a nightmare. Will you be OK?"

"I should be fine now. You're home. Safe. That's what I needed to know."

"Flip your pillow to the fresh side. Go back to sleep, Jo."

"You too, Benjamin. Sorry about this."

"Not a problem. Happier dreams now. I'll dream about your kisses."

"'Night." She hung up and set the phone aside. She flipped her pillow to the cooler side and settled in, thinking about kissing Benjamin. Much more pleasant dreams followed.

~*~

Ben yawned and stumbled to the kitchen. His parents had returned to his house the previous night, and he'd spent the weekend setting up his new computer. His only reprieves from work had been his date with Jo and going to church. Then Jo had called him in the middle of the night. He was glad she felt she could do that. He recalled times when she'd have a rough day at work, either in the bar or on the road construction crew, and how if it was bad enough, she'd have nightmares and he'd comfort her. He wondered if she'd suffered from that after the shooting as well.

He still loved her. Could he live with the danger her career entailed? It wasn't really part of their original dream of having children and her staying home while he worked. It would have been a sweet reward after all she had done to help him in those early years before the money started to roll in. By then she was long gone, due to his own foolishness and the legal challenges. It was a moot point. She wasn't falling into his arms again that easily. It was a foolish fantasy to entertain.

Since the roads were clear he went for a run outdoors. When he returned, he found a bleary-eyed Molly in the kitchen.

"The coffee is hot." He handed her a cup.

Molly held hers close and leaned against the counter. "This morning Geoff starts patrolling with Jo again as his partner."

"That's good, isn't it?"

"Yeah. Benny, I really like this guy. He's even offered to come to Romania with me in February to experience my passion for orphans."

"Cool."

"I know, right? I got a good one. I'm eager to start the next chapter of my life."

"What chapter is that?"

"Settling down with a husband and kids."

"Do you envision Geoff as the man you'd share that dream with?"

She nodded.

"Please pray for Jo and me. I've come to the conclusion that I want her as my wife again. She's not so open to the idea, but she's at least letting me date her."

"Want me to talk to her? Or perhaps Geoff?"

"No!" Ben blurted out before putting a finger to his lips. "If she feels pushed or manipulated, she'll have nothing to do with me. She'll think I'm doing it even if I'm not."

"Fine. Can you give me a ride to work? I'm assuming Mum and Dad will want my car again."

"Nah. I don't anticipate going anywhere today. They can take mine."

"Great. I have to get ready. Thanks." Molly skipped to her room and shut the door behind her.

Ben went to his own room and prepared for work.

Stepping back into the kitchen later, he found his parents. Mom was making scrambled eggs. "Good morning, Mum." He gave her a kiss on the cheek. "Dad." He patted him on the shoulder before refilling his coffee mug. "Did you make enough for me?"

"Yes, dear," Mom said, as she put plates in front of him and his father. "Eat up!"

Ben rose to get some salsa out of the refrigerator, as well as a bottle of ketchup. He handed the ketchup to his dad before dumping some salsa on his own plate. He dug in. "Mmmm, sharp cheddar. Good call, Mum."

Molly rushed out of her room and grabbed a bag out of the fridge, presumably her lunch. "Bye! I'm off. See you later. Thanks again, Benny." With that, she was out the door to the garage.

"What was she thanking you for?"

"I told her you could use my car today if you wanted."

"But we left our Christmas gifts in the back of her van. We were going to wrap them while you two were gone today."

"You could have just put them in your room. I doubt she'll look back there. We aren't little kids anymore. We won't search the house for hidden presents. It'll probably be safe enough where she works."

"You'd better hope so." His mother shook a spatula at him.

Ben took his plate to the sink, rinsed it, and put it in the dishwasher. "Let me know if you need my car." He filled up his coffee. "I'm off to work. I'll be in my office." Ben disappeared as quickly as he could.

He was glad they were in the dark about Jo. He feared anything could happen to disturb the new relationship springing up between them. It was too new, too…sacred. Yeah, that was a good word for it. Fragile and sacred. He shut the door to his office and settled down to work. Easier to say than do when thoughts of Jo continually interfered with his coding.

31

STRESS WOULD NOT BE HARD TO TAKE IF IT WAS CHOCOLATE-COATED.

ANONYMOUS

Captain Jenkins took Geoff and Jo aside. "This week I have you riding together in one squad. Jo, I know you were shook up with that accident, and Geoff, you've not been back for long. Don't think of this as a setback but as a reward. You get company for the week."

Geoff nodded. "That's fine, sir."

Before they got in the car, Jo motioned that Geoff could drive. "You OK?"

She shook her head and frowned. "The accident. I had a nightmare about it. Called Benjamin to make sure he was OK."

"Does Ben show up in your nightmares often?" Geoff asked.

"I had one after the shooting, and after I'd seen Benjamin again. It was him on the ground instead of you."

"And who was Ben in the one you had last night?"

"The guy I tried CPR on who died at the scene."

"I'm sorry. Those are hard."

"Yeah."

Geoff swallowed hard. "I would suspect your feelings for Ben are pretty strong, if the thought of losing him would terrify you so much."

"I don't want to talk about Benjamin."

"You brought it up."

"Fine. How are you and Molly?"

"Jealous?" He grinned and started the squad car.

"No! I'm happy for you. Two people I adore and care about are dating—and that's a good thing."

"We're doing well. It probably sounds trite, but I think I'm in love."

"She's wrapped you up like a burrito," Jo teased. She was glad to divert attention away from her confused heart.

"Has she always loved kids?"

"As long as I've known her, it's been the thing she's most passionate about—providing homes for orphans. She ended up doing international work, but I'm sure she'd be just as good working on local adoptions too. Every Child A Home is blessed to have her on their staff."

"Yeah. And I'm blessed to have her in my life. Would you think me foolish to propose so soon?"

"If you love her and she loves you? Not at all. I think you'll be perfect together."

"Thanks for the vote of confidence."

They drove for a while before stopping for coffee.

"Can I confess something to you?"

"What?" Geoff asked.

"I'm beginning to wonder if this was the right

career field for me."

"Why?"

"I get too emotionally scarred by the accidents, the shooting. I'm not sure I'm psychologically able to cope with this."

"They gave you evaluations. You're fine. Are those things hard? Absolutely. That's what makes you human and a good law enforcement officer. You care about the people you're serving. It's not about writing tickets—it's about keeping the roads safe for everyone, helping people when they are vulnerable, and rescuing those in trouble. It's a noble cause, and you're highly skilled. I'm grateful you are my partner."

"Thanks. Still…"

"What else would you do?"

She sighed. "I'm not sure. With my training I could be an inspector at the weigh stations or work at the Department of Motor Vehicles."

"They get about as much love as we do on most days," Geoff quipped. "Don't sweat it. And don't make any hasty decisions based on your emotional response. What you went through would cause anyone to cry or have nightmares. It's an unfortunate part of the job. Imagine how the paramedics and emergency medical technicians feel when they can't save someone. They have more training and equipment, but they are not God, and neither are you."

"Got it. That's what I needed to hear. Thanks."

"Anytime, partner." Geoff turned on his lights and siren. "Got a speeder. Let's go."

~*~

Benjamin had been grateful that a few times this past week, Geoff and Jo had joined them for dinner despite long work shifts. But he was glad Jo was so good and dedicated to her career; he wanted her to be happy and joyful. He also prayed they could grow together in the newfound faith they shared. He was thrilled he could clear up one debt from their past. To share his monetary success and help her was a financial obligation he'd never fulfilled as a husband.

His parents had taken a train to spend a few days sightseeing in Chicago. That left him and Geoff with the opportunity to romance their gals without parental supervision. It was good to be full-grown, responsible adults.

He still thought it funny that after dinner, Molly would claim the living room with "her" television, asking Jo and him to go to the basement. At least the furniture was decent down there.

Ben led Jo down the stairs, and she collapsed on the couch. "Thanks for letting me change here instead of going home. I couldn't imagine spending another minute in that vest."

"I'm glad you wear it at work, but I admit I'd rather hold you close without it." Ben turned on some music and sat next to her.

She snuggled up to him, and he turned on the gas fireplace with the remote. An area rug and a small tree occupied the space. "This room has potential."

"Yeah. I considered getting a treadmill down here.

I could run anytime, whether the gym was open or not."

"Would you do it, though?"

"I think so."

They sat comfortably listening to the holiday tunes.

"Something weird happened the other day," Jo finally spoke up.

"Really? What?" Ben asked.

"I was balancing my checkbook, and my student loan payment hadn't been taken out. So I went online and discovered the loan had been paid in full. I called in, but they couldn't give me any information on who did it."

"That's kind of cool." He kissed the top of her forehead.

"It's also weird. Whoever did it would have to know my social security number and password." She pulled away from him and turned to face him, shaking her head. "You didn't do this, did you? I warned you not to try to manipulate me or pressure me into marrying you."

Ben pulled away, surprised at her withdrawal. "If I were pressuring you, wouldn't I have bragged about doing it? What makes you think I have that kind of money to throw around, anyway? How much did you owe?" He didn't want to lie.

"Don't play sly with me. It had to be you. You're the only one who knew that information, because some of those loans were taken out while we were still married."

"Wouldn't that legally make them my responsibility as well?" Ben bristled. How had one innocent act of generosity turned so bad?

"Not once we divorced," Jo stood.

"My name was on the ones we took out while we were married. I had some as well. But don't worry. Mine are paid off. If something happens to me, they won't be coming after you for the money."

Jo's breathing grew labored. She was gearing up for a fight.

Ben rose to his feet. "Listen. You left our marriage and took some of what we had in savings. I owed you far more than that for all you did to support us while I went to school and got my business up and running. I failed, but that didn't need to be something you paid for. I'm glad your loan is paid off, but don't berate me about manipulation and pressure. All you've done is kiss me and push me away. What kind of mixed message is that?"

Tears sprang to his eyes. Grief over his past sins and failure to win Jo back now, all tumbled inside his chest. "I love you. I've loved you since I first met you. That never died, no matter how hard I tried to bury it. Obviously, you don't feel the same way. I suppose it's better that I realize this now. Go ahead and leave. Again. I'll leave you alone as you wanted." He turned off the fireplace and music before taking the stairs two steps at a time.

He entered his office, kicked the door closed, and locked it. He didn't bother with the lights. Collapsing into his office chair, he gazed out at the dark night. A drink. He'd give his right arm for a drink right now. He paced the floor for a minute before picking up the phone and calling Roberto.

"Hey, Ben, what's up?"

"Is this an OK time to talk?"

"Are you in trouble?"

"Not legal trouble. I broke up with Jo. All I want right now is to go out and get hammered."

"The pain cuts deep, doesn't it?" Robbie asked.

A door closed. Jo must have left.

A knock came to his door.

"Benny?" Molly asked.

He covered the phone receiver. "I want to be alone," he barked out.

"Ben, the fact that you called is a good thing. The pain is real, and it's OK to admit it. I'm sorry that happened. Wanna talk about it?"

"Jo accused me of manipulating her. She deduced that it could only have been me who paid off her student loan. I never intended for her to find out it was me. How is that pressure? I thought I was doing something nice for someone I loved."

"Wow. Ouch. That hurts. Listen, you can't control how other people think and act. And you can't allow Jo's emotional blaming to stick to you. Your motive was pure. Walk in that truth. I'm sorry that it caused a divide between you when you hoped for much more. I'd like to say maybe it's for the best, but I don't know that it is. A drink won't make it better or take away the problem. It might create new ones. You are a new creation in Christ. You don't need to live like you did in the past."

"So how do I move past this?"

"Time. Prayer. Friends. How about I pray for you now?"

"OK." He bent his head, tears still making paths down his cheeks.

"Heavenly Father, You know how Ben's heart aches right now over losing Jo and how that taps into all the pain from the past. We ask that You wrap Your arms around him. Comfort him by the power of Your Holy Spirit. Give him peace in the midst of his pain, and the assurance that You are still at work in his life. We trust You, Lord, even when we don't understand what You're doing. Help Ben face the pain without the alcohol and continue to function and do work that honors You. We love You, Lord."

"Amen," Ben whispered. "Thank you. I've never had to make a call like this before. Not that I probably didn't need it at times, but I appreciate it."

"You'll be all right? No thoughts of drinking now or otherwise hurting yourself?" Robbie asked.

"I won't hurt myself or drink. I can't say I'm fine, but I think I'll be able to go to bed and face tomorrow. Right now, that's enough of a win for me to grab."

"Good. Call any time."

"Thanks. Good night." Ben hung up the phone.

Jo had tried to call, but he ignored it. He didn't even listen to the voice mail. It was over. It needed to be. He couldn't be jerked around like a yo-yo. Either he was worth trusting or not. Apparently, in Jo's eyes, the answer was negative in spite of his best intentions. He took a few deep breaths, opened the door, and went to his room to go to bed.

Somehow he managed to avoid his sister and Geoff. He wasn't feeling social right now. He hit the pillow a few times, as if that would punch down all the hopes and dreams that kept pushing themselves forward to be acknowledged.

~*~

Geoff offered to let Jo drive the next morning, but she shook her head.

"You OK? Am I going to be able to count on you out there?"

"I'll have your back. I'm fine." She straightened her spine as she buckled herself in. "Let's go."

"Molly and I were worried about you and Ben last night."

"No need to worry. I'm sure Benjamin Wentworth 'sticking-my-nose-where-it-doesn't-belong' Elliot is just fine."

The aggression in her voice startled him. "Did you need to hit the punching bag this morning?"

"No. Just drop it. OK? Benjamin and I are over. Done. Finished. Kaput. Terminal."

"Wow."

"Just drive, Geoff," she growled.

~*~

Jo returned home that night and paced in her apartment. Somehow, Benjamin thought paying off the student loan debt was his responsibility.

You should be grateful he did that.

Why? He had no right to try to buy his way into her life after all that had happened. That's what it felt like. A bribe. An attempt to control her.

But he'd never really controlled her, had he? He'd welcomed her making her own choices and wanted her to do what she wanted. Then and now. She didn't have to be a waitress, but they both enjoyed the great tips she'd gotten, and the free drinks… Oh, but that was so long ago. Her insides were twisted up so badly she wanted to burst. Could she really trust him? She didn't want to be seen as a gold-digger, as it appeared that he'd really risen high financially. Knowing Benjamin, he'd been thrifty enough to have a good chunk in the bank. She probably could quit her job and take time to figure out what she really wanted if she were to marry him again.

What if it wasn't Ben?

Had he really manipulated her as she'd stated?

Right. Marriage. Again. To her former husband? Who did something like that? It was impulsive and foolish to even consider it. No. It was better to walk away from any hope of a future with him when she was already so confused about what she wanted in life. Interesting how that had never bothered her until she'd run into Benjamin again.

How would she get along, since almost everyone she knew was connected to Benjamin? She remembered Renata. Somewhere she had the woman's phone number. She dug it out of the pile on her desk and dialed it.

"Hello?"

"Renata? This is Jo March. We talked between services a while back and you told me to call to chat sometime. My dad was the State Trooper who found your first husband."

"Right. Sure. This is a good time. Did you want to talk on the phone or come over?"

"If it's OK, I'd like to meet face to face."

"My husband is at work, and the twins are hopefully down for the night. You're welcome to stop by." Renata gave Jo the address. "I'll make some tea for us."

"Sounds wonderful. Thank you."

Jo changed clothes, got in her car, and headed to the address Renata had indicated. The lovely woman opened the door and invited her in.

"Welcome to our home. Let's go to the family room. Liam is having a little tummy time there. He'll be ready to go to bed soon, at least for a few hours." Renata settled into a chair close to the baby. "What can I do for you, Jo?"

"I'm having a hard time, and I recalled how bad things had been for you. I was wondering what your secret was."

"Secret? To what?"

"To falling in love again after so much pain."

"There's no secret. I had to live through it. I tried to run away from the pain but that didn't work. Healing takes time. I wasn't looking to fall in love, but Tony proved himself over and over. He respected my boundaries and was a great friend. Most of all, he trusted God. In the meantime, I had to do some healing from my past, and that wasn't easy. I'm grateful for the church and the people there who helped me. Not only do I serve on a worship team, but I also attend our Mothers of Preschoolers group. Where is this question coming from?"

"I was dating my ex-husband." Jo went on to explain what had torn the marriage apart and how God had brought them back together and how she'd blown up last night. A tear escaped, and she brushed it away with her hand.

Liam cried. "Hold on to those thoughts. I'll be right back." Renata scooped up the baby and left the room.

Had it been a mistake for Jo to come here and spill her guts to a stranger? She wanted someone who was impartial. Renata had gone through a horrible time with her physically abusive husband, who had put her in the hospital and killed their unborn baby before he was shot in a hunting accident up north. It had always amazed her that people had been so supportive of Mick and called Renata horrible names as she lay healing in the hospital from her physical and emotional wounds.

Renata tiptoed back into the room. "We should be fine now." She sat down. "I'm not an expert on romance or love, but Jo, if he never told you about paying the loan and did that on his own, not to gain notice, how does that make him a manipulator? Did he admit he did it?"

"Not really, but he didn't deny it either. Benjamin was never very good at lying."

"How did things end between you this time?"

"He told me he was tired of me being hot and cold, wanting kisses and refusing to consider marriage."

"Kisses can be powerful. I refused to kiss Tony until our wedding day. On the cheek, sure, but not on the lips. It was worth waiting for and kept the physical urges to a minimum. We could make our decisions based on our friendship and how God was leading us, instead of on our hormones."

"So I messed up by allowing kisses?"

"Not necessarily. What works for me isn't for everyone. I understand that. It sounds like you were giving him mixed messages. Why even date him if you don't think you could have a future with him?"

"How could I ever trust him again?"

"You listed a variety of things he has done to prove himself trustworthy, Jo. But what have *you* done to prove you wouldn't just run away again? It sounds like he was taking the bigger risk on you. That—is love."

More tears fell down Jo's cheeks.

Renata shoved a box of tissues her way. "Listen, I'm sorry to be the one to say those things, but maybe that's why you called me. You didn't want someone with a hidden agenda giving you advice. It sounds as if others have been trying to tell you what to do. That can make it hard to listen to God speaking to you."

"I'm new in my faith. I'm not sure He'd even want

to speak to me."

"Oh, Jo. He does. Maybe you should get away by yourself this weekend and seek Him without the distractions of your partner, parents, ex-in-laws, and Ben and Molly. Did I get the names right?"

"Yeah, you did."

"Let me pray for you." She reached out and took Jo's hands in her own. "Lord, You are a good God who delights in giving us the desires of our heart—when we finally know what those are. You understand Jo's heart even when she is confused. Please give her clarity as she seeks You. Give her peace to follow where You lead her, especially as it pertains to Benjamin. I ask that You would also give Benjamin peace, as it sounds as though his heart is hurting too. Jesus, even though this is confusing right now, I ask that You make all things clear in Your perfect time."

"Amen."

Renata enveloped her in a hug. "Don't ever doubt God's love, Jo. That is one thing you can depend on—always." She pulled back.

"Thank you."

"Let me know what happens. I'll be praying for you." Renata walked her to the door.

"I will. Thank you. And good night."

"'Night, Jo." Renata closed the door.

Jo made her way to her car, started it, and drove home. Get away for the weekend? But where? She called her brother.

"Hey, Jo, what's up?"

"You still own that little cabin in the woods?"

"Yeah, but it's shut up for the winter now that deer hunting season is over."

"All I really need is heat, right? I could bring water with me. I just want to get away to pray."

"You're more than welcome to it. There's plenty of cut wood. Dress warm. Even with the fireplace, it's usually chilly in there. Especially if it's windy. Cell reception is poor, and there's no Wi-Fi or electricity."

"Yeah, I remember how to rough it. Thanks. I'll head up there in the morning. Just for one night."

"If you need anything, there's a phone three miles away. The address is in the cabin."

"Great."

"You OK?"

"I think I'll be fine, but I'd appreciate your prayers."

"Got 'em. Stay safe, Jo."

"I will. Remember—I carry a gun and know how to use it."

"Hopefully it never comes to that."

"Right. Good night."

She hung up and began to pack her things for early departure. Suddenly she started to feel better. She had a plan.

32

NEVER LET FEAR, PRIDE, OR EGO DICTATE YOUR NEXT BATTLE PLAN.

T. BLAUER

"Benny?" Molly's voice was tentative and eager.

"Huh?"

"We have some news to share," Geoff said.

"OK." Ben dropped the dishcloth on the edge of the sink. "What is it?"

"Geoff proposed to me today, and I said yes."

Ben forced a smile. "Wow! That is the best news I've heard in a long time. Congratulations, sis!" He stepped forward to wrap his sister in his arms for a bear hug, lifting her off the floor, spinning her around. When he set her down, he reached out a hand to Geoff, who pulled him in for a hug. "I couldn't ask for a better man to be my brother-in-law, or to take care of this handful."

The men parted.

Geoff grinned as Molly hugged her fiancé tight.

"I'm sorry things didn't work out with Jo," Molly said.

Ben sighed. "The past needs to stay there, Molly. Lock that particular skeleton in the attic, please." He turned and grabbed a white box. "Celebratory truffles, anyone?"

"Are those the dark chocolate and peppermint ones?" Molly asked.

Ben grinned and nodded. "Yup."

Geoff and Molly helped themselves to chocolates as Ben led them into the family room. "So, have you set a date?"

Geoff grinned. "We haven't even discussed that much yet, but we're planning to take a trip to Romania in February. Maybe we could get married before that and spend our honeymoon there."

Molly's mouth dropped open. "What a fabulous idea!"

Ben waved a hand. "Wait. Does that mean you're living here until then?"

Cringing, Molly nodded. "It's really only eight weeks or so. Is that a problem?"

"No. I'm really happy for you two."

"Want to join us for dinner to celebrate?"

Ben shook his head. "No. That should be something for the two of you. When will you tell Mum and Dad?"

"When they return to town."

"Tomorrow morning, I need to head up to Minneapolis for some contract work. I don't anticipate being back until Thursday evening."

"But that's Christmas Eve!" Molly exclaimed.

"True, and if all goes according to plan, I should be able to make the late candlelight service at church."

"This feels wrong." Molly pouted.

"Listen. There are plenty of boxes of chocolate. They are all labeled, and the ribbons are attached. Take what you need for your party at work."

"OK. Thank you." Molly rose to her feet, dragging Geoff with her. She leaned over to give Ben a kiss on the cheek. "We're going out now. In case I don't see you before you leave in the morning, just remember that I love you. Drive safe. I'll be praying for you."

"Thanks, sis. And congratulations, guys. I really am happy for you."

"I want you happy too, Benny."

"I know. God's not ready to give me my happily-ever-after yet. I need to be patient." He shrugged. "Maybe I had my one shot and ruined it. I can't beat myself up over that. There's a new year around the bend. I'll leave my heart in His hands."

Geoff patted him on the shoulder. "Best place for it to be. We'll be praying."

~*~

The next morning, Ben took an extra-long run, showered, and packed his bag for his trip to Minneapolis. He hadn't told Molly that he was working with the FBI up there. Will would be coming up tomorrow. He could have waited a day, but he just couldn't handle going to church and seeing Jo. Not yet. This way he didn't have to be under the scrutiny of his parents either. He'd left a note for them about his trip but didn't mention Jo. He trusted Molly would share the truth. As for a car? He suggested that for this week they rent one, as Molly needed hers to get to and from work. He didn't need to feel bad, since he was already saving them the hotel expense.

He groaned as he drove. If Geoff and Molly waited until before the trip in February, would his parents hang around that long too? Maybe he could encourage the couple to get married sooner—say New Year's Eve? Maybe he should email his sister about that. He chuckled at what her response might be. Given the sparks between Molly and Geoff, an earlier wedding might be advisable anyway.

He remembered those days with Jo as they had prepared for the wedding. He also remembered their honeymoon and the bliss of time alone with no work or pressures.

It still bothered him that she'd gotten that angry about him paying off her loan. A loan he partially shared responsibility for anyway. He had benefited from those loans, as they helped pay for tuition, rent, and food. It saddened him that they were happier when they were poor. Now he'd achieved all they'd ever hoped for, but it meant nothing without being able to share it with the one person he loved.

He finally arrived at his hotel and settled in for the night. He opened his Bible. Job, chapter 37: 5.

God thunders wondrously with his voice;
he does great things that we cannot comprehend.
For to the snow he says, 'Fall on the earth,'
likewise to the downpour, his mighty downpour.
He seals up the hand of every man,
that all men whom he made may know it.

Then the beasts go into their lairs,
and remain in their dens.
From its chamber comes the whirlwind,
and cold from the scattering winds.
By the breath of God ice is given,
and the broad waters are frozen fast.
He loads the thick cloud with moisture;
the clouds scatter his lightning.
They turn around and around by his guidance,
to accomplish all that he commands them
on the face of the habitable world.
Whether for correction or for his land
or for love, he causes it to happen.

Ben wasn't a Job by any means. He'd suffered the whirlwind of financial losses and his wife had left him, sure, but much of that was because of his own foolish choices. He was healthy and had bounced back and had a good career now. These verses reminded him that God was wonderful and inscrutable. Ben considered himself an intelligent man, but there was no way he could out-think God—especially in relationship to Jo March. God was in control, and all of Benjamin's attempts to woo Jo were just that. His attempts.

God, if You really want Jo and me to be together, You will need to be the One to make that happen. I'm powerless to change her heart or her mind. But You, God? You are the King of love, and I'm sorry I tried to do anything without seeking You first. Forgive me. Bless Jo even if it means she is never to be a part of my life again. I leave her—and any possible 'us'—in Your capable hands.

~*~

The drive north was long, but once Jo arrived at her brother's cabin in the woods and had the fire going, she unpacked her sleeping bag and pillow to place them before the fire. She'd be cozy tonight even as the wind howled outside.

Renata had been correct. She'd been holding Benjamin to a standard she'd never met herself and had accused him of her own failings. He'd never pressured her. He'd protected her, provided secretly, and loved her.

And what had she done? Played yo-yo tricks with his heart.

She really wasn't that fickle, was she? She'd always loved Benjamin. She was ashamed at how she'd failed him three years ago and then gone and done it all over again. Would he ever listen to her apology? Would he ever open his heart to her again? He might have felt he didn't deserved it three years ago, due to his own perceived failures—but this time there was only one person to blame. Her.

He'd not responded to her emails and texts and hadn't answered any of her phone calls. Not that she could blame him. She really didn't want to hear from herself either. But would God? Renata assured her God's love was faithful and trustworthy. And He understood her heart even when she didn't.

She opened her Bible. Psalm 139. She started reading, but it wasn't until verse seven that the words seemed to jump off the page.

O Lord, you have searched me and known me!
You know when I sit down and when I rise up;
you discern my thoughts from afar.
You search out my path and my lying down
and are acquainted with all my ways.
Even before a word is on my tongue,
behold, O Lord, you know it altogether.
You hem me in, behind and before,
and lay your hand upon me.
Such knowledge is too wonderful for me;
it is high; I cannot attain it.
Where shall I go from your Spirit?
Or where shall I flee from your presence?
If I ascend to heaven, you are there!
If I make my bed in Sheol, you are there!
If I take the wings of the morning
and dwell in the uttermost parts of the sea,
Even there your hand shall lead me,
and your right hand shall hold me.
If I say, "Surely the darkness shall cover me,
and the light about me be night,"
Even the darkness is not dark to you;
the night is bright as the day,
For darkness is as light with you.

Jo sighed. She couldn't hide from God, and what had she done? She'd even tried to hide from the love He'd graciously brought back into her life, healing and reframing the past. She pulled out her journal and began to write. She had so many things to confess to her Heavenly Father who knew it all, but to clear her thoughts from the traffic jam that was stalling her movement into a better tomorrow, she needed to write it out. And pray. And hope that maybe Benjamin, like God, would give her another chance.

~*~

Jo drove home from the cabin in a far better state of mind. She didn't know what God would do, but she was at peace. She needed to beg Benjamin's forgiveness for her outburst of anger. Renata had been correct. He hadn't deserved that, and never even admitted to paying off the debt. He'd been correct. Some of that debt had been acquired during their marriage. He did have a responsibility to help pay it off. She'd just never realized it, nor would she have been inclined to ask him to do it. It was a gift she'd flailed at him for. Why? Her own pride? Mostly her fear of trusting herself to trust him, when ultimately her trust needed to be in God—not Benjamin.

That was something new for her and hadn't been a part of their marriage. Could God make marriage better between them? She could only hope so. If God even wanted her to marry him. She still wasn't sure and had no clue whether Benjamin would even look at her twice now, given the way she'd wounded him.

The week ahead would be a long one. She and Geoff were working evenings. They'd miss Christmas Eve church services and celebrations with family. Well, at least for her.

Benjamin worked days. There was little to no time to connect with him.

She'd written him a letter that she'd put in the mail when she got back to town. She doubted he'd open an email or answer a phone call at this point. She hoped that if nothing else, he'd at least forgive her. She'd need to trust God with that, along with everything else.

33

YOU NEVER KNOW HOW MUCH YOU CAN DO,
UNTIL YOU TRY TO DO MORE THAN YOU CAN.

T. BLAUER

Ben arrived at the FBI offices early in the morning and began working with the information technology department, training them on his program. He'd been trying to hack their other software and had devised fixes for the system he would install. By late afternoon, the majority of the work was done.

Will had arrived and together with another forensic accountant pulled Ben into helping them with their case by following the money trail.

The numbers boggled him, and he didn't need to understand much of what was going on to recognize it was a big deal. If the guys they were pursuing were to learn who was doing it—each of them could be a target. Was he getting paid enough for that? He took a deep breath and let it out.

"You OK?" Will asked as they took a break.

"Yeah. The enormity of what you're fighting is just a little frightening."

"Part of the job. Seeking justice isn't always pretty

or without risk. People don't like a light shining on their sin. They hide in the dark, and you provided a new flashlight for us to detect them. It's important work. Are you sure you don't want to join the FBI?"

Ben shook his head. "I don't think so. I'm glad I can help you, though. Not all my systems have this profound of an impact. They streamline companies, enhancing productivity, and helping to prevent embezzlement. Obviously, one of my strengths now."

"After what you went through with Doug? Understandable." He nodded to some chairs, and they sat. "Can I ask you a more personal question?"

"I don't have to answer but go ahead."

"You and Jo? I know you left early yesterday, but she wasn't at church either. Geoff and your sister acting sweet, and I noticed some bling on her left hand."

"What's the question? Geoff and Molly are engaged. I'm thrilled for them. As for Jo and I, there is no 'and' in that equation. There's Jo. There's me. Not together. Her choice."

"You're just letting her go like last time?"

"You don't understand. I tried to woo her. I dated her. I cared for her when she was sick. I don't know how much more I could have done short of handcuffing her to me and dragging her to the altar. I don't want to win a bride who can't stand the thought of being with me."

"I could have sworn she loved you."

"She never said the words."

"Did you?"

Benjamin nodded. "Making me the fool." He sighed. "Can we leave this to never be discussed again?"

Will frowned. "Sure. Sorry, dude. I really thought—"

"Yeah, well, so did a lot of people. Me included. We were wrong." Ben headed back to the office and grabbed a cup of coffee as if drinking that would ease the ache in his chest.

~*~

Jo mailed her letter on the way to work. She walked in and spied Geoff there, grinning from ear to ear. "Something's up, partner. What is it?"

Geoff showed her a photo of him and Molly, with the stunning ring on her left hand. "She said yes."

Sorrow warred with joy for her friend. "Congratulations. I'm so happy for you. You and Molly seem well-matched."

"You don't think we're moving too fast?" Geoff asked.

"You are asking the wrong person that question, Geoff."

"Yeah. Sorry about you and Ben."

Jo sighed. "It is what it is."

Captain Jenkins came to give them their assignments.

Jo was on her own again, as was Geoff, although they'd be driving a similar area of the highway between Madison and Milwaukee. The roads were expected to be slippery at times, and traffic-heavy with the holiday travelers.

"Be careful out there," the Captain admonished before they headed to their cars.

"See you on the road, partner," Geoff said as he got in his patrol car.

Jo saluted him. "See ya."

~*~

The rest of the week was mundane. Speeding tickets. Flat tires. Helping motorists who ran out of gas. A few fender-benders, but thankfully nothing tragic. Jo prayed it would stay that way. This wasn't the worst way to spend her days…or nights. She liked driving the squad car and helping people out. If only it would stay that simple…and safe.

She feared it wouldn't.

~*~

Benjamin was beyond exhausted, but he was determined he'd make it home before midnight on Christmas Eve. The traffic was heavy, forcing him to go slower than he wanted. After he made it past Madison, he headed east on the interstate.

He had a weird feeling that someone was following him. He moved over to the far right lane to let people pass, but one sport utility vehicle stayed two cars behind.

Many were traveling to the greater Milwaukee area for the holidays. Traffic had thinned out a lot, though. It was after ten o'clock, and not as many cars were on the road. But this one stuck to him with every move he made.

He pulled off to use the restroom at a gas station, and the other car pulled off too. He couldn't see who it was as they never got out. Strange. Perhaps he was being paranoid after his work with the FBI and the break-in. There wasn't anything he had that was of value to anyone.

The FBI had the program and were taking it from there. They might have him go to other offices in the new year, but their own IT guys would likely be able to handle it without him now.

Fluffy flakes of snow began to fall on his windshield. He headed back out onto the highway and the truck sped up behind him. He was already going the speed limit in the far right lane. Not many cars were around.

A popping sound startled him. He struggled to maintain control of his SUV, as something went wrong. Another pop followed. His car hit the gravel and spun, flipping as it went into the ditch. What sounded like gunshots followed, but Ben wasn't sure. The airbag exploded in his face, and he slipped into blackness.

~*~

Jo saw the incident from the westbound lane and radioed it in. Hopefully, Geoff wasn't too far away. She found a turn-around, and with lights on and siren blaring, she sped toward the SUV, which had flipped into the ditch but landed right-side-up.

Rescue vehicles had already been dispatched. Another vehicle had stopped to render aid. But someone outside the vehicle turned to fire as she pulled up behind it.

"Car 9. 10-32. Man with gun. Shots fired," she radioed. "10-78. Need assistance." *Please hurry.*

She opened the door. "Stop! Put down your weapon!"

He aimed, and she shot back, hitting the assailant.

A second person ran to the damaged truck with a gun raised.

She went around the back of her patrol car and aimed at the man, just as he fired at the driver's side of the vehicle.

This wasn't an accident. It was attempted murder.

A squad car pulled up behind hers and Geoff was by her side in a flash.

Jo ran over the snow-covered grass to where the second shooter had gone down. He was dead. She shuddered as she recognized Doug—Benjamin's former business partner, the man who had ruined things for her and Benjamin years ago.

She kicked the gun away and moved to the car.

The occupant was limp and had been hit with a bullet, but she couldn't determine exactly where. She turned on her flashlight to see better, and horror filled her heart.

Benjamin!

"Geoff! Get over here now!"

The car was still running and the engine steaming.

All they needed was a fire on top of this.

Geoff slid down the snow-covered side of the ditch to come up beside her. "What've you got?"

"It's Benjamin. He's been shot."

Spots flared in front of her vision.

Geoff grabbed her. "Snap out of it, Jo. Do your job. Can you get in the passenger side? Get the car turned off and see about keeping him stable until help arrives. I'll grab a blanket. The ambulance will be here soon."

A sheriff's deputy arrived and began directing traffic past the accident scene.

Jo fought to get in the passenger door, which had been damaged in the crash. She finally broke the window and climbed in that way.

Geoff brought her a blanket to put over Benjamin.

"Benjamin? It's Jo. Can you talk to me?" She held his hand. There was no response, but he at least had a pulse. "It'll be OK. We'll get you out of here." She applied pressure against the darkening spot on his coat. She kept up a steady monologue of assurances to him. How could she have ever denied loving this man? Her conscience smote her.

Soon the paramedics were there, and with the Jaws of Life and a backboard, they extracted Benjamin from the vehicle.

Geoff dragged her out of the opened-up side of the SUV, pulling her away from the scene to let others work.

Jo shivered. Her hands were red with blood. She wiped them off in the snow until a paramedic handed her a towel. "Thank you."

"Go sit in your car. Now," Geoff barked. "I don't want you passing out on me."

"I'll be—"

"Go. No arguments."

Jo obeyed and climbed into the warm squad car. Leaning her head forward, she prayed. Nothing like an accident to show her how she really felt. *Lord, let him live. Please!*

When the FBI arrived on the scene, she realized Benjamin might have been targeted in more ways than one. Could this have been related to the work he did for the FBI? She called Will. "Hey, sorry to interrupt your Christmas Eve."

"It's fine. I came home from church a little while ago and was about to head to bed. What's up?"

"Someone tried to kill Benjamin tonight. Remember Doug? He's dead. We haven't identified his partner. Benjamin's on the way to Froedert Hospital. He's been shot."

"He's still alive?"

"Yes. I was first on the scene."

"Jo—I'm so sorry."

"Just wanted you to know. I need to work a few more hours yet before I can get to the hospital. Geoff is also on duty. Someone should be there for Molly and her parents after they've been informed."

"Who is calling them?"

"My boss."

"OK. Got it. I'll be praying for him—and for you. I can't imagine finding someone I loved—"

"Love. Don't use past tense. He's not dead."

"Fine. I'll be there, Jo."

"Thanks, Will."

Geoff and Jo worked the accident scene until the bodies and cars were cleared away. They stopped for a break at a local gas station, each grabbing a cup of coffee.

"Will you make it, or should I call Captain Jenkins and request you be taken off duty?"

"I have no claim on Benjamin. Not with the way I left things. I'll go after my shift is done. Do you want to go and be with Molly?"

"She called. She was crying, but she understands I can't come in yet. Ben will likely be rushed into surgery, so there's not much any of us can do right now except pray. I can do that while I drive as well as you can."

"Right."

"You ready to get back at it? Not that much longer before dawn. The roads should be pretty empty, so perhaps the rest of the shift will be uneventful."

"I pray so. It's not a very merry Christmas, is it? Thanks, Geoff." Jo got behind the wheel of her squad car and hit the road in the opposite direction of her partner. Was this why God had brought her to this place? To be able to save Benjamin? Had she saved him? She had no way of knowing, so she tried to shut out thoughts of the worst-case-scenario, to no avail. If Benjamin didn't survive, where would that leave her? Could she keep doing her job, knowing she'd failed? Her longing to be reconciled with him burst inside her, but there was nothing more she could do right now.

She prayed the rest of the shift would go quickly.

34

CHOCOLATE NEVER DISAPPOINTS; IT LEAVES ITS LOVER WANTING MORE.

ANONYMOUS

Geoff stood by Jo as she was ready to leave the station. "Heading straight to the hospital?"

Jo looked down at her uniform. "I got a little dirty. I think I'll go home first, shower, and change."

Geoff looked down at his own uniform. "I didn't get quite as messy as you. Molly's waiting for me, so I'm going as is."

"That's fine. I'm not sure how receptive any of them will be upon my arrival. Maybe you can pave the way."

"You never said what happened."

"I was an idiot."

"Are you now?"

"No. Now I'm afraid I'll lose the one person I love most in the world."

Geoff swallowed hard. "I'll try to pave the way for you."

"Thanks, partner. The good news is neither of us got shot."

"And thanks to your marksman skills, Ben is still

alive. If you hadn't gotten that shooter before he fired again, Ben might not have had a chance. You were the hero tonight."

"I wish that felt as good as it sounds."

"You did the job you were trained to do. There was no way you could have known any of that would happen."

"Thanks for the vote of confidence. Hopefully, his family will see it that way too."

"I have your back, partner. See you at the hospital."

~*~

Jo wept as the water poured over her in the shower. Her two nightmares had come to life tonight—Benjamin being shot, and in a car accident. How could she move forward in life without him knowing she loved him? Would he even accept her now after how she had acted?

You saved his life last night.

Benjamin didn't know that. He hadn't been aware. She wasn't about to use that to gain his favor.

Just as he didn't use paying off the loan to gain yours.

All right, God. You got me there.

She drove to the hospital and grabbed some coffee on the way. She'd need all the help she could get after the long night she'd had.

Geoff had given her information on where they'd be and had called to give her the scoop on Benjamin's recovery. He'd survived surgery but hadn't awakened yet.

She walked into the waiting area expecting to be shunned. Molly and Mr. and Mrs. Elliot all rushed at her to envelop her in their arms, murmuring thanks for saving Benjamin's life. She looked over to Geoff and mouthed a thank-you.

He saluted her with his coffee cup.

Soon they settled her into a chair and all began speaking at once.

Geoff shushed them. "Give the poor girl a break. She's had a rough night." He took her hands to see where they'd been scraped raw from digging in the snow to get the car door open. She tugged her hands back and tried to cover them up with the cuffs of her sweater sleeves.

A nurse bustled to the waiting room.

They all turned their attention to her.

"Is Jo here?" The nurse looked at Geoff, who pointed to Jo.

The nurse's eyebrows rose, and she smiled. "It would only make sense that a handsome young man like that would want a pretty girl to come visit him first."

Jo stood and turned to the Elliots. "Are you OK with this? I can let you go first. He is your son."

Mrs. Elliot grinned. "But you're the love of his life. Go and be with him, Jo."

Geoff shoved her toward the door to the ICU.

Jo followed the nurse to the room, where Benjamin was hooked up to several machines.

"He's breathing on his own. Talk to him. He was

only awake for a minute, but maybe you can bring him back."

Jo went to the bed. "Benjamin. It's Jo. I'm here. I'm so sorry. I love you, and I think I've always loved you, but I was too afraid, and I made you suffer for it."

"Shhh," he said as his eyes flickered open. "I love you too. So, will you marry me?"

"If you'll still have me."

"I do." He gave a silly grin.

"Ask me again when you're not on pain medication. I won't hold you to this declaration."

"It's the most honest one you'll get."

"Your sister and parents are here, worried sick over you."

"You weren't?"

"I almost passed out at the scene. Geoff helped me stay on task. When I realized it was you, it was my worst nightmare come to life."

"Shhh. Just turn the pillow over. You'll sleep fine."

Jo smiled. "I love you, Benjamin Wentworth Elliot."

"And I love you, Jo March."

"Is it OK if I kiss you?"

"I would like that very much."

Jo leaned over and did just that.

~*~

A day later they moved him to a regular room.

Benjamin was looking forward to Jo's visit. He'd missed Christmas completely.

Will stopped in. "Hey, buddy. How are you feeling?"

"I've been better. Any news about what happened?"

"It doesn't appear that Doug and his cohort had any ties to the work you've been doing for us. He was recently released and obviously was stalking you, waiting for his chance. We were able to talk to someone from prison. Doug was filled with rage over having been caught. He thought he was too smart for that. This smacked of revenge. Notes found at his mom's house indicated he planned to kill you. He was also behind that break-in. Even if he had found anything of importance in your office, he didn't have any connections to feed the information to. He was never able to break your password either."

"If I keep working for you, am I safe?"

"What's this 'if' you're talking of? Of course, you're safe." Will shook his head.

"Well, I really want to be sure of that. I don't mind doing the training, but I prefer to be as behind the scenes as possible in any further projects."

Will shook his hand. "Understood. You want to be with Jo and have your happily-ever-after. Hard to do when your life is in danger."

"No hard feelings?" Benjamin asked.

"No way. Jo has always been yours. I'll need to look elsewhere for a wife, if that's what God has planned for me. I need to get going. Get well, and don't forget to invite me to the wedding." Will gave a salute and left.

Benjamin sighed. At least he wasn't in any danger. He didn't want anything to get in the way of his wooing Jo. He looked at the clock on the wall for the millionth time, eager for her to arrive.

Before Jo would visit, he expected his parents to come by with the gifts from under the tree and some sweatpants for him, so he could be more comfortable instead of wearing the silly gown the hospital gave him.

He didn't really care about the gifts. He was weak as a kitten and his head ached, but he was happy. Jo had agreed to be his wife.

Finally, Geoff and his family arrived. His sister gave him a hug and informed him she'd completed his secret errand just as he'd requested.

"Where's Jo?" Benjamin asked.

"She said she'd be here," Geoff assured him. She'd been on duty again last night, working with Geoff. The poor guy looked beat.

Jo bustled into the room. "I think someone transposed those numbers just to mess me up."

Molly gave her a hug. "Well, you're here now."

Gifts were exchanged, and somehow Jo had managed to bring gifts for everyone except Ben. He pouted. "What, nothing for me?"

"I have something for you, but it kind of depends on what yours is." She grinned.

Ben pulled out a white package wrapped in a red ribbon instead of the usual blue that signified his truffles. "Here you go."

Jo sat on the bed, facing him. "Are you sure?"

He nodded.

Jo loosened the cloth ribbon, and it fell away. She lifted the top part of the box to reveal a box of his exquisite homemade chocolates. The top one had a diamond wedding band stuck in it.

"I refused to take the pain meds today. So please give me your answer so I can take the meds. Will you marry me, Jo March? As soon as possible?"

"Yes, Benjamin Wentworth Elliot. I will marry you all over again. This time forever."

Ben reached for the box, pulled out the diamond, and licked off the chocolate.

"Hey, that was part of my truffle!" Jo protested.

He grinned. "You want it—come and get it." He placed the truffle between his teeth.

"You're on." Jo bit the truffle that stuck out of his mouth and then kissed him in the process. "Mmmm. Now that is one way to eat chocolate I've never tried before."

Ben took her hand and slid the ring on. "Soon. Please?"

Molly jumped up and down. "Double wedding!"

Ben shrugged. "I'm OK with that, but I don't want to wait until February."

"I'd be willing to marry my gal soon as you're up for it, Ben," Geoff said with a grin. He hugged Molly close and kissed her.

"We'll have to see how soon the doctor will allow certain activities before we set a date," Jo said.

"It'd better be soon, or I'll become a very difficult patient."

The nurse bustled in. "You mean you'll be worse than you already are?"

Everyone laughed, and soon the other nurses rallied around to congratulate him on his upcoming marriage.

"What about my gift?" Benjamin asked.

Jo went around the corner to grab a package and had to help him unwrap it. Inside was a carved wooden box with Big Ben on it. The velvet-lined interior held photos of the two of them from the past.

"Wow. Jo. Thank you. I will treasure this forever."

Jo leaned forward and whispered in his ear, "Merry Christmas, my love."

He turned to meet her lips in a gentle kiss. "Merry Christmas."

35

CHOCOLATE HAS FINESSE—THE CHARM TO SEDUCE AND INDULGE AT ANY TIME, DAY OR NIGHT.

ANONYMOUS

Jo could hardly believe it. For a second time, she was marrying the man of her dreams. They weren't the same people they were years ago. God had transformed them both and she was grateful.

Her mother dabbed her eyes as she fluffed out Jo's dress. "Oh, sweetheart. I'm so happy you and Ben are getting married again."

"Thanks, Mom. That means a lot."

"I hear the music. I'd better get seated." She grabbed some more tissues to squeeze in her hands. "I'll probably need these." With a kiss to Jo's cheek, Mrs. March left the room.

Her father was there in his wheelchair. "I don't know why you want me to do this. I feel silly. I'll probably roll all over that beautiful dress."

"Don't be silly, Dad. I wanted to ask you something."

"Sure, honey. The wedding won't start without you." He winked at her.

"Would you be upset if I stopped working as a

State Patrol Officer?"

"What? Why? You're good at what you do. But you know I'll support your choices, whatever they are."

"Well, I'm not quitting yet, but thinking about possibly starting a family. I don't feel right doing that while in this career."

"Some women do it, but you know firsthand the challenges that come with the job, and the risks involved. Whatever you and Ben decide, we'll love and support you."

"Really?"

"Of course. You know your mother is eager for grandchildren. To be honest, so am I."

Jo grinned. "Benjamin and I haven't decided anything yet, but we'll let you know when we do."

Molly popped in. "Come on! They're waiting for us!"

"Great. Are you ready to meet your groom—again?" Dad grinned.

"I am. Let's go." She bent over to give her father a kiss on the cheek, and they took off for the entrance to the church sanctuary.

Jo's joy exploded as she stood at the back of the sanctuary with Mr. Elliot. Molly and her father would go first. This was more exciting and nerve-racking than the first time around at the county courthouse, when she'd been oblivious to how hard life could be.

Benjamin still had some healing to do and appeared pale. He'd lost weight, but his eyes twinkled at her from across the distance.

Molly had loaned her a necklace.

Something borrowed.

He is mine. All mine.

Forever.

The music started. Molly and her father walked down the aisle, and then Jo and her Dad followed. Soon the women stood side by side with their respective grooms. Poor Benjamin would be able to tell in an instant how anxious she was. Her palms were sweaty from gripping her flowers too tight. No way would she wipe them on her satin gown. She handed off the blue flowers to her mother.

Something blue.

Pastor Dan gave a short message and spoke the vows. Benjamin put her old wedding ring back on her finger, with a new second band littered with diamonds he'd not been able to afford back then.

Something old.

Something new.

Benjamin's eyebrows wiggled as Pastor Dan invited the men to kiss their brides.

Her husband placed his hands up by her face so tenderly that she sighed and leaned in for a gentle kiss that promised far more.

They turned to Molly and Geoff and exchanged hugs, and together the four of them went down the aisle. Molly and Geoff first—she was the older twin, after all—and then Jo and Benjamin.

Joy welled up inside her as she held her husband's hand. Benjamin was hers once again, now and forever. She wouldn't make the same mistakes she had in the past. Hopefully, she'd learned from them.

Both sets of parents were overjoyed. Mr. and Mrs. Elliot had spent the last night in a hotel so Benjamin and Jo could honeymoon at the house. His parents were leaving for their home in London that night. Jo's parents and brother were returning to Green Bay that evening.

Tomorrow, Jo and Benjamin would fly south. All Jo knew was that it would be warm. She could hardly wait.

Molly and Geoff would travel in a few weeks to Romania and were already starting the paperwork to pursue adoption.

Jo turned to Benjamin and kissed him again as guests congratulated them. She planned to keep him around for good this time. Through better or worse. Richer or poorer. In sickness and in health. She'd failed before, but she'd learned from her mistakes.

~*~

Benjamin snuggled next to Jo in the car. "You are beautiful. You know that whatever happens from here on out, I'll support your choices."

Jo frowned. "Whether I stay or leave the State Patrol?"

"I'll admit I'll miss you when you work, but yes. Even if I need to become a stay-at-home dad so you can fulfill your dreams."

"But also if I want to be a stay-at-home mom?"

"Whatever you want. I trust God to watch over us

both in whatever we do. And rest assured, I'll not be doing anything remotely dangerous with my work."

Jo snuggled closer. "I think we can talk about all this where it's much warmer in a few days."

"I agree. We have other, more important things to do." Ben chuckled.

When they arrived at their house, Ben wasn't physically strong enough yet to carry his bride over the threshold. Instead, he happily dragged her into the empty house and stopped in the hallway for a kiss. He pointed to the ceiling, where a sprig of mistletoe remained from Christmas.

They now had a chance to start a fresh life together.

Will had given him a card before the wedding. "Thank you for your able assistance. I can now say you are no longer an idiot. Congratulations."

Ben hoped that Will would someday soon experience the joy he had now. This time, Ben was determined not to mess it up. He went to the kitchen to get some truffles to bring back to the bedroom. Before he could return, his wife appeared.

Wow. He loved being able to think of her as his wife again.

"Coming to bed, dear?" Jo asked. She walked into the kitchen wearing a dainty chocolate-brown lace negligee.

"You bet." He might not be able to carry his wife over the threshold, but the doctor had at least given him permission for this.

My sacrifice, O God, is a broken spirit; a broken and contrite heart you, God, will not despise. ~ Psalm 51:17

The joyful feeling of salvation is tempered by the reality of past sins. The sacrifice Jesus made for all mankind shows the magnitude of what God's love for us. With each of our sins, helped to crucify Him and pierce the nails through His body on the cross. We need absolution and forgiveness. When we commit sins and then seek forgiveness, God grants mercy to those with a contrite heart. Others on the walk in faith may be at a different place in their relationship with God, they may be less at peace or more in tune with our Lord than we are. We have to love them as they are, and help them to achieve the happiness we experience in loving Jesus. And we can still rejoice because they are part of the family of God.

In **Truffles and Traffic**, the protagonist has suffered a setback in her working life. As she struggles to overcome, she encounters someone from her past. Anguish over his decisions separated them, but now he claims he's turned his life over to God. Wary of allowing her broken heart to be shattered again, she has to decide to trust him…and God.

Have you ever been so wary of the people who've hurt you that you find it difficult to forgive or to trust them again, even if they claim to have changed. It's a difficult place to be, especially if the person in question has promised before to change, and has only hurt you again and again. While it's important to protect yourself sometimes, it's just as important to realize that we all sin, you included, and you (like the rest of us) have let down God on multiple occasions…and yet, He forgives endlessly and repeatedly, whenever you ask, as many times as you ask. So, the next time you're faced with having to trust someone who says they've changed, be on guard in case they haven't, but also give them a chance to prove they have changed. You might just be surprised and in the end, gain a friendship you thought was lost forever.

LORD, HELP TO HEAL MY BROKEN SPIRIT, AND TO SHOW OTHERS THEIRS CAN BE HEALED, TOO. IN JESUS' NAME I PRAY, AMEN.

ACKNOWLEDGEMENTS

It would be impossible to thank everyone who has helped me on my journey, so I apologize in advance for those I will miss. It doesn't mean you are any less valuable and, thankfully, God keeps better track of those things than I do and His "well done, good and faithful servant" has more merit than any thanks written here.

So here it goes. Special thanks to:

Benjamin Lodwick – for being my real life happily-ever-after.

Kristen (Hammer) Hardin – for begging and pleading with me to write a book with truffles! Yum! And for being a beta-reader.

Marti Crockatt – for being a beta-reader and giving me helpful feedback!

Heidi Burns – for your friendship, support, and many cups of chai and chat!

Doris Pollard Wichern – I'm sad that you never got to read this story but am grateful for always believing and supporting me. I miss you.

Lisa Lickel – thanks for being such a wonderful mentor, friend, and shoulder to cry on when the publishing process throws me those curve balls. And for being brutally honest in helping me make this manuscript better.

Community Church Fond du Lac – for being an inspiration for Orchard Hill. We're not perfect—but I've seen great things in our church family, and I'm proud to be associated with you all.

Anonymous Wisconsin State Patrol Officer – who gave me insight and information to help me write this story. I hope I did it justice.

Sally Shupe – my faithful editor. Thank you for finding all those silly errors!

Leah Daniels – for whetting your whistle on copyediting. I wish you a wonderful career in this! Thank you!

M. Jamie West - for being another editor who never fails to make my writing shine. I'm grateful for your work on this manuscript.

Jeff Rockel – for being a fresh set of eyes to catch mistakes and make this story better. I appreciate your encouragement and support.

Nicola Martinez – my beloved editor-in-chief, who convinced me that even with the challenges I faced during this manuscript, I could write, and it would be all the better for the blood, sweat, and tears that went into it. I'm grateful for our friendship.

BIOGRAPHY

Susan M. Baganz is living her own happily-ever-after with her husband Benjamin. She chases after two Hobbits and is a native of Wisconsin. Susan writes adventurous historical and contemporary romances with a biblical worldview.

Susan speaks, teaches, and encourages others to follow God in being all He has created them to be. With her seminary degree in counseling psychology, a background in the field of mental health, and years serving in church ministry, she understands the complexities and pain of life as well as its craziness. Her favorite pastimes are lazy…spending time with her husband, snuggling with her dogs while reading a good book, or sitting with a friend chatting over a cup of spiced chai latte.

You can learn more by following her blog: www.susanbaganz.com
Her Twitter feed: @susanbaganz
Or her fan page:
www.facebook.com/susanmbaganz.

Thank you

We appreciate you reading this Prism title. For other Christian fiction and clean-and-wholesome stories, please visit our on-line bookstore at www.prismbookgroup.com.
For questions or more information, contact us at customer@pelicanbookgroup.com.

Prism is an imprint of
Pelican Book Group
www.PelicanBookGroup.com

Connect with Us
www.facebook.com/Pelicanbookgroup
www.twitter.com/pelicanbookgrp
To receive news and specials, subscribe to our bulletin
http://pelink.us/bulletin
May God's glory shine through
this inspirational work of fiction.
AMDG

You Can Help!

At Pelican Book Group it is our mission to entertain readers with fiction that uplifts the Gospel. It is our privilege to spend time with you awhile as you read our stories.

We believe you can help us to bring Christ into the lives of people across the globe. And you don't have to open your wallet or even leave your house!

Here are 3 simple things you can do to help us bring illuminating fiction™ to people everywhere.

1) If you enjoyed this book, write a positive review. Post it at online retailers and websites where readers gather. And share your review with us at reviews@pelicanbookgroup.com (this does give us permission to reprint your review in whole or in part.)

2) If you enjoyed this book, recommend it to a friend in person, at a book club or on social media.

3) If you have suggestions on how we can improve or expand our selection, let us know. We value your opinion. Use the contact form on our web site or e-mail us at customer@pelicanbookgroup.com

God Can Help!

Are you in need? The Almighty can do great things for you. Holy is His Name! He has mercy in every generation. He can lift up the lowly and accomplish all things. Reach out today.

Do not fear: I am with you; do not be anxious: I am your God. I will strengthen you, I will help you, I will uphold you with my victorious right hand.

~Isaiah 41:10 (NAB)

We pray daily, and we especially pray for everyone connected to Pelican Book Group—that includes you! If you have a specific need, we welcome the opportunity to pray for you. Share your needs or praise reports at http://pelink.us/pray4us

Free Book Offer

We're looking for booklovers like you to partner with us! Join our team of influencers today and periodically receive free eBooks and exclusive offers.
For more information
Visit http://pelicanbookgroup.com/booklovers